ONE THOUSAND NIGHTS

CHRISTINE POPE

DARK VALENTINE PRESS

ONE THOUSAND NIGHTS

ISBN: 978-0692281482
Copyright © 2014 by Christine Pope
Published by Dark Valentine Press

Cover art by Nadica Boskovska. Cover design and book layout by Indie Author Services.

To learn more about this author, go to
www.christinepope.com.

For Adrian

PROLOGUE

A desert wind blew, dry and hot, the last gasp of the *ser-accar* before the blessed rains of winter arrived to bring with them the short season of green, of growth. Beshalim Kel-Alisaad, Hierarch of Keshiaar, stood beneath the shade of a great canopy held up by four burly servants, but the cover it provided did nothing to keep the perspiration from sliding down his back beneath the heavy embroidered robes he wore. Still, he knew he could show no sign of discomfort, could do nothing but stand there, still as a statue, as she was brought out onto the flat, scorching expanse of the approach to his palace.

Ah, she was still so beautiful, hair whipping like black silk in the gusts of the *ser-accar*, profile pure and perfect. Her sojourn in the palace dungeons did not seem to have marred that exquisite face, just as the shapeless garments she wore could not conceal the lush curves of her body.

Besh wished he could close his eyes, could turn away so he would not have to see what happened next. But such weakness was not a luxury he could afford, even though otherwise he was the most powerful man in a thousand miles. His left fist knotted at his side, concealed in the folds of his heavy robes. It was the only expression of the agony he was now experiencing that he would allow himself.

The watching crowd was silent, but he sensed the hunger within the people who stood there. Not to see justice done, precisely, although that was part of it.

No, they were here to see blood.

The executioner was a great, bald man, holding the curved sword of his profession. He waited, scalp shining in the merciless sun, as the two guards brought her to the dais. Azeer Tel-Karinoor, the Hierarch's chancellor, stepped forward. If the heat bothered him, he showed no sign of it as he lifted the scroll he held and read in his clear, ringing voice,

"Hezia Kel-Alisaad, for crimes of high treason and gross adultery, the sentence is death. The light of the sun will no longer shine on you, and your name will be spoken no more. The crimes you have committed against our sovereign have cast you utterly beyond redemption, and God himself has turned His back on you. You have indulged the flesh, and your flesh will be no more. So is the judgment of our great Hierarch. Stand now, and meet your fate."

Those shoulders, once so proud, slumped a little. But then her chin lifted, and she cried out, "I am guilty of nothing but love! Besh, please—"

At such a casual use of his name, the crowd began to murmur. It was not seemly to address the Hierarch in such a manner at any time, let alone in so public a place, by a woman who had no rights left to her, especially not those of a wife.

Tel-Karinoor's lips thinned. "You are guilty of treason." A curt nod at the two men flanking the condemned woman, and they thrust her to her knees in front of the executioner. "As the Hierarch wills it, so it will be done."

No, he had not willed it. When she had been caught in her deceptions, had begged and pleaded for her life, for him to understand…even then he had not wished for her death. It would have been so much better to release her from the marriage, and banish her and her accursed lover—the one whose name Besh would never allow himself to speak again—forever from the borders of Keshiaar. But while the Hierarch had many powers, changing the laws of his land to accommodate an erring consort was not one of them. She must die, as any traitor would. All of her rank and titles had been forfeit once her adultery was discovered.

He stood silent, watching, knowing he could not look away, could do nothing to show any sign of weakness. If only he could forget the sound of her laugh, the sweet honey of her lips. It had been an arranged marriage, as such things always were, but he had loved her. That was why the betrayal cut even more cruelly.

She had not loved him, had instead loved the one person she should never have even thought of in such a way, the one man whose involvement compounded her transgression a thousand times and more.

The executioner's sword flashed in the sunlight as he grasped it with both hands and lifted it over his head. It had to be a strong and sure blow, to make the cut in one sweep.

Besh pulled in a breath of the scorching air, then gave the barest of nods. This thing could not be stopped now, so best to get it over with quickly. He would not let himself think of her fear, of how her heart must be pounding in her perfect breast. To think of such things would rob the fragile strength that held him in place now, doing that which custom expected of him.

A glitter of steel. A faint whistle as the sword cut through the air. And then a thud as her graceful head was severed from her neck, followed immediately afterward by her body slumping forward and collapsing on the wooden dais.

It was done.

The executioner lifted her head by its gleaming black hair, and the crowd erupted in cheers. Besh swallowed the taste of bile in his throat, holding himself ramrod straight, and raised one hand, as if to acknowledge the skill of the swordsman.

And now, custom satisfied, he could leave this cursed place, take refuge in his apartments. There was already talk of finding him a new wife, for Hezia had not given him an heir. He would let his advisors manage that. Let them find him a princess if they liked. He knew he must provide Keshiaar with a son, and perhaps some day he would force himself to perform the act necessary to produce the required offspring.

But he knew he would never love again.

CHAPTER ONE

The ambassadors from Keshiaar appeared on a wet morning in Fevrere, their unheralded arrival sending the entire palace into a frenzy. Ashara had come to my chambers to tell me the news, although in truth she did not have very much to report.

"And Lyarris, almost at once they were closeted with Torric in his office, and not in the audience hall, so it must be some secret matter. I will have to pry it out of him whenever he reappears," she added, green-gold eyes dancing.

I had no doubt that she would. They hid very little from one another, my brother and this wife of his. "Good, for I will admit to some curiosity. It is certainly not a time of year to be traveling."

"No, so it must be *very* important." She paused, one hand going to her stomach, although it still looked flat as ever to me.

"Are you feeling quite well?" I asked. "I can call for some water, or cider."

"Oh, no, I am fine," she replied quickly. "The illness comes and goes, but today I am well enough. It is just—I am still trying to convince myself that it is all real."

It would be very real some six months hence when that child entered the world—kicking and screaming, no doubt—but I thought I understood what she meant. After all, it had been quite the rapid progression for Ashara, from nobleman's daughter reduced to scrubbing the pots in the house that should have been hers, to Empress, and now mother to the next Emperor. Well, if the child was a boy, of course.

"It is still new, I suppose," I told her. "But of course everyone is very excited."

As they should be. That the Emperor would wed such a girl at all, especially one whose family was tainted by magic, had been the subject of a good deal of gossip. But since she was such a good, sweet young woman, and because she had shown she understood her duty very well by getting with child only a month after her marriage, the populace was willing to forgive her somewhat questionable past.

"And I more than anyone," she said, cheeks pink. After a pause, she lifted her hand from her stomach and went on, "That is, perhaps except for Torric. At any rate, I must go, for now Lord Hein is in quite the frenzy, trying to revise the plans for tonight's feast and entertainment so that they will be suitably impressive. We can't have the ambassadors from Keshiaar thinking we are hopeless provincials, after all."

"I doubt very much they would think that." True, Keshiaar was a great empire, the only one in the world to rival ours here in Sirlende, but provincial? No, I did not believe they would have that opinion of us. Then I added, "Well, I should not keep your from your appointment with Lord Hein. I am sure the two of you will concoct something that will quite turn the ambassadors' heads."

"Now you are teasing me," she protested, but her eyes were dancing. "But that is all right, for I love you anyway. And you will understand me when I say I am somewhat relieved that your mamma is down with the ague, for at least I will not have to worry about her interference. It makes things so much easier. But now I must go."

Which she did, after giving me a quick kiss on the cheek. Her two maidservants trailed after her and shut the door to my suite. I did not precisely sigh, but I did think of how much things had changed. Only a few short months ago, I would have been the one to consult with Lord Hein, if my mother was not well enough to manage the task. But while I was still the Crown Princess and accorded all the respect due that position, I was not the Empress.

And a good thing, too, because that is not something I would wish on anyone, I thought. Ashara has managed admirably, but the novelty of court life has not yet worn off for her. As for me, I will be glad when Thani and I are able to make our own announcement. I will press for a short engagement, so that we can be together and away from Iselfex as soon as is seemly.

Oh, how I wished my beloved were here with me now. But he had gone back to his estates for a fortnight, saying he could not utterly abandon Marric's Rest for court. Though I missed him dreadfully, I understood his reasoning. He was fairly new to the management of his estate, and leaving it for too extended a time would not be politic.

In the meantime, I would have to revise what I had planned to wear to dinner. It was supposed to be a quiet evening, no more than fifty sitting down to table with us, followed by a harp concert in one of the smaller chambers, but of course that would not do to entertain the noble ambassadors from Keshiaar.

As I went to survey my wardrobe, my maid Arlyn at my side, I couldn't help wondering again exactly why those ambassadors were here.

I had no chance of learning the true reason for their mission during the course of that evening, for the conversation was all light and inconsequential—discussions of the weather, of the next growing season, whether the price of silk would rise or fall. And although I shot a questioning glance at Ashara as she and Torric entered the dining hall, she only gave the slightest lift of her shoulders, followed by a shake of her head. Apparently her confidence in "winkling" those secrets out of my brother had been misplaced.

During that dinner I caught one of the ambassadors giving me an oddly appraising look, as if I were a horse at a fair that he wanted to buy. Frowning, I glanced away from him at once, and told myself I must be imagining things. After all, he was a foreigner, of a different cast of feature than the people of Sirlende, and no doubt I was misreading his expression, although I thought he looked vaguely familiar, as if I had seen him before on a previous visit to the palace.

Even so, I was glad when the meal was over and we had all moved into the ballroom. Lord Hein and Ashara had apparently decided that dancing was a more enticing pastime than sitting and listening to music, and of course the members of the court had no reason to decline attending such a pleasant event. It was still a small enough affair, perhaps slightly more than a hundred people in attendance, but with them milling about, I was more or less shielded from the view of the senior Keshiaari ambassador.

Or at least I thought I was. As the musicians struck an introductory chord, he approached me and bowed deeply. "Your Highness."

I curtseyed in return. "Ambassador Sel-Trelazar."

"You would honor me, Your Highness, if you would be my partner for the *padrane*."

Surprised, I could not help but ask, "You know our dances, Ambassador?" Yes, his face was somewhat familiar, but I could not recall him ever participating in one of our dances during one of his previous visits.

"Oh, yes, Your Highness. This is not my first journey to Sirlende, you know, and I have been to South Eredor as well, where the amusements are similar. I think you will not find me too clumsy-footed."

There was nothing much I could say to that. Certainly I could not decline his invitation. So I smiled, and curtseyed, and allowed him to take my hand and lead me out to the dance floor, where we took up our positions directly below my brother and Ashara. Her eyebrows lifted as she took in my dance partner, but after Torric sent her a warning glance, she adopted a pleasant, noncommittal smile and looked away.

For myself, since Thani was not here, one dance partner was as good as another. And Ambassador Sel-Trelazar proved to be true to his word, light on his feet and making nary a misstep. He was not so very old as I had thought—perhaps in his latter forties. The beard made him seem older, I supposed; in Sirlende it was not the fashion for men to wear beards. Certainly it seemed rather impractical to me, as Keshiaar, lying far to the south as it did, was quite fiercely hot. But the one the ambassador wore was trimmed closely enough that I could see the clean line of his jaw underneath the beard, and overall I thought him a rather fine-looking man, with his strong dark brows and long, elegant nose.

The dance was a slow and stately one, the traditional opening for a ball before the musicians progressed to more lively tunes. Because of this, it allowed for conversation in a way that some of the other pieces did not. A double-edged sword, as it meant I would not be able to retreat into silence the way I might if I were dancing, say, the linotte.

"And did you have a good journey, Ambassador?" I inquired. "I have heard that the seas can be quite treacherous at this season."

"As to that, God must have smiled on us, for the passage went smoothly enough, save for one stormy day as we came around the Melinoor Peninsula."

"I am glad to hear it," I replied. Yes, I had read that the Keshiaari people believed in one god, as did those in South Eredor, although it was not the same god. It was not something I had made much study of, preferring history and geography to religion, and I decided to let the reference pass. "Your business must be very important indeed for you to come to us at this season, though."

His dark eyes twinkled. "Ah, Your Highness, I fear I cannot tell you more. That is something His Majesty will have to discuss with you."

I found I did not much like the sound of that. My gaze slipped to Torric, who had seemed preoccupied all evening, and had done his best to avoid speaking with me. Not so difficult, what with the ambassadors to entertain and so many nobles of the court in attendance, but such behavior was unlike him. Perhaps he was doing his best to keep his distance because I knew him all too well, and might be able to guess at the ambassadors' true mission here if I spent too much time in his company.

All this passed through my mind in an instant. Hoping my hesitation was not obvious, I told the ambassador, "As I'm sure he will, once he has a spare moment."

An expression I couldn't quite read passed over Ambassador Sel-Trelazar's face. "Yes, His Majesty has many things to occupy his time. But I think he will make time for you in this."

I could only nod, and soon after that the dance ended, and I was able to make my escape and have a servant bring me a much-needed cup of wine. There were undercurrents here that I did not quite like, but try as I might, I could not determine what could possibly be the source of my unease.

Except perhaps my brother, who smiled and charmed as he always did, and danced with his wife and many ladies of the court, but never me. He seemed to make sure he always had a group of courtiers around him, or at least Ashara and her dear friend the Lady Gabrinne, lately married to Duke Senric. It was as if Torric was doing everything in his power to put up a barrier between the two of us, and I found I did not much like it.

I did not like it at all.

The next morning rain pattered against the windows, and my chambers felt dark and dull despite the many candles Arlyn had lit to drive back the gloom of the day. She brought me my breakfast, which I only picked at. The unease of the evening before had not dissipated after a good night's sleep. If anything, it had only grown worse.

"What do you wish to wear today, my lady?" Arlyn asked, hovering in front of the enormous cabinet that housed my wardrobe.

"You may choose, Arlyn," I told her, for in that moment I truly did not care. It was supposed to be a quiet day, although now that the ambassadors were here, I guessed that my brother would put on yet another entertainment this evening—a grand concert, or perhaps a play, although I was not sure the ambassadors would approve of such an amusement. I had heard their people were very strict, and did not approve of women putting on costumes and enacting made-up stories, let alone sharing the stage with men.

All in all, Keshiaar sounded like quite a harsh place, and I was glad to be here in Sirlende, where we were more liberal in our beliefs. True, women did not have the same freedoms as men, but at least they were allowed to go about on their errands unaccompanied, if that was what they wished, and could even manage their own businesses—as long as they were not the type of business deemed unsuitable for a woman. Running an inn or managing a bake shop or working at embroidery were all considered seemly occupations, while overseeing a factory or building a house most definitely were not.

"The wine-colored velvet, my lady?" Arlyn asked, holding up the gown in question. "And your garnet ensemble?"

That seemed well enough, so I nodded. "That will be fine, Arlyn."

And so she helped me into my chemise and my gown, then brushed and curled my hair. As she was setting the delicate diadem of garnets and gold on top of my head, a knock came at my door. Arlyn murmured an apology to me and went to answer it. Outside stood one of the footmen. He handed her a folded piece of creamy paper, and said, "For Her Highness."

She bobbed her head and thanked him, then shut the door and came back over to me. "This is for you, my lady."

"Thank you, Arlyn." I took the paper from her and unfolded it. The heavy black handwriting was unmistakable—Torric's. The message was brief enough: *Come to my*

chambers at eleven o'clock. There is something we need to discuss.
~T

Ah, perhaps the mystery would at last be cleared up. I thought I should be relieved, but again that shiver of misgiving went through me, and somehow I guessed I should not be quite so eager to hear what my brother had to say.

But as I could not refuse an audience with the Emperor—even if that Emperor also happened to be my brother—I knew I could only go and hear him out, and discover that all he wanted was to discuss the opening of a new trade route, or dropping the tariffs on imports of Keshiaari silks. We had had such talks in the past, for he was not the tiresome sort of man who believes a woman cannot provide good counsel. Now, though, I thought such commonplaces were not precisely what he had on his mind.

At a few minutes to eleven, I left my suite, accompanied by Arlyn, and made my way from the East Tower to the sumptuous chambers Torric now shared with Ashara. As I entered, though, I could see no sign of my sister-in-law. My brother stood in front of the hearth, staring down into the fire, which was crackling cheerily away.

"Torric," I said, after Arlyn had shut the door behind me.

He turned, but offered me no smile of greeting. "Ah, Lyarris. Good." An off-hand gesture toward a pitcher and two goblets that sat on a side table. "Some mulled wine?"

I thought it a bit early for such refreshment. However, something in his expression told me I should not demur, so I went and picked up one of the goblets. "I sense that you have something on your mind."

"Is it that obvious?"

"To me, yes." I sipped some of the wine; it had been mixed with cider, and so was not quite as potent as it might otherwise be. "It is not usually your way to spend an entire evening avoiding me. Tell me, what do those ambassadors want, precisely?"

"Direct as always." He took up the second goblet; however, I noticed he did not drink, but merely held it, as if he wanted to absorb some of its warmth, although the room was certainly comfortable enough. "Yes, Lyarris. They have come to me with a...proposition."

"Oh, dear, that sounds ominous," I remarked, hoping to coax a smile from him with my light tone.

But his expression remained sober. "I fear you will think it so. It appears the Hierarch's consort has...died...and he seeks a new wife. Of course his advisors' first thought was of you, as you hold a rank befitting a son of desert kings."

I could only stare at Torric blankly, his words somehow not taking on any shape that made sense. At last I found my voice. "But of course you told them I was already engaged."

Then he did lift the goblet and take a large swallow of the mulled wine. Not looking at me directly, he replied, "Your engagement is not formal. It has not been announced."

"Well, it will be! We had meant to say something earlier, but you wished to announce Ashara's pregnancy first, which is as it should be. But for all intents and purposes, Thani and I are betrothed." These protests tumbled out one after the other without my even stopping to take a breath, as if I knew I had to utter them as quickly as I could before Torric could come up with some other argument. Yes, it was true that the Duke of Marric's Rest and I had not yet published the notice of our engagement, but that was merely a formality.

Torric drained the goblet and poured himself some more of the mulled wine. "No, you are not engaged. Not formally." This time he did face me, the handsome, familiar features tight with strain. "Do you not think I don't know what I am asking of you? But this—this is an opportunity I had never dreamed would be yours. The Hierarch's consort! The two greatest empires in the world joined! How can you pass that up for a mere duke?"

Anger flared in me. "He is not 'mere' to me, Torric. He happens to be the man I love. Or does that count for nothing with you?"

"Of course it does," he replied, clearly exasperated. "But I need you to think like a princess, Lyarris, not a woman in love."

"Indeed?" I snapped, not bothering to hide the fury in my voice. "That is rather disingenuous of you, brother, considering you threw your entire empire into an uproar so that you might choose the woman of your heart, and not a foreign princess. Or is it simply that only a man is deserving of such considerations, whereas a woman must do as she is told?"

"Oh, for all the gods' sake!" He paused then, clearly struggling within himself, and set down the goblet he held. When he spoke again, his tone was gentler. "Yes, I did overthrow convention to take Ashara as my wife. And I had hoped that you would be able to find a similar happiness in your own marriage. If it were anyone else, I would have sent them packing. But this is not some petty princeling's piddling second son. This is the Hierarch of Keshiaar who has asked for your hand. It would be utter insanity to refuse him."

Logically, I knew his words were only the truth. But my heart was already given to someone else, and it cried out at the cruel request my brother was making of me. I could not do it. I simply could not.

As I stood there, tense and quiet, Torric approached me and took my own goblet from my hands, then placed it next to his on the table. "I will not ask you for an answer now. I only told the ambassadors I would speak with you. They seemed surprised by that, but agreed to wait."

"Of course they were surprised," I said bitterly, "for in their own land I have heard that a woman has no true will of her own, and must do everything as the men in her family bid her."

"Oh, then they are a sensible people," Torric replied, his tone teasing. But he sobered abruptly when he saw no answering smile on my face. "Take this," he added, and pulled a small pouch from the inner pocket of his doublet.

Uncertainly, I took it from him, felt a hard oval shape within. I drew it from inside the pouch and saw that it was a miniature portrait, set in a frame of cunning enamel work picked out with cabochon garnets and turquoise. The man depicted in the portrait was young, although perhaps a few years older than my brother, dark as all the people of Keshiaar were, but with even, regular features. His eyes were a surprising shade, almost amber, striking against the swarthy skin.

"He is…handsome," I managed.

"Yes, he is. I would not ask such a thing of you if he were old, or ill-favored, or anything less than someone deserving of the Crown Princess of Sirlende."

Irritation flared again, and I shoved the miniature back in its pouch. "Do you think me so shallow that I can be swayed simply because the man in question is not objectionable in appearance?"

"Of course not!" Abruptly, Torric pulled off the circlet he wore, and ran his hand through his hair. It was a gesture familiar to me, one he resorted to when frustrated. "Again, I am not asking you to decide anything today. Just please— think on the matter."

I felt I could not bear to look at Torric for a second longer. "I could ponder the matter forever and a day, and still it would not change my mind. I cannot—I will not sell myself to someone just so you can improve your trade agreements with Keshiaar!"

And with that I stormed away from him and burst out into the corridor, startling Arlyn, who appeared to have been indulging in a flirtation with one of the guards who always stood watch outside the Emperor's chambers. She knew better than to ask any questions, though, and merely trotted along after me as I took long, angry strides back to my own chambers, where I slammed the door and then threw the miniature in its pouch onto the nearest table.

After that, there was really nothing to do but burst into tears.

Some time later I heard a gentle knock on the door to my suite. By then I had more or less recovered myself—or at least I had ceased weeping into the pillows on my bed and had gone back out to the sitting room, where I made myself take a seat at the desk and pretend to look over some of my writings from the day before. Not that I cared two figs in that particular moment about the tale of a talking bear and two sisters, a story related to me by one of Arlyn's fellow serving girls, but at least by shuffling the papers, I had forced myself to some semblance of calm.

Through all this Arlyn had hovered in the background, clearly worried by my apparent breakdown, but too well trained to do anything but wait it out. When that knock at the door came, she hurried over to answer it with an alacrity that would have amused me at almost any other time, but now only made me want to shake my head.

Standing outside was Ashara, flanked by two ladies-in-waiting and several guards. The set of her mouth told me how much she disliked having such a retinue follow her wherever she went, but for the Empress such things were expected, and therefore nonnegotiable. I myself had managed to dispense with such a gaggle of followers, save for my maid, some years earlier, telling Torric that I simply could not bear to have those women spying on everything I did. That announcement had caused quite an uproar in the household, for of course my mother, the Dowager Empress, thought it the grossest breach of protocol. But Torric had prevailed, and I was left blessedly alone. Ashara, however, had not been allowed that luxury.

"May we speak?" she asked formally.

"Of course," I replied at once. I knew precisely why she was here, and I did not wish for such a conversation. But I also knew to turn her away would only set tongues wagging. "Arlyn, go and fetch us some tea, if you please."

That would get her safely out of the way for a while. In actuality, she would go out and relay the request for tea to one of the upper-level maids, who would then pass it down the chain of command until the order arrived at the kitchens. But at least she would remain outside until the tea in question appeared, and that should take several minutes. And Ashara's retinue would not be allowed to follow her into my chambers, but rather would have to loiter in the hall until Her Majesty's business was concluded.

She came in and paused, and one of the guards moved forward to shut the door behind her. I could see the relief pass visibly over her face before she moved forward and took a seat on the divan before the fire.

"One would think you would be used to all that, after three months," I said.

"I doubt I ever shall, but I will endeavor to hope that it will become slightly less obtrusive as time wears on," she replied, a little smile at the corner of her mouth telling me that she had recognized my teasing for what it was. Then even that faint smile faded, and she added, "I suppose you know why I am here."

"I can guess. Torric knows that I am angry with him, and so has sent you as his ambassador, thinking that perhaps you can persuade me where he has not."

A shake of her head, those amazing dark copper curls shimmering in the firelight. "Well, that is what he asked of me, but it is not the real reason I came."

"It isn't?" I inquired in some surprise. Oh, Ashara was not overly meek, and had stood up to Torric on more than one occasion if the situation warranted it. But they were usually of one mind on everything, and so they rarely disagreed. For some reason, I had thought for sure she would have sided with my brother on this matter.

"No, of course not!" she burst out. "Lyarris, you are the sister I always wished for. Surely you cannot think I would support sending you away to marry someone simply because it was politically expedient! I told Torric as much, and he said that while he admired my idealism, such sentiment had no place in politics."

"He is right, you know. I should be thinking coldly. I should be remembering my place as the Crown Princess of Sirlende, and doing what is best for the empire." Suddenly my legs felt as if they could not support me any longer, and I sank down on the divan next to her. "But oh, Ashara, I cannot do it! Perhaps if I did not love someone else—perhaps if my heart were not already given—I could have made myself submit to such a scheme. Torric seems to think that because this Hierarch is not so many years older than I, and comely, it would be easier."

"It is because Torric is a man," Ashara replied, fine eyebrows drawing together even as she reached out to pat my hand. "And your brother. That is, in his mind he feels that he had some hand in drawing your attention to Sorthannic Sedassa, and so because he had done so once before, he can now redirect those attentions to the ruler of Keshiaar."

"It is not the same thing at all!"

"Well, I know that, and you know that, but…." She let the words trail off, and I saw some curiosity in her eyes. "And how is it that you know he is comely?"

Without replying, I stood and went over to my desk, where I had set the little pouch containing the Hierarch's portrait. I pulled out the beautiful jewel-like piece and brought it back over to my sister-in-law, then laid it in her hand.

Her brows lifted, and she gave a nod. "Ah, well, if this portrait is anything close to a true one, then I can see that he is quite handsome. And, as you said, if you had not already given your heart to someone else, perhaps that would be enough. But, circumstances being what they are…." She shook her head. "I will attempt to talk some sense into your brother, make him see that just because the formal announcement has not been made, it does not mean you have not already bound yourself to Lord Sorthannic."

"He will only try to browbeat me with arguments about trade agreements and such," I said with some bitterness.

"Well, he can try. However, I will tell him that trade agreements are all very well, but they do not keep a woman warm at night."

"Ashara!" I exclaimed, somewhat shocked that she would utter such a thing. Heat flooded my cheeks. Of course I knew they were a very affectionate pair—too affectionate, some might say, and remark that such obvious love between the Emperor and his wife was not seemly—but I had not expected her to ever allude so openly to those sorts of relations.

"Oh, what point is it trying to avoid such things?" Her gaze slid toward her belly, and she ran one hand over the skirts of her copper-colored velvet gown, although she was slender as always, showing no sign of the child she carried. "I rather think it would be disingenuous to imply that my relationship with the Emperor is not intimate. At any rate," she went on, getting to her feet so she might move closer to the fire, "it is not as if the Keshiaari ambassadors know that your engagement to Lord Sorthannic is not precisely formal."

"Oh, I think they know that very well," I said darkly. I loved Ashara, and she had a quick mind, but she had not yet lived at court long enough to know that everything the imperial family did—or did not do—was common knowledge. And even if it were not, well, lands with far less influence and wealth than Keshiaar had their spies here in Sirlende, so of course I could expect no less of that desert empire.

A certain knowing light entered her eyes, and she gave a brief nod. "Well, if that is the case, then I think it best that you write to his lordship. Have him come to you here in Iselfex. Do not tell him the reason why, only that it is urgent. He will come, will he not?"

"Yes," I replied immediately. True, Thani had been back at Marric's Rest for not quite a fortnight, but I knew he would return to the capital if I asked. And it would be so much easier to face down my brother if it were the two of us doing it. "That is an excellent idea, Ashara. I will dispatch a letter to him at once." On a sudden impulse, I went to her and gave her a quick hug. "Although Torric is being rather pig-headed about this particular matter, I do have to admit that he showed extremely good judgment when he chose you."

Her cheeks flushed slightly, but she laughed and gave an airy wave of one hand. "Oh, well, when the alternative is the Lady Brinda Aldrenne, that makes the choice somewhat easier, does it not?"

I gave a mock shudder. "I suppose that is true."

Arlyn returned at that point with the tea, and we moved the conversation to more innocuous topics. I had no idea how much of the reason for the ambassadors' visit had already begun to circulate through the palace, but I saw no reason to give the gossips any additional ammunition. And after an appropriate interval, Ashara excused herself—no doubt to return to Torric and gravely inform him that I was intractable when it came to the Hierarch's suit, and that the ambassadors had made this long journey for nothing.

I loved her for that…but I also knew my brother would not give up so easily.

CHAPTER TWO

What precisely passed between Ashara and my brother, I did not know, but he did not renew his appeals for me to accept the ambassadors' proxy proposal. They were, I could tell, getting anxious—sidelong glances sent in my direction when they thought I was not paying attention, overly florid panegyrics to the exotic beauties of their homeland. However, as they were, if nothing else, consummate professionals, they seemed willing to sit through the concerts and balls and lavish supper parties as if attending such events was the only reason they had traveled more than a thousand miles at the tail end of a long, cold winter.

I had sent the letter to Thani, and now I could only wait. Two days' hard ride for a messenger to reach Marric's Rest, and most likely three for the return trip. That meant I could expect my betrothed—for I did think of him in such a way, no matter what my brother might say—sometime the day after tomorrow. Although Torric had left the matter alone, his expression was eloquent enough. It spoke of his disappointment in me, that I could not see past the folly of my heart to make the decision that would be in the service of my homeland.

From time to time, I would withdraw the miniature portrait of the Hierarch from its pouch and gaze on his features. Why I did such a thing, I was not sure. Perhaps to somehow apologize for rejecting him? Despite the foreign cast to his features, he did have very kind eyes. They appeared to watch me and understand the reasons for my refusal. And I seemed to note a certain sadness there, which I supposed was to be expected, as he had recently lost his wife. Torric had not said why; I assumed she must have died in childbirth, or perhaps of some illness native to that fierce desert land.

I saw nothing of cruelty or dissipation in that face, and that was why I secretly hoped for him to find a bride among his own people, someone who could make him happy. Something about those calm, dark features made me wish him no further sadness.

Which was foolish, of course. A miniature portrait no larger than a few inches from top to bottom was not precisely a good measure of a man's appearance, let alone his character. Most likely I had spent so many hours writing down stories and fairytales that I had begun to let my imagination run away with me. I had no doubt that the Hierarch viewed this whole transaction as merely that—a political arrangement, bartering favorable trade agreements and treaties for a highborn bride. It was the way of such things, after all.

Over the past few days, I had more or less managed to avoid being alone with the senior diplomat, Ambassador Sel-Trelazar. The junior ambassador, named Amil Nel-Karisoor, seemed more interested in sampling the delights of the imperial court—including its ladies—than pressing the suit of his monarch. But Sel-Trelazar, I feared, was not one to be so distracted, especially on an evening when my brother had decreed there should be cards, and dice. Gambling was one of the main pastimes of the court, but I had always disliked it. Too many disgraced themselves by falling into debt, all for foolish games. It was expected, though, and my brother, a canny and cautious gambler himself, had little pity for those who found themselves in difficulty.

"Should I outlaw the practice, simply because a few fools have no self-control?" he had snapped at me once when I had mentioned that perhaps more wholesome entertainments might be instituted at court.

And so I was feeling impatient, not merely because I disliked his choice for that evening's diversion, but also because I was expecting Thani to be here on the morrow, a day that could not come soon enough. In the meantime, I knew I had to continue this charade, until at least such time when he and I could present a united front and declare to everyone, ambassadors included, that we were betrothed, and there would be no match made with the Hierarch.

As that thought passed through my mind, another came to supplant it.

I realized I had not even been told his given name. Perhaps that was something a prospective royal bride did not need to know.

"Your Highness."

Startling slightly, I realized that Ambassador Sel-Trelazar had approached me as I stood there abstracted, my thoughts far away. And he had fairly caught me, for nearly everyone else was occupied with some game—the men gambling, the ladies watching, some openly encouraging, others laughing and gossiping amongst themselves whilst fortunes were lost and won.

"Ambassador," I replied, once I had recovered myself.

"My lady, if it is not too much of an imposition, may I have a word in private?"

That sounded dangerous, but there was no way for me to demur without seeming rude. I arranged a gracious smile on my face and said, "But of course, Ambassador. If we step through those doors, we will be in one of the smaller salons. It should be quieter there."

He pressed his hands together and bowed from the waist—a gesture of obeisance from his homeland, I supposed. I inclined my head in return, extending a hand to indicate the door through which we should pass. Ever polite, he opened it for me, then closed it behind the two of us once we stood in the salon.

It was cold in here, for, expecting this room to be ignored in favor of the gaming in the great hall, the servants had only kept a banked-down fire going, barely more than glowing embers. I saw Sel-Trelazar shiver, and thought of how uncomfortable it must be for him, used as he must be to far hotter climes.

But then he straightened, as if casting aside his discomfort, and said, "My lady, many thanks to you for agreeing to speak with me alone. There are some things I wish to say to you that I would prefer other ears not hear."

This piqued my curiosity somewhat, and I replied, "It is no problem at all, Ambassador. Please, tell me what is on your mind."

He smiled, teeth seeming very white in the half-light of the room and against his dark beard. "Truly, Highness, the tales of your beauty and graciousness were not exaggerated."

Court speech, empty words. He had to have been trained in such things. But there was an odd diffidence to his stance, as if he did not quite know the best way to say what must be said.

"You are very gracious, Ambassador," I said. "However, I do not think you drew me aside merely to pay me compliments."

"And perceptive as well," he said. "Yes, Your Highness, if my only aim was to praise you, then it would be easy to do so in the company of others." A pause, and he watched me carefully, dark eyes intent on my face. "Your brother has told you why we have come here."

"Yes." Again the image of the face in the portrait flashed across my mind, those sad amber eyes.

"I understand your reticence, my lady. It is no small thing to give up everything one has known and travel more than a thousand miles to be with a man one has never met."

"No, it is not," I replied, wondering at his openness. Usually a diplomat would not have stated such a thing quite so baldly.

He gave me a knowing nod. "And I wonder, Your Highness—how much of the matter has His Majesty shared with you?"

The question puzzled me. "Not a great deal. That is, he said that the Hierarch's wife has recently passed away, and so, after waiting a certain interval, he now seeks a new consort." I hesitated, then added, "While I feel for his loss, I must tell you that I am not free to accept his suit. My understanding with the Duke of Marric's Rest is known to all in Sirlende."

"Yes, that." He glanced away briefly, as if to take in the heavy dark furniture, the portraits and landscapes hanging on the paneled walls. "His Majesty seemed to indicate that it was not yet a formal betrothal."

"In terms of announcing it publicly, no, but at Midwinter the Duke did ask me to be his wife, and I accepted his suit. Surely that should be straightforward enough."

"Yes, Your Highness. I understand that. But...."

"But?"

"Perhaps it would be better if we sat down." He swept a graceful hand toward a pair of velvet-upholstered chairs near enough the fire that we should be more or less comfortable there.

Well, I had agreed to this meeting, and so to refuse to take a seat in his company would be rude. I nodded, then moved toward one of the chairs and sat. As I had thought, it was warmer here, the faint scent of wood smoke somehow comforting, warm and homely, especially when contrasted with the melange of perfumes and colognes and hair rinses worn by the crowd of nobles in the hall next door.

Once I had arranged my skirts and folded my hands on my lap, Sel-Trelazar seated himself as well, his posture straight, hands set squarely on the arms of his chair. "My lady, I fear your brother tried to shield you from the facts of our Hierarch's consort's demise to protect you, but I believe you should know the truth of the matter, so that you may make your best decision."

Curious. I recalled Torric's strange hesitation when he said, *It appears the Hierarch's consort has...died....* Surely if it had been an ordinary death, he would have simply stated the facts. "And what is the truth of the matter, Ambassador?"

He sighed. Or rather, a long breath escaped his lips as his fingers tightened on the arms of his chair. "Hezia Kel-Alisaad, the consort of the Hierarch, was found to be an adulteress. The only penalty for such an act of gross treason is death, of course."

"Of course," I murmured, mind reeling. No simple death in childbirth or from a fever, then.

The gods only knew what was in my expression in that moment. Sel-Trelazar went on, the words coming quickly, quite unlike his usual measured, graceful delivery, "It was an arranged marriage, as such things are, but His Most High Majesty truly cared for her, so the betrayal was doubly cruel."

Ah, well, that explained the unknown sadness I had seen in the painted eyes of the miniature portrait. A good artist, then, to catch that which the Hierarch no doubt wished to conceal. I said slowly, choosing my words with care, "Ambassador, while I truly feel for His Most High Majesty's loss, I still do not see why the circumstances of her death should change my mind."

A heavy nod, as if he had expected such a reply. "Your Highness, I know what it is I am asking of you. But I have also seen that you are a great and noble lady, one of a pure heart. Truly, when I came here, I thought only of securing a suitable wife for the Hierarch. But now I believe—I know— that to have such a consort such as you would do much to heal the hurt he has suffered."

"I fear your confidence in me may be rather misplaced," I replied lightly, but something in his words had evoked an odd ache somewhere within my breast. The stakes for refusing this offer might be higher than I had imagined.

For the first time he smiled. "I do not think so, my lady. I have had the very great honor of spending many years in His Most High Majesty's service, from the time he ascended to the throne when he himself was little more than a boy, and—may God forgive my impertinence—I believe I know something of his nature. You are wise and beautiful and honorable. Surely you could never have even contemplated giving in to your baser desires the way Hezia did."

The tone of his voice—and the informal manner in which he said her name, with no honorific—told me all I needed to know of his opinion regarding the late consort. Not that I could entirely blame him, for certainly adultery on its own was a terrible enough transgression, but adultery when your spouse also happened to be the ruler of your land was immeasurably worse. For of course the royal lineage was traced through the male line, and if a child was of uncertain parentage, then all would be thrown into chaos. It was, as the ambassador had said, the very worst kind of treason.

Perhaps it should have been within me to find some sympathy for this unknown Hezia, to wonder at a love so fierce that she was willing to risk death for it. However, I found I could not, for my mother, who had made no secret of her dislike for my father, nonetheless remained faithful until the day he died. Surely she had more reason than most to stray, as he certainly did not do anything much to hide his numerous affairs. But she hadn't, had lived in such a way that it was impossible to think she would engage in such an activity.

Not that I mean to imply that I admired her, because her own disappointment in being denied the match of her heart in order to marry the Emperor had led her to develop the most bitter of tongues, a tongue she did not scruple to guard, even with her own children. Or perhaps especially with her own children.

"No," I said at last. "I know nothing of the late consort's character or family, but I was raised so that such a thing would be unthinkable to me." As Sel-Trelazar began to give me an approving nod, I added quickly, "That is not to say I am in agreement that I would be the best match for your Hierarch. My heart is given to another. Surely the last thing you want is to have him married to yet another woman who is in love with someone else."

"It is the last thing I want, Your Highness, and I thank you for being frank with me."

My thoughts from earlier in the day, when I had gazed upon the Hierarch's portrait, rose in my mind once again. "May I ask something, Ambassador?"

"Anything, most noble lady."

"What is the Hierarch's given name? I have not yet heard it spoken."

A smile, and he replied, "It is Beshalim Kel-Alisaad. Those who have been granted the right to address him familiarly call him Besh."

I nodded. It was simple, easy to recall. And I thought I liked how it sounded as I repeated it in my mind. *Besh*. "Thank you, Ambassador. It helps, I think, to know something of him beyond his title."

My reply seemed to give Sel-Trelazar some hope, and I worried that in asking for the Hierarch's name, I had allowed the ambassador to think that my mind was not yet completely settled on the subject. I opened my mouth to tell him it was not so, but he forestalled me by saying, his steepled his fingers under his bearded chin, "It is not for me to speak of where you have chosen to give your heart. All I can say is that His Most High Majesty is a man of a generous nature, and a man of learning and discernment. I have heard that you, too, my lady, are a scholar of some renown. I think you would find that you have more in common with the Hierarch than you might imagine. Truly—and I have traveled the world, and seen many wondrous things and met many people—I cannot think of anyone better suited to be his consort than your noble self. Would that circumstances had been different, and you had been free to become his wife long ago."

There was little I could say to that, as certainly I did not have the ability to go back and change the past. True, I had been promised to the Earl of Fallyn's son at a very early age, a betrothal that came to nothing when he gave his heart to someone else. Such a thing would normally have mattered very little, but as the Earl was a great good friend of the crown, my father had released the Fallyn heir from the contract, leaving him to follow his heart, and me quite unattached. If that engagement had never been made, then most likely my father would have attempted to have me betrothed to the young Hierarch, for certainly it was a far better match at almost every level.

Perhaps in a perfect world matters would have been arranged so. However, we had to attend to things as they stood here and now, and not as they might have been. The ambassador was looking at me with such hope that I kept my tone as gentle as I could as I replied, "Yes, Excellency, it does sound as if His Most High Majesty and I would have suited very well. But I cannot change the past. All I can do is make the best choices I can going forward to the future." I stood then, and he rose a second later, disappointment clear in the slump of his shoulders.

Then he straightened, and said, "Yes, Your Highness. I will pray to God that you will make the right choice here. May He shine His light upon your path." He bowed formally, in the Sirlendian fashion, and I inclined my head. It was clear that the audience was over.

He left me then, returning to the light and noise of the main hall next door. But I stood there in the dim salon for some time afterward, my thoughts churning. What he had said weighed upon me more heavily than I had expected.

Why that was, when I had already made up my mind, I could not determine.

The shallow clamor of the evening seemed even more tedious after my conversation with the ambassador, and after a scant half hour in the hall, giving false smiles to those who approached, and wishing Torric had thought of any sort of diversion for the evening rather than gaming, I sought him out and told him I wished to retire early.

"Are you quite well?" he asked, an expression of concern flitting over his features.

"Yes, of course, but I have something of a headache and would like to return to my chambers. No doubt a bit of peace and quiet is all I truly need."

His brows drew together at that comment, as if seeking to find yet another dig at the gambling going on around us, but then he seemed to shrug. "Very well. Things will go on for some hours yet, and no need to have you weary yourself unnecessarily."

I smiled then and thanked him, and informed Lord Hein that I would be retiring for the evening. At once he sent an escort of four guards to see me to my rooms. Silly, really, safe in the heart of the capital as I was, but no princess of the realm could take a single unaccompanied step when the palace was filled with guests. At least I was well used to it by now.

After they had followed me upstairs, and seen me safely installed in my suite, I let out a breath and pulled the diadem from my head. Arlyn, who had been dozing on the divan in front of the fire, came to with a start and got to her feet at once.

"A thousand apologies, Your Highness! I was only resting my eyes and—"

"It is no matter, Arlyn," I said gently, stopping the flow of words before they could get started. "It is enough that you help me out of this dress and brush my hair for the night. After that, you may retire."

"Of course, Your Highness," she replied, then followed me to my bedchamber so she might unlace the heavy velvet gown and store it safely in the wardrobe, and take off my silken chemise and replace it with a warmer linen one for sleeping. After she had brushed my hair and braided it deftly into its nighttime plait, I bid her a good night's rest, and she went, yawning, to the small room off my own where she had her own bed.

I, however, was weary but not sleepy. Gathering up my heavy brocaded robe from where Arlyn had draped it across the foot of my bed, I went back out to the sitting area and prodded the fire with the poker, reviving enough of the flame that it began to crackle again merrily, sending some much-needed heat into the room. On a side table sat a pitcher of water and a heavy glass goblet, and I poured myself some and drank, glad of the simple liquid after the heavy wines served at the reception.

Driven by an impulse, I set down the goblet, then moved across the room to my desk, where I had left the Hierarch's portrait in its pouch, sitting on top of some of my papers. I withdrew it and cupped it in my hand, and gazed down at his features once again.

Besh Kel-Alisaad, who had been betrayed by the woman he loved.

A wave of pity went over me then, strong and unexpected. I attempted to push it away—after all, pity was no better a basis for agreeing to a marriage than the colder exigencies of treaties and trade agreements.

And yet....

I shook my head, crossing to where I had left the water. Perhaps the dregs of the wine I had drunk with dinner were still playing with my mind, making me whimsical and foolish. Deep within, I knew that was not true. I had had only one glass, and that hours ago. No, I was as sober as I would ever be.

You love Thani, I told myself. *That is the one thing you should hold on to in all of this.*

Yes, I did care for him. He was handsome and kind, and one of the better judges of human character I had met. He did not share my love of books and learning, preferring the sturdier pursuits of hunting and raising horses, or the quieter pastimes of growing vines and making wine, but that did not lower him in my estimation, instead raising it. Unlike so many other men I had met, he did not wish to be an idle nobleman, losing himself in foolish court pursuits. We had often shared a laugh together when poking fun at some of the sillier courtiers and their escapades. Not so anyone else could hear, of course, but as our own private jokes.

Surely that was more than most noble couples shared. But there were times I wished I could discuss something I had read with him, or ask him to look over my writings and give his opinion. The one time I had made such a request, he had only laughed and said, "I am not a scholar, Lyarris. I generally left such things to my sister. She always had her nose in a book."

I let out a sigh and closed my fingers around the portrait, feeling the smoothness of the enamel frame and the hard shapes of the cabochon gems press into my flesh.

Sel-Trelazar's words echoed in my mind: *His Most High Majesty is a man of a generous nature, and a man of learning and discernment....*

No, I could not let myself think of that. I must think of Thani, the way he had pressed his lips against mine at the Midwinter feast as we hid ourselves in an alcove, seeking to escape the gossip and prying eyes that sought to learn the extent of our connection. That, and also recall the warm, rich sound of his voice as he had asked me to be his wife. In that moment, I had thought myself to be the happiest woman in the world...a happiness that did not dissipate even once the glow of the celebration and the wine we had drunk wore off. I truly believed he was the match of my heart, or at the very least the best match I could possibly make. For if I could not wed a foreign prince, then at the very least my husband must be a duke. And there were not so many of those in Sirlende, especially of a suitable age and temperament.

Could it be that I had fooled myself into thinking I was in love with Sorthannic Sedassa, simply because I knew I had no true alternative?

Oh, gods, would that the ambassadors had never come, and I had never heard Beshalim Kel-Alisaad's sad story! For I would have married the Duke of Marric's Rest with a calm heart, knowing that I could do no better, that perhaps the true match of my soul did not exist.

Now, however….

My fingers seemed to open of their own accord, and once again I gazed down into the face of the Hierarch, this Beshalim Kel-Alisaad.

Besh. Surely if I were his wife, he would allow me to address him in such a fashion.

And when that thought passed through my mind, I knew I was lost.

CHAPTER THREE

Thani arrived at the palace early the next afternoon, just as a few flakes of snow began to fall from the sky. He came with the smallest contingent that custom allowed, some ten of his men-at-arms, and again, as custom dictated, he went to pay his respects to my brother the Emperor first, so I had an extra measure of time to pace nervously before the fire, rehearsing the words I would say, and knowing as I did so that no matter how elegant and practiced they might be, it would not matter in the end. I was about to hurt the man I thought I loved, and who had said he loved me, and nothing could change that.

I had not mentioned any of this to my brother, given no hint of what was passing through my mind. Thani should hear of this first from me, and although my brother was a consummate diplomat, I could not trust him to keep a secret of such magnitude from the Duke. Some measure of his excitement at having his sister agree to marry the Hierarch of

Keshiaar might slip out, careful as he was, and as much as I understood that what I had to tell him would wound Thani immeasurably, it would hurt far worse to hear the news from someone else.

And so I lingered by the fire, and then went to my desk and attempted to pick up my writings of a few days ago, only to push them aside when I realized I could not possibly hold my scattered thoughts to such a task. Arlyn sat quietly in the background, embroidering a pair of gloves for me. I knew she must be wondering what was amiss, what could possibly have caused her mistress such unaccustomed agitation, but of course I could not confide in her, either. Perhaps Ashara would have lent a sympathetic ear. Again, though, I wanted no inkling of my decision to be known by anyone except Thani until I had spoken with him.

At last came a knock at the door to my suite, one I had been both expecting and dreading. Arlyn went to answer it, and I heard Thani's deep voice greeting her.

My blood seemed to go hot, and then cold, but I made myself rise from my chair by the hearth to go greet him.

He was so very tall, and so handsome, that I felt my resolve falter. I had said nothing to anyone; it was not too late to put my madness of the last few hours aside and forget those moments of doubt. But no. I would not allow that to happen. In the black hours of the previous night, I had made my decision. I cared for Thani, I knew that to be true. But was it a love to stand the test of time? The kind of love that would make a woman risk death, as the late consort of the Hierarch had?

When I had searched my soul, examined the deepest reaches of my heart, I realized the answer to both those questions was no.

"Arlyn, you may leave us for now," I said. The words were calm and in command, betraying no trace of my inner turmoil. Well, that was something.

She bobbed a curtsey and left. Normally an unmarried woman would never have been allowed to be alone with a man thus, but Thani's and my engagement, although not formally announced, was still common enough knowledge amongst the members of the court and our servants that our being left unattended was not terribly scandalous.

As soon as she had closed the door behind her, Thani came to me and took my hands in his. The feel of those strong fingers around mine, rough with the calluses of a man who spent a great deal of time in the saddle or holding a sword or jousting lance, made me want to weep. But I would not allow myself that weakness. I was the Crown Princess of Sirlende, and I would deliver the unwelcome news as graciously and painlessly as I possibly could.

"What is it, Lyarris?" he inquired. "For you said very little in your letter, only that you wished to see me at once. But now that I am here, I can see you are greatly troubled."

"Is it that obvious?" I essayed a weak smile, one I feared did not fool him at all.

"Perhaps not to those who do not know you well, but—"

"But you cannot be counted among their number," I finished for him. Preparing for this interview, I had had wine and light, savory cakes brought up, although the thought of eating anything made my stomach clench. I pointed toward the refreshments and said, "Some wine?"

His eyebrow lifted, as if he guessed that I was only offering him the drink to stall for time. He did not comment, though, save to say, "Thank you, yes."

I poured for him and then gave him the goblet. He took it from me and drank, a small, measured sip, a courtesy.

Then he waited, watching me. "Whatever it is, surely you can tell me."

No, I am not sure I can. I picked up my own goblet, although I only held it and did not drink the wine Arlyn had poured into it earlier. But delaying would only make things worse, so I drew in a breath and said, "We have had a visit from several ambassadors from Keshiaar."

One dark eyebrow lifted. "Indeed? It is surely not the time of year for that."

"No, it is not," I agreed, thinking of the snow that had begun to fall outside. "But they felt their mission was urgent enough to risk a sea passage at this season."

"And was it?" He did drink this time, his blue eyes, so striking against his dark hair and tanned skin, watching me carefully.

"Yes, I believe it was." I turned the goblet in my hands, feeling the smooth silver against my palms, the coolness of the liquid within. Perhaps I should have sent for mulled wine, given the snowy day outside, but I had not known for sure how long it would have to sit before Thani came to me. "They came here to say that the Hierarch's consort has passed away, and that he wishes my hand in marriage."

A deep, terrible silence, one in which those blue eyes did not blink, but only remained fixed on my face. Finally he replied, "And of course they were told that you were already promised to someone else."

"Yes, they were."

"Well, how is that not the end of the matter?" He continued to stare at me, then said, "What is it you are not telling me, Lyarris?"

"I—" Suddenly my mouth was dry, dry as Keshiaar's fabled deserts, and I lifted my goblet and took a swallow of wine. "Thani, my brother did tell them I was not—not free to accept their offer. And I told the senior ambassador, Sel-Trelazar, the same thing."

"But?" Thani prodded, his expression telling me he did not believe that to be the end of the matter.

"But—but I have thought on it, thought on it at great length."

"And so you have decided to agree to their proposal," he said heavily. His knuckles whitened as his fingers clenched on the goblet he held. I could see the thin silver buckle under their pressure.

"Y-yes," I faltered.

"I see." The words were spoken quietly, but I could hear the anger running beneath them, like the faint, dangerous spark that sets off a forest fire. "You realized that to be the wife of a duke was nothing, when you could be the consort of the Hierarch of Keshiaar, queen of one of the world's greatest realms!"

"No, that is not why," I said at once. I could bear his anger, but I could not bear to have him think me greedy and grasping, desiring only to be raised to such an exalted height, high above all other women.

"Pray tell me why, then," he retorted, before lifting his goblet and finishing the rest of its contents in a single swallow. "For unless the Hierarch himself came here to make his suit, and you looked into his eyes and fell madly in love, I confess I cannot understand how you could ignore everything that has passed between us to accept this proposition!"

Oh, how could I explain this to him, when I could barely explain it to myself? "Thani, I—"

"Sorthannic," he corrected me. "For only those who care about me may use that nickname."

Ice went through me then, despite the heat from the fire only a few feet away. "Very well. My lord, I studied my heart. I care for you. I do. I think perhaps we could have made a good marriage, despite our differences in temperament. But after everything, I have come to realize I cannot love you the way you deserve to be loved. And that is not fair to you. Not fair at all."

Again a terrible silence fell. He stood there, staring at me as if I were a stranger, as if one of those strange, fey creatures of legend had invaded my body, turning my heart cold as stone. Finally, "And yet you think you can love this Hierarch, a man you have never seen, never met?"

"Such matches are not made for love," I said wearily. "This is something I have been raised knowing. I was taught to do my duty. When I met you, I thought—I thought perhaps my fate might be different. Now, though, I realize I would be doing you a disservice. You will find someone else, and be happy. And I—I will do what is good for Sirlende. And perhaps this Hierarch and I will learn to live with one another after a time. I have been told that he is a man of learning, and so at least we will have that in common."

"Meaning we do not, I suppose," Thani said, setting down his goblet. I noticed that he did not bother to refill it. "As I am only a simple man, one who cannot possibly hope to understand you."

"That is not what I said—"

"Perhaps not. But I think perhaps it is what you meant. Very well, Your Highness. I see your mind is made up, and so I will waste no more breath trying to change it." He straightened, his fine chin lifting. "I will see myself out."

With that he strode to the door, not sparing a single glance back at me. It shut behind him, and he was gone. And I—

Well, I stumbled to the divan, sank down upon it, and buried my face in my hands.

Some time later a summons came from my brother. He wished to see me in his private chambers. Immediately. No "when it is convenient," or "at your leisure." This summons did not surprise me.

I had been expecting it.

So I set aside the book I had been pretending to read, and allowed the two footmen to escort me to my brother's suite. No one paid me any mind as I passed through the corridors, save to curtsey or bow, or murmur, "Good afternoon, Your Highness." After all, I visited my brother often, and although most of the time I did so with only Arlyn as my escort, it was still not so unusual for me to be accompanied by a foot-man or a guard or two. To everyone around me, I was sure I looked placid and calm as always. Inwardly, though, I was writhing. No taking back what I had said to Thani, but oh, how I wished that interview had gone differently.

I saw no sign of Ashara when the footmen guided me into the sumptuous reception chamber in the imperial suite, and guessed that Torric had requested that she be elsewhere—perhaps consulting with Lord Hein over that evening's enter-tainments, or, gods forbid, spending some time with my mother. I would not wish that on anyone, and hoped fer-vently it was the former.

No sooner had the footmen retired to the foyer, shut-ting the door behind them, than my brother stepped forward from where he had been waiting by the enormous hearth of carved black marble, and said, "It is most curious. The Duke of Marric's Rest has sent word that he will not be staying in the palace, and instead is having his house here in town opened up…and also that he regrets it highly, but he cannot attend the supper this evening."

"Indeed?" I managed, although once again I found my throat dry, and the word barely croaked out.

"Indeed," Torric replied, dark eyes glinting. He paused a few feet away from me and added, "I was hoping you could cast some light on the Duke's unusual behavior. For surely a man does not make a journey of a hundred miles in bleak

Fevrere to see his betrothed, only to turn away at the last moment?"

"No, he does not." I drew in a breath, then said, "I believe he is angry with me because I told him that I had decided to marry the Hierarch of Keshiaar."

If I had told my brother I intended to abandon my crown and run off with a troupe of jugglers, I do not think I could have elicited a more startled reaction. His eyes widened, and he exclaimed, "You what?"

Now that I had said it, I felt a bit better. Not much, but a little. Uttering the words gave a shape to my intent, made it more real. "You heard me, Torric." My gaze shifted past him to an elegantly carved table placed against the wall, where a silver pitcher of water sat, surrounded by a set of matching goblets. I went there and poured myself some water, only halfway wishing it was wine. The liquid was cool against my throat, a welcome relief.

There were not many times in my life I could recall seeing Torric positively flummoxed. In fact, I thought perhaps this might be the only one. He stood there in the center of the chamber, jaw working as if he meant to say something but could not quite decide what. At last he closed his mouth, crossed over to me, and poured himself his own goblet of water. "Damn tepid stuff," he said. "I should've had the footmen bring up a bottle. But Ashara heard from one of her ladies-in-waiting that her younger sister's new doctor insists that women with child should not drink anything stronger than cider, and so Ashara has said we should not have wine in our chambers." He lifted the circlet he wore, ran a hand through his hair, and then replaced the finely worked band of gold, a gesture I had seen him make often enough when he was trying to work through something in his mind.

"It is good that she is taking such care," I said, glad of a reason to talk about anything but what had just passed between Thani and myself.

"Yes, of course." Then Torric shook his head. "But enough of that. May I ask whence has come this remarkable shift in your opinion of a marriage with the Hierarch?"

"You may ask," I told him, attempting to keep my tone light, as if I were teasing.

He was my brother and I loved him, and we were far closer than many siblings, as we'd only had one another as a bulwark against our mother's harsh tongue, but there were some things I could not imagine myself saying to him. Especially not what I had seen in my heart when I looked deep within it the night before, and realized that Sorthannic Sedassa could not make me truly happy. Not that I expected such a thing of the Hierarch, either. In that case, though, it would be a match made for politics, and no one truly expects love to come from such a union.

And of course I could never confess to Torric that, somewhere deep inside my soul, I hoped perhaps my case might be different.

Now, though, his face darkened, and he said, "I will not lie and say I am not happy to hear this, for of course it is great news, much more than I could have ever hoped for. But I also do not want to think of you sacrificing yourself for this, throwing away something you insisted you wanted. Just two days ago you stood in this very room and claimed you could never marry the Hierarch. So I think you may forgive me for wondering whence has come this sea change."

I lifted my goblet and drank deeply of the water therein, then poured myself some more. "Then let us say I thought the matter over with some care, and realized perhaps Lord Sorthannic and I would not suit quite as well as I had first thought."

Torric let out a sigh at that reply. His dark eyes scanned my face, and at last he gave a reluctant nod. "And somehow I fear that is all I will hear from you on the matter, unless Ashara winkles it out of you."

Despite everything, I could not help but smile, as she had said almost those same words just a few days earlier about her husband. "Perhaps. For you know, Torric, there are some things that women only wish to confide in one another. Is it not enough that I have agreed to the marriage?"

"It would be…if I were certain you were not sacrificing your happiness to do so. I don't want you to feel as if you were forced to this conclusion."

"I most certainly was not," I said stoutly. "I came to it on my own, and therefore you should accept my decision and question me no further."

He fell silent then, studying me as if he sought to discover the truth in my face. At last he said, "Then have I your leave to summon the Keshiaari ambassadors and tell them the news?"

"You do. I am sure they will be pleased."

"That is an understatement." Unlike those ambassadors, my brother did not look pleased at all. His brow was still puckered, as if he were worrying at the problem in his mind, trying to discover exactly what it was that had compelled me to accept the Hierarch's suit.

"Do not look so troubled, brother," I said, again taking care to keep my tone light. "Have I not always said that I wished I could go upon an adventure? I cannot think of a greater adventure than becoming the Hierarch's wife."

Of course the word spread through the palace like wildfire through a summer-parched meadow. I believe my brother did have time to speak with the ambassadors in private before they learned of my decision through less than official channels, but even so it was a close call. Ashara came to me within the hour, eyes wide and disbelieving.

"After everything you said just the other day, you have thrown off Lord Sorthannic to accept the Hierarch after all?" she demanded, after unceremoniously shooing all of her ladies-in-waiting out into the hallway, where they would be forced to be precisely that in deed as well as in name.

"Yes," I said wearily. My head had begun to ache, and I wished I could hide in my chambers until it was time to depart for Keshiaar. That day, though, was still some time off, as I knew my brother would not permit me to undertake the sea passage until calmer waters prevailed, most likely sometime in early Averil.

"But...why?"

"Because I realized I do not love Lord Sorthannic the same way you love my brother. I wish with all my heart that things were different, but as they are not, would it not be false of me to cling to the Duke of Marric's Rest, merely as a way of avoiding a political marriage?"

Quietly she sat and appeared to digest that statement. After a pause, she said, "But you seemed happy enough with him—"

"I was. Or rather, I thought I was. He is a good man. I cannot dispute that. And because he is a good and worthy man, he should have a wife who is as besotted with him as he is with her. Don't you see?" I added, and sank down on the divan next to Ashara, holding her gaze, hoping that she would see the truth in my eyes. "It is because of how I see you look at my brother, and the way he looks at you, that I know something of what two people can share. And now that I have such knowledge, I cannot ignore it. I know I do not feel that way toward Lord Sorthannic."

"And you—you think you will feel this way about the Hierarch?" Her tone was dubious, even as she turned from me slightly so she could retrieve his portrait from where I had left it sitting on one of the tables flanking the divan where we sat.

"No, I am not that foolish. But at least he seems to share some of my interests, as he is a man of learning. It is more of a basis than many such matches have."

She nodded absently, staring down at the portrait. Then her fingers tightened around the little jeweled frame. "But it is so very far away," she said quietly, and I thought I heard the quiver of tears behind that near-murmur.

"It is," I agreed, feeling a certain tightness in my own throat. For I had always wished for a sister, and now had one, and soon I would lose her, along with everything—everyone—I knew and loved. It would have been one thing for the wife of the Duke of Marric's Rest to come visit her relations in the capital, and quite another for the consort of the Hierarch of Keshiaar to make such a journey. A thousand miles and more. Once I had made the journey to that faraway land, I did not believe I would ever come back.

"But I think I understand," she said at last, and now her tone was firmer, that hint of tears gone. Yes, she was my dear sister-in-law, but she was also the Empress of Sirlende. She had learned quite a few things these past few months. "You do not wish to be false to the Duke, but in breaking the engagement, you have also removed the one impediment to your marriage with the Hierarch. So it would not be truthful of you to continue to deny the match."

"That is precisely it," I replied, relieved that she understood so clearly. "And perhaps you can pass on that insight to my brother, as I fear he believes I have gone mad, even if it is a madness that suits his purposes."

She actually laughed a little at that, then lifted her shoulders. "I will do what I can. But I think as long as you know the truth in your heart, that is the most important thing."

Yes, I had seen that truth…or at least what I perceived to be that truth. I could only hope that I would not wake on the morrow, and discover that it had changed once again.

But I did not. Oh, yes, I ached for the hurt I had caused Thani, and the realization that I would not be his wife twinged as well. Under that, though, was an odd sense of relief, as if I had somehow known all along that our match was never truly meant to be.

And after that, I did not have much time for rumination, for of course that evening before dinner Ambassador Sel-Trelazar had to pay his respects and shower me with praise for my discernment, my beauty, my graciousness in accepting his master's suit. My mother even paid me a visit soon afterward, almost happy for once, clearly pleased that I had made the correct decision at last in agreeing to be the queen of a far-off land, rather than stay here and be the wife of a duke…especially a duke whose mother had the ungracious temerity to be a commoner.

So much planning, so much to do! The junior ambassador was dispatched with the news at once, to return to his homeland so that preparations could be made there against my arrival. He did not look overly pleased to be sent away so quickly and required to abandon the pleasures of the Sirlendian court for a treacherous sea journey in mid-Fevrere, but there was no help for it. It was his role to go ahead, and then Ambassador Sel-Trelazar and the rest of their retinue would accompany me once that same voyage was deemed safe enough for me to attempt.

In the meantime, the ambassador took it upon himself to instruct me in the Keshiaari tongue. It was difficult, but not impossible, for I already knew the common tongue spoken in both the lands of North and South Eredor, and Purth and Farendon, and I had taught myself Selddish as well, though no one beyond the borders of that secretive land bothered with it. Sel-Trelazar seemed pleased with my progress, and said that by the time I disembarked in Tir el-Alisaad, the capital of Keshiaar, I should be speaking his language like a native.

More than that, a new wardrobe was ordered, for the ambassador assured me that my gowns of heavy velvet and brocade would not do well at all in his homeland's warm climate, and so garments made up to his specifications were constructed for me. I wondered at them, at the gossamer-fine shirts, meant to be layered under the short-sleeved tunics of thin silk, edged in costly embroidery, with billowy trousers to be worn underneath. I had blushed at first to even con-template wearing such a thing, but then I realized that truly they were more practical—and comfortable—than my layers of hose and petticoats and knickers, not to mention the bone reinforcements that had lately begun to be stitched into the bodices of gowns. All this I gazed at, and wondered how truly different things must be in Keshiaar, for their garments to be so unlike ours.

I already knew something of that land's histories and cus-toms, for of course I had studied those amongst reading books on North and South Eredor, and Farendon and Purth as well. Never had I thought I would travel to that distant realm, let alone become wife to Keshiaar's ruler, but at least I was not completely unfamiliar with its traditions. No complicated nobility, with its layers of barons and earls and dukes. Only the Hierarch, and below him what seemed like an uncounted number of princes, all of them claiming that title because of their connection to the royal family of Kel-Alisaad.

A hot, inhospitable place, but one with vast mineral wealth. And not all dry and dusty, for the great river Al-sheer wound through the country, emptying into the same Carulan Sea that touched the coast of Sirlende, albeit many, many leagues away. The winter was their welcome time, when the rains would come and all would be green, if only briefly.

This I recalled, and so much more, but of course reading such things in a book could not match experiencing them in reality. As the days ticked down and the preparations for my departure continued apace, I found myself seized by an ever-increasing restlessness. I wanted to see these things for myself, to taste those strange fruits and the spices that grew in that warm, unfamiliar clime, to see the great city of white marble where the Keshiaari court made its home. All these things occupied my thoughts, but none more than the ruler of that land. What would his voice sound like? His laugh? Was he grave and quiet, or possessed of a teasing humor, like my brother? Of course, when that thought passed through my mind, I realized that the Hierarch probably did not have much to tease about, what with the manner in which he had lost his wife. But still, my mind kept casting forward in time, and I became impatient with the daily routine of my present life. It was as if, now that I had made the irrevocable

decision, I only wished to be gone. Yes, there was the interminable packing of those items I could bring with me, and
the gifting of those things I could not—Ashara had no use
for my gowns, as our coloring was not at all similar, but they
were gratefully accepted by her stepsister Shelynne—but still
it seemed as if the time was passing more and more slowly,
dragging out far longer than it should.

At last, some ten days into Averil, the harbor-master at
Marten's Point came to the palace, gravely informing my
brother that the seas had calmed, and it was, in his estimation, safe for the Crown Princess to make her sea journey.
I trembled at the news, for as much as I had longed for the
weary waiting to be over, now that the moment was here,
I realized there was no going back. Very soon, everything
would change.

The night before my retinue would leave for Marten's
Point and the great ship that awaited us there, Torric held a
great feast in my honor. Lord Hein made sure all my favorite dishes were served, for of course there was a very good
chance I would never taste them again. Looking on everyone, all those faces I had known since my childhood, I found
myself having to hold back tears. How dear they all seemed
to me now, even blustery Lord Keldryn and my cold, sharp-
tongued mother. But I had committed myself to this thing,
and I would see it through to the best of my ability.

So I smiled, and ate until I felt near to bursting, and
exchanged blithe words with my brother and dear Ashara,
now growing quite large with child, and went to bed that
night knowing it would be the last time I would look out the

window of my suite at the lights of Iselfex, or see moonlight reflected in the waters of the River Silth. I did not weep, for the Crown Princess of Sirlende could not been seen embarking on a journey to her new homeland with puffy eyelids and pale cheeks.

And the next morning I embraced my brother and my sister-in-law for the last time, as the doctors had deemed it unwise for her to make such a journey, and I could not ask my brother to leave her alone, if even for a few days. So we made our farewells, and offered brave smiles that probably fooled no one. And after I dutifully offered a cheek to my mother's cold kiss, bowing my head as she instructed me to always behave as befitted a princess of Sirlende, I at last rode away to Marten's Point, the harbor where I would take ship and leave my homeland behind forever.

CHAPTER FOUR

The scent of salt caught me first, wild and unknown, and with it came a wind unlike anything I had felt in Iselfex, rough and cool. That wind whipped around us and tugged at my carefully arranged curls, seeming to promise the one thing I had never experienced in all my life.

Adventure.

Not that we had met any on the road, of course. Ours was a large party, some fifty strong, although only a little more than half that number would actually be sailing to Keshiaar. Most of them were servants and guards who had traveled with Ambassador Sel-Trelazar. I had my own small retinue, four women servants to attend my wardrobe and such, although Arlyn was not one of them. She had tearfully told me that she could not bear to leave Sirlende, especially for such a "dreadful hot place, begging Your Highness's pardon," and of course I would never force her to make such a sacrifice. I wished her all the world's luck, and made sure that after I left, she would have a good place in the household of the Duchess of Gahm, Ashara's great good friend.

Torric had wanted me to bring along several ladies-in-waiting as well, but I declined, thinking that if Arlyn had not wanted to make the journey, I certainly would not ask such a thing of the daughters of our barons or earls. No, the attendants I had with me were women without any close family, those who had said they did not mind leaving their homeland, as they had little to tie them there. With that I had to be content, although some small part of me wished for a familiar face to accompany me on this journey.

The ship waiting for us was Sirlendian, a light, fast caravel used for plying the trade routes between Keshiaar and my homeland. It was not the vessel Ambassador Sel-Trelazar had traveled in to get here; that one had taken his junior compatriot on ahead, so that all might be prepared for my arrival. Perhaps it was foolish, but I found myself glad it was a Sirlendian ship that would bear me hence. Somehow I felt I would not quite be leaving all of my home behind, traveling thus.

Captain Talaver was its commander, a tall man in his fifties with a beard so thick and full, he would have been right at home in Keshiaar. He bowed low when I stepped aboard, my meager retinue following behind me with my wardrobe and other necessities. "Your Highness, you do my humble ship a great honor."

"It is a beautiful ship, Captain," I told him, for it was, with its bright blue sails and prow carved into the likeness of a leaping dolphin.

"*Merwinna* will not steer you wrong, Your Highness. She'll get you to Keshiaar and your betrothed before you can blink."

"Ah, that would be a good trick," I replied. "The normal span of time will be quite sufficient, but I do thank you."

He laughed then, and began issuing orders for the disposal of my possessions and the dispensation of the rest of my party, and within a remarkably short span of time I was settled in a lovely cabin aft, with cunning carvings of more frolicking dolphins around the doors and a single round window—a porthole, I think he called it. Two of my attendants would sleep in there with me, while the other two had to make do in a smaller cabin one deck below us. I did not know where the ambassador and his party would be housed, but I supposed I would find out soon enough. Although the ship was not small, it was not so large that I did not think we would feel ourselves very much in one another's laps by the time we reached Tir el-Alisaad.

But then I heard shouting from above, and the ship seemed to move beneath me. They must be casting off. I knew I could not miss my last glimpse of Sirlende, so I bade my two attendants come with me up to the deck, where we made our way to the high platform there. From that vantage point we had an excellent view, and, more to the point, we were mostly out of the way of the crew, who were occupied with unfurling the great azure sails and maneuvering them to catch the freshening breeze from the west. That wind, I knew, would drive us all the way to Keshiaar.

I turned then, facing the town of Marten's Point, and the green hills which surrounded it, and the white sand of its crescent-shaped harbor. Somehow I doubted I would ever see hills that green again.

"Goodbye, Sirlende," I murmured. My eyes stung, and I would not begin to guess whether that was because of the sharp, salt-laden air, or because I knew I would never see my homeland—or my brother, or Ashara—ever again.

To my relief, I found that sea travel rather agreed with me. Oh, it took me some time to gain my sea-legs, and until then I tottered about, unsure of my balance, but at least I did not spend the entire voyage retching into a bucket the way poor Halda, one of my maids, did. Even after four days at sea, she could keep nothing down but water and hard biscuits, and so of course I excused her from her duties until we were safely back on dry land.

For myself, though, I could only marvel at the expanses of open water all around us, with no land in any direction. I had read of such things, but until one can see them for oneself, the notion of the open sea does not seem quite real, like something out of a fairy story. As were the dolphins that swam alongside the ship, jumping in and out of the blue, blue water, guiding us along our way. We were very lucky, for the weather held during almost the entire voyage. It was only as we came around the Melinoor Peninsula at the far southern end of Purth that we hit a squall, and were tossed about quite fearfully. But then the sun came out once again, and the wind settled, until a few days after that we drew close to land again, and the white spires of Tir el-Alisaad came into view.

My heart seemed to catch then. Finally, after a month and a half of waiting, and another two weeks on the ocean, I had come to Keshiaar.

Or at least, to its docks, where a runner was sent to the Hierarch's palace to inform him of our arrival. As good a ship as Merwinna was, I rather longed to be off her at that point, to feel solid earth beneath my feet again. But we must wait until a suitable escort arrived, Ambassador Sel-Trelazar informed me.

"This meager party will never do to accompany the betrothed of His Most High Majesty to the palace," he said.

As I could tell he was quite serious, I nodded gravely, thinking that even in Sirlende a troupe of some twenty-five should have been sufficient to go the two miles or so from the docks to the royal residence. Perhaps it was just as well, for I found myself needing that time to acclimate myself to the heat, which seemed to encroach upon the ship as soon as it was stilled at the dock, with no more strong ocean winds to combat the dry, hot air that seemed to spill down upon the city from the deserts that stretched on three sides around it.

But I waited, clad in my new Keshiaari garments and glad of them, feeling them like a whisper of gossamer against my skin. I had told my maidservants not to bother with curling my hair, as I had no idea what the fashion for such things was here, and I guessed the hot, dry winds might defeat their best attempts. Besides, I thought perhaps it would be best to meet my betrothed with no such artifice between us. Well, not much, anyway. Karenna had insisted on touching just the faintest bit of rouge to my lips, and I had decided to let her—mostly because the beeswax ointment used to bind the pigment felt as if it would give my mouth some protection from the sun.

After almost an hour had passed, a great clamor rose up from the docks, and I saw a large group of men-at-arms wearing curiously curved helmets and long crimson coats approaching through the crowds, which parted immediately to let them through. In the center of the group were ten large, burly men in white, carrying what seemed to be the Keshiaari version of a sedan chair, although this one was far more ornate than any I had ever seen, painted and gilded, with a curious carved knot on top, almost like a pinecone, but far more intricate. And I somehow doubted that such a thing as a pinecone had ever been seen in Keshiaar.

"Your escort," Ambassador Sel-Trelazar murmured to me, quite unnecessarily.

I nodded, though, and waited until the contingent had made its way to the quay where Merwinna was docked. Captain Talaver, I noted, stayed out of the way; he had done his duty by bringing me here, but he had no part in the events which were about to unfold.

One of the guards stepped forward and clasped his hands together, then bowed from the waist. "Amassador Sel-Trelazar, we are here on behalf of His Most High Majesty to see that his intended bride is conveyed safely to the palace."

"I thank you," Sel-Trelazar replied. "Here is Her Serene Highness." He turned to me and bowed as well, far more formal than he had been on the journey here, when we had had a number of lively chats about the oceans and ships, in addition to his continuing to instruct me in the Keshiaari language and customs. "If Your Highness will take her seat in her chair?"

I nodded, then stepped forward, allowing myself to be handed up into the sedan chair. Although their customs were not mine, I knew enough to follow along, to play my role. Just before the guard closed the silken curtains, obscuring my view, I saw the ambassador give me a reassuring nod. Good thing, for my stomach had begun to feel quite fluttery, as I wondered what they would do with my maidservants, or my luggage, or—but no, that was foolish. Sel-Trelazar had it all in hand. My task was to sit here in the stifling gloom of the sedan chair, and feel those burly men turn it around and convey me away from the docks, into the heart of the city.

Oh, how I wished they had not closed the curtains! For not only was it quite unbearably hot, but, more importantly, I could see nothing of my surroundings. Perhaps the Hierarch did not wish his affianced bride to be gawked at in the streets of his capital. Although I could just barely understand that reasoning, I did not find it quite fair that I should be denied a glimpse of my new home. Also, though I had certainly fared well enough on the ocean's tossing waves, I could not say the same for my current mode of transport. Some cloying perfume seemed to cling to the draperies that enclosed me, and that, combined with the heat, made my stomach begin to churn. I swallowed and shut my eyes, willing myself not to be ill.

For won't that make a good impression, I scolded myself, *having you appear in the Hierarch's palace spattered with your own sick?*

The mental image that produced was enough to force back some of the nausea, and I held on to the edge of my seat, feeling the carved wood bite into my fingertips. To distract myself, I shifted, then lifted just the barest edge of the curtain to my right. Surely it couldn't be all that bad to allow myself just a peek. I could tell the streets were crowded simply from the babble of voices around me, speaking words I could not yet understand. Yes, the ambassador had been instructing me in the tongue of this land, but to hear so many voices at once, all clamoring together—well, of course I couldn't possibly begin to separate them into coherent syllables.

I caught a quick glimpse of buildings of pale brick and white stone, bodies packed together, their clothing similarly light in color, perhaps to ward off the rays of the fierce sun overhead, black hair gleaming in the harsh, bright light. And beyond that, a quick impression of a group of market stalls huddled up against a building, with fresh fruit and vegetables shimmering in hues of green and red and yellow, and gold glinting in a woman's ears as she laughed and tossed her head.

All that I caught in a single brief flash before one of the men carrying the sedan chair apparently noted the gap in the concealing curtains, and twitched it shut again. He did not look at me, but the disapproval in his stance was clear enough.

Ah, well. I could only hope that once I was properly installed as the Hierarch's consort, I might be allowed to see something of the people who would then be my subjects. Surely he didn't intend to keep me this cloistered at all times?

After an interminable jolting ride through the streets of Tir el-Alisaad, the sedan chair finally halted someplace that felt marginally cooler. The curtains parted, and I saw Ambassador Sel-Trelazar beaming at me and flanked on either side by five of the crimson-wearing guards. He appeared none the worse for wear, and so I guessed he must have been provided with a mount for the journey to the palace, even though I had not spied one before I was stuffed into that awful chair.

"Your Highness," he said. "Welcome to your new home. If you will allow me to guide you a little longer, I will take you to your suite, where you will meet your new servants."

"My new servants?" I inquired, puzzled. "But what of Karenna, and Halda, and Jensi and Shendra?"

"Oh, they are being brought to your quarters as well. But four is certainly not enough to service the Hierarch's betrothed, and so they will be supplemented with women from the palace. But here, allow me."

He extended a hand, and I took it gratefully, descending to the ground with rather an ungraceful jolt. Well, after that long voyage, and the sedan chair trip that followed, perhaps I could be excused for not being at my best.

All that was forgotten, though, as I looked around me, remembering to close my mouth, as gaping like a peasant getting her first glimpse of the Iselfex grand market was most likely not behavior befitting a princess. But even I, accustomed to the splendors of my brother's court, had not been expecting anything as splendid as this.

Buildings of white marble surrounded us, all of them constructed with colonnades to provide shade from the bright sun. The columns supporting the roofs of the colonnades were carved into the semblance of slender women, their upraised hands touching the ceilings of the covered walkways, which appeared to be painted in intricate patterns of blue and ochre and red. In between the columns were enormous alabaster planters, each with an elegant evergreen trimmed into a stylized diamond shape. And out beyond the shaded colonnades was a garden with colored gravel walks and more evergreens, and flowers whose names I did not know, but which cast their sweet perfume in all directions, so it seemed to drift on the hot air. In the very center was a white marble fountain several times the height of a man, water splashing over its fluted basins, and reflecting the mosaics in shades of blue that shimmered under the midday sun.

All this I drank in as quickly as I could. Perhaps, despite my best efforts, my mouth had fallen open slightly, for the ambassador said, "Truly, the palace of His Most High Majesty is one of the wonders of the world. But now, Your Highness, if you will permit me?"

I nodded. "Of course, Ambassador."

Perhaps the briefest smile, one that came and went behind his beard so quickly I couldn't be sure I had not imagined it. Then he led me through a massive arched doorway, and into a long hallway of marble cunningly inlaid in the shapes of flowers and twining vines, with more of those alabaster planters on either side, although now they were occupied by graceful, feathery-looking plants I could not identify. And oh, the frescoes on the walls, and the intricate mosaic ceilings overhead! My senses were quite dazzled by the patterns and colors I saw around me, so different from the grand but dark splendor of the imperial palace where I had grown up.

These hallways were quite busy, with servants in white scurrying about, and men in long silken robes like the ones I had seen both the Keshiaari ambassadors wear, so their appearance was not quite as foreign as it might otherwise be. I did not see many women, but knew that was to be expected; it was the Keshiaari way to keep the sexes far more segregated than they were back home in Iselfex, and so they would not be wandering idly about the palace, but kept to their own quarters, save when all might gather for a great feast in the evening.

Down one hall, and another, and then up a great curving flight of stairs, and finally down another corridor, one which ended in a set of massively carved doors in some pale wood I did not recognize. Two of the guards hastened forward to open them, and Ambassador Sel-Trelazar bowed to me once again.

"Here I must leave you, for I am not permitted within Your Highness's quarters. But if you should need anything, only send word through the servants, and I will meet with you in one of the audience chambers. Fare you well, Your Highness."

Panic seized me then, for he was the only familiar thing in my world in that moment. How I wished I could reach out and seize his silken sleeve, beg him to stay with me, if only for a few minutes longer. But that was certainly not how the

Crown Princess of Sirlende should behave, and so I merely bowed my head and said, "Thank you for all your advice and support, Ambassador. I hope it will not be too long before I see you again."

He must have seen something of my nervousness, for he said, "I have been told that His Most High Majesty has a welcome feast planned for this evening, and I am honored to have been invited. So it shall not be very long at all, my lady."

I flashed him a relieved smile then. Knowing I could not delay any longer, I turned away from him, and allowed the guards to shut the heavy doors behind me just after taking up their positions on either side of the massive lintel. The sound seemed terribly final, as if providing the final division between my former life and the one I must live now.

Taking in a breath, I made myself turn around and survey my new surroundings. The antechamber was large, with more of those intricately beautiful mosaics on the ceiling and frescoes on the wall, the floor this time alternating red and white marble faintly veined with gold. Despite this splendor, the room was sparsely furnished, decorated with only a few carved tables topped by blown-glass vases in jewel hues and filled with creamy fragrant flowers. The windows had carved lattice-work covering them that allowed something of a breeze to come through but blocked out much of the light and heat of the day.

"Greetings, Your Highness," said an unfamiliar feminine voice in Keshiaari, and I looked away from the window to see a tall woman in the off-white clothing of a servant, just as the ambassador had described, standing outside a doorway that must lead to the inner rooms of the suite. She was tall, and rather forbidding in appearance, with her long, strong nose and equally pronounced chin. Her brows were thick and black, and pulled together somewhat as she surveyed me. "I am Miram, the keeper of your chambers and your person."

That was what she said, but my mind translated it as "maid," or perhaps a combination of chatelaine and lady's maid. "Greetings, Miram," I replied.

She clasped her long hands together at her waist and bowed. "Your things have been brought hence already, Your Highness. Perhaps if you would wish to survey your rooms, to see if they are to your liking?"

And if they are not? I thought, with a wry twist of my lips, one which I fought to hide. But I merely said, "That would be very good, Miram. Thank you."

Her mouth tightened almost imperceptibly, although I could not quite decide what I had said to provoke her disapproval. Was I not supposed to thank her? Quickly I wracked my brains, trying to recall what Ambassador Sel-Trelazar had told me about exchanges with the servants, but in that moment I could not remember what he had said.

"This way, Your Highness," she said, spreading her hand to indicate the rooms beyond her.

Chin high, I advanced into the sanctum, seeing more mosaics on the ceiling, although the frescoes here were less geometric and instead painted in the shapes of stylized flowers that twined in and around one another. This was quite obviously a sitting room, furnished with several silk-upholstered divans, and with rugs patterned in shades of blue and rust and soft green on the floor. I noted there was no fireplace—not that surprising, if it was this warm already in early May. Beyond that I spied a sumptuous bedchamber with a large bed covered in soft terra-cotta-colored silk and hung with gauzy drapes of the same color.

I also noted my own serving women in there, unpacking my wardrobe and bustling about, and I felt my spirits lift somewhat. So they had been brought here. I had no idea why I would ever think otherwise, but perhaps it was merely my weariness and discomfort at being in a strange place. Even though I did not know them well, at least they were a small piece of home, one I still had with me.

"As you see, all is being taken care of," Miram informed me. "Tonight His Most High Majesty, may God praise his name, is holding a great feast in your honor. We must lose no time in preparing you."

"Indeed?" I said in some surprise. Not that I was any stranger to spending hours and hours getting ready for the banquets and balls and musicales back home, but as I thought it could not be much more than one or two in the afternoon, I had a hard time imagining exactly what they had in mind for me.

"Indeed, Your Highness. We must begin right away." She clapped her hands then, and three young Keshiaari women came out of one of the side chambers, their embroidered slippers slapping on the marble floor. "Guide Her Highness to the bath chamber, and begin getting her ready for the feast."

They all bowed, hands pressed together at the waist, and then pointed toward the bedchamber. I knew there was little

I could do to decline, and so I followed them into the room where I would sleep, and then past that to an elegant tiled room where an enormous tub had been built right into the floor, with steps leading down. It had already been filled with water—I did not want to think what a monumental task that had been—and scented with rose petals.

Light hands plucked at my garments, peeling them away one by one. As I had had my own maid attend me ever since I was a child, I was not overly modest about allowing women servants to see me undressed, although it did feel strange to do so in front of a group of girls I had just met. I quickly moved to the tub and descended the steps into the water, feeling it soft and warm around me, only a few degrees warmer than the air itself. To my surprise, the servant girls peeled off their own clothing as well, save the thin blouses they wore under their tunics, and came into the water with me, each one taking a limb and scrubbing it well, as if I had brought something of the stink of the ship's confined quarters with me. Perhaps I had; once I got over the shock of the situation, it did feel rather good to have them use soft brushes on my arms and neck and legs, and to wash my hair not once, not twice, but three times with some sort of foaming concoction that smelled of a sweet spice I could not identify.

During all this, I saw nothing of my own maids, and guessed that Miram had instructed them to stay occupied with the disposition of my wardrobe, for whatever reason. After I climbed out of the tub and was dried off from head to toe, soft rose-scented lotion was rubbed into every inch of my skin, and one of the maids handed me a robe of soft, shimmering red silk. Thankful, I took it from her and wrapped it around myself, then sat down at a dressing table and had my hair polished with silk until it gleamed like glass. Two of the maids pulled some strands back from my face and coiled them into a knot at the back of my head, but they left the rest of it to hang down as it was. I saw no sign of a curling iron, and was glad, for I had always hated the interminable sessions of winding my hair around the iron, attempting to torture my stick-straight hair into the long spirals currently in fashion at court.

But that was certainly not the end of the preparations. My nails were stained with some sort of red paste, which was also applied to my lips, and the outlines of my eyes traced with black powder. Finally, it was time to get dressed, this time in the most sumptuous of the costumes I'd had made back in Sirlende, of shimmering silk patterned in red and gold, with embroidery of gold and pearls around the neckline and the cuffs of the short sleeves. Underneath was a light shirt of sheer linen, and the usual billowy trousers in a muted shade of red.

I had thought they would bring my own jewels, but Miram brought forth a carved wooden box and opened it, saying, "A gift from His Most High Majesty."

Certainly I was no stranger to fine jewels, but I couldn't help letting out a small gasp as I gazed down at the wondrous pieces held within that chest. How he had known I would be wearing gold and red, I had no idea, but gleaming within was a necklace of finely worked gold and enamel, set with hundreds of faceted garnets and tiny pearls, with matching earrings and bracelets and an exquisite piece that sat on top of my head and had a teardrop-shaped garnet that hung directly in the center of my brow.

And rings of gold and garnet for my fingers, and even for my toes, as the footwear they brought me was not the flat embroidered slippers I had expected to wear, but sandals of gilded and woven leather that slipped between my toes and fastened around my ankles. It felt odd, to have my feet exposed in such a way, but I had to admit that it made sense here in the sheltered confines of the palace, especially when one considered how warm it was.

At last I was arrayed to Miram's satisfaction, and realized that somewhere in all that time the bright heat of the day had gradually dwindled to a warm lavender-tinted twilight. I also realized that I had been so caught up in all the fuss, I had not stopped to wonder where my intended husband was in all this. Of course I had expected to be provided with my own chambers, at least until we were wed, but I would have thought that he'd come to greet me. Or was I not of that much importance, just something else to be fitted in somewhere during his schedule for the day? But this feast was supposedly in my honor....

I shook my head, and heard the dangling jewels of my headdress jingle faintly. "Am I not to meet my affianced husband before the festivities begin?"

Miram's brows drew together. "That is not the custom, Your Highness. He will see you tonight, at the feast, and then you will be married."

"I—what?" I gasped. Not that I had expected a lengthy betrothal, of course, especially after the Hierarch had already waited several months for me to come here. But tonight? I felt a flare of anger toward Ambassador Sel-Trelazar in that moment. He should have told me this was what would take place. For whatever reason, though, he had said little of what would actually happen to me once I arrived at the palace, instead instructing me on the foods of his land, the celebrations and festivals, the way everything would come to a halt in the palace every day at precisely nine in the morning, as that was the time legend said their god had sprung from the sands of the desert, and given his blessing upon the people of Keshiaar.

"Yes," she said, her tone implacable. "And now it is time to go. His Most High Majesty will not be pleased if you are late to your own feast."

She clapped her hands again, and the maids helped me to my feet, performing small adjustments to the fall of my tunic, the placement of my headdress. At last she gave a stern nod, and guided me from the bath/dressing chamber out to the sitting room, and then the foyer. The guards standing duty snapped to attention. Through some unspoken exchange, they seemed to know what to do, for they opened the door, allowing me to step out, then shut it behind them. Clearly Miram's duties had been discharged, and she would remain in my chambers.

"Your Highness," one of the guards said, pointing a gloved finger down the corridor.

I had the absent thought that he must be terribly warm in that quilted tunic and those gloves. However, I knew better than to ask.

Lifting my head, I walked serenely in the direction he had indicated, striding forward to the feast.

To my husband.

CHAPTER FIVE

The great banquet hall was on the ground floor of the palace, an enormous chamber that surely could seat five hundred—at least, it appeared that many were in attendance. There were a great many doors, so that they could be opened to catch the evening breeze as necessary, and I realized that was why there were no candles that might be blown out by such drafts, but oil lamps of glass suspended from bronze fixtures overhead.

I wished I could look about more, but I knew to stare would be considered provincial at best. I only caught a confused glimpse of men in high-necked robes and women in garments similar to mine, all of them dark-haired and dark-eyed like me, but with skin several shades darker. I was glad to see the women there, for I think some part of me feared that they would be excluded from this occasion as they were from so many other public events. But perhaps a banquet in the palace was not deemed "public," and therefore was not off-limits. Even so, I could not help but note that the men and women did not sit side by side, as they would at a banquet in my homeland, but were strictly segregated, the women seated on the left of the hall, the men on the right.

As the guards paused just inside a door near the head of the hall, I saw a tall, somewhat thick-set man, probably of an age with Ambassador Sel-Trelazar, although with a fuller beard that already showed a good deal of grey, come forth and bow deeply from the waist, hands clasped together.

"Your Highness, you honor us with your presence. I am Azeer Tel-Karinoor, His Most High Majesty's *visanis*—what in your homeland you would call a chancellor."

"And you honor me with your name," I replied, glad that, despite my current rather agitated state, I had not forgotten that simple courtesy.

He bowed again. "Your Highness, allow me to guide you to your place at the high table."

I smiled my thank-you, following him as he led me from under the colonnaded perimeter of the hall to a grand table on a dais. Despite its size, there were only two places set there.

Oh, gods. So it would only be the two of us, this promised husband of mine and I, on display for all to see? Well, I had spent my entire life on such public display, although in Sirlende at least we shared the imperial table with other high-ranking members of the household, or noble and honored guests.

"You will stand until His Most High Majesty enters and invites you to sit," Azeer murmured in my ear, and I gave a tiny nod of acknowledgment, grateful that he had offered me that much guidance.

But what a strain it was to stand there in front of everyone, to have all those unfamiliar eyes upon me, some curious, some faintly hostile—mainly from the women, and I guessed it was because they would rather have had one of their own standing here, and not a foreign princess.

And having one of your own turned out so very well last time, I thought, compressing my lips so I would not allow myself an ironic smile.

Then a murmur seemed to spread through the crowd, and I saw everyone rising to their feet from the carved and gilded chairs in which they sat, bowing, hands clasped before them, as a tall man clad in black entered through the back of the hall.

Because the dais where I stood was raised some two feet higher than the rest of the hall, and because all those in attendance were currently bent more or less double, I could see him clearly, my gaze traveling the length of that enormous room and fixing on his face.

Oh, as handsome as he had been in that portrait, the unknown artist who had painted it had done him no great service, for he was so very much more striking in person, with high, sharp cheekbones, a sensual mouth and fine chin, and thick black hair waving back from his noble brow. From that distance I could not make out the color of his eyes, but that hardly mattered. He was still so much more than I had imagined, as I had not dared hope he could even match that portrait, let alone outshine it so decidedly.

Somehow my legs managed to keep holding me up, even though my knees at that moment felt very much like jelly. I stood straight, chin high, knowing I was there to represent Sirlende, and so could show no sign of weakness—no sign that the very sight of him somehow seemed to heat the blood within my veins.

He approached, expression solemn, no smile of greeting. I could not begin to guess whether this was the custom, or whether something about me had displeased him. Perhaps the junior ambassador, Amil Nel-Karisoor, had been too effusive in his praise of my beauty. If he had, there was certainly nothing I could do about it now—and neither could the Hierarch himself, as he was the one who had extended the offer of marriage in the first place, and to refuse me now would cause such an insult that relations between the two empires would be forever strained.

These thoughts passed through my mind as the Hierarch made his progression through the chamber, and I fought to keep my expression cool and serene. I could not let him see how nervous I was, how much I feared that he would not find me pleasing. To have given up my homeland, hurt the man who had hoped to marry me, and traveled a thousand miles for nothing? No, I could not allow myself to even contemplate that possibility.

At length the Hierarch ascended the dais and stood next to me, then surprised me by bowing. Caught off guard, I curtseyed, then hoped I had not offended him by responding in the manner of my own land, and not his.

"Lyarris Deveras," he said quietly, then took my hand and raised it briefly to his lips. Just that tiny brush of his mouth against my flesh was enough to send shivers running down my spine, despite the lingering heat in the chamber, where it felt as if very little of the day's warmth had yet abated, despite all those doors opened to let in the evening breezes. When he raised his head and his gaze met mine, I saw that his eyes truly were amber, striking against the heavy black lashes and the straight dark brows. He continued, in perfect Sirlendian, "Truly, my ambassador did not have sufficient words to describe your beauty. I owe Sirlende a very great debt, for it has sent its greatest jewel to me."

They could have been empty words of flattery, but in that moment I did not care. It was enough to hear his praise, uttered in the words of my homeland. I did not know why I should be surprised that he could speak Sirlendian. After all, Ambassador Sel-Trelazar had said his ruler was a man of great learning.

Finding my voice, I replied in the Keshiaari tongue, "And Sirlende is equally in Keshiaar's debt, for allowing Your Most High Majesty to be bound to one of its daughters."

The amber eyes danced a little. "Beautiful and learned? That was far more than I had dared hope for, but it seems God has pitied His humble servant and has sent him the perfect bride. Please, my lady, sit, and take your ease."

I did as he requested, glad of the chance to sit down, and a second or two later he followed suit, settling himself in a throne-like chair, of which mine was a slightly smaller replica. Throughout our exchange, the assembled company had remained standing, and bowed at the waist—I hoped there was no one with a bad back among them—but after the Hierarch had seated himself, they appeared to take that as the signal to resume their own seats.

At once a pair of servants stepped forth from the shadows, each carrying a gold-plated pitcher set with onyx and jasper. The serving man poured a measure of wine into the Hierarch's goblet, then waited as his ruler took a sip and finally nodded. Next to me, the serving woman stepped forward and poured for me as well, and then in unison they stepped back off the dais and disappeared behind a carved wooden screen, perhaps set there to conceal the passageway into the kitchens.

The Hierarch lifted his goblet toward me, and I grasped mine and raised it toward him as well. This much at least was not that different from the sort of toast we might offer back in Sirlende.

"To my lady bride," he said, his voice not loud, but carrying through the hall, as everyone had remained silent even after they were seated. "And to our most beneficent union with the great empire of Sirlende!"

He clinked his goblet against mine, afterward drinking of its contents. I echoed his movements, and took a swallow of the wine. It was cool, perhaps kept in a storeroom underground so it should not grow too warm, and spicier than the wine of my homeland, dark underneath, rich and heady. I warned myself to be careful and not drink too deeply of it, for I feared the combination of the wine and the heat could prove to be my undoing.

All throughout the hall, everyone lifted their goblets and toasted us as well. That seemed to be the signal for the feast itself to begin, as at once servants began hurrying in from all directions, carrying heavy platters and bowls all in beaten silver and gold, and set with semi-precious stones. Truly, I had always known that Keshiaar was a rich kingdom, but now, looking upon the casual use of such costly materials, I began to realize what that meant.

The food was rich and varied and strange, but as Ambassador Sel-Trelazar had instructed me somewhat in the popular dishes of his homeland, I had something of an idea what to expect—roasted lamb and beef, sharply seasoned and tasting of garlic, the vegetables roasted as well, a small white grain called rice that we did not have in Sirlende. In truth, everything I tasted seemed pleasing enough to the palate, once I had grown a bit more accustomed to the unusual combinations of seasonings, so unlike what I was used to.

Beside me, the Hierarch ate as well, but I noticed he watched me as I consumed my meal with no hesitation, no raised eyebrows at what had been set before me. "You have had Keshiaari food before?" he inquired, setting down his gold-plated fork so he might drink some more wine.

"No, Your Majesty, but your ambassador described it very well to me, so I might have some idea of what to expect. It is all quite delicious."

"I am glad you think so. And your chambers—you find them adequate?"

"More than adequate, Your Majesty. All possible comforts have been seen to, and Miram seems wonderfully capable."

He ran his finger over the edge of the goblet he held, then nodded. "I am pleased to hear that. I do apologize if all this took you aback" —a gesture toward the company with his free hand— "but it is our custom for a husband to not look upon his wife until the wedding feast."

I did think it odd that the feast should come first, and the ceremony afterward, but of course I would not say such a thing to him. Neither would I comment on the strangeness of not even looking upon one's future spouse until the day of the wedding. In some ways, perhaps that was best, if the marriage was arranged anyway; it certainly gave the parties involved far less time to back out of the arrangement. But I only smiled at him, saying, "Your Majesty, no apologies are necessary. I am the stranger here, and will follow your traditions to the best of my ability."

In answer, he smiled as well, and I saw how that expression illumined his face, bringing light to his extraordinary eyes. My heart gave an odd little thump when I saw how he looked upon me, and I could not believe my good fortune, that not only was he handsome and well-spoken, but kind and gentle as well. I began to hope that perhaps I truly had done the right thing in coming here. No one at court had questioned my breaking off my engagement with Lord Sorthannic, for the majority of them were cool and calculating at heart, thinking continually of how they might advance their own positions, and so jilting a mere duke so I might wed an emperor made perfect sense to them. But I had tasked myself for it, even as I knew I had done the right thing, for I hated to think of how such an abandonment must have hurt the man I truly had thought I loved.

Now, though, I felt my pulse race in a way it never had with Thani, and the blood rose to my cheeks as I hurriedly reached over to take another sip of wine and so hide my confusion. Whether the subterfuge was effective, I could not say, for the Hierarch replied to my comment by murmuring, "Nevertheless, I know it is not your custom, and perhaps was something of a shock. But I am very pleased to see you managing so well."

And what would you have done if I did not? I wondered. Thank goodness for the privacy of one's own thoughts, for I could ponder such a thing in one second and in the next say in a jesting tone of voice, "All the same, Your Majesty, I do hope there are not too many more surprises awaiting me this evening."

He did not respond in kind, however. The light in his eyes dimmed, and he answered coolly, "Not too many, I think," before turning back to his neglected meal.

Oh, dear. It seemed I had mistaken his easy manner for true friendliness…or perhaps I had offended him. I knew him not at all, and so I could not guess which was the case, or whether his response stemmed from some other source altogether. But as I could not take back my words, I followed his example and picked up my own fork, then forced myself to eat a few mouthfuls, although my appetite seemed to have deserted me. Even with that, I made sure my expression remained serene and pleasant. Luckily, that was a skill I had perfected over the years. No matter what might be roiling one's thoughts at any given time, a princess of the imperial house knew better than to let those thoughts be reflected in her countenance.

And after this there was still the wedding, and after that....

My stomach clenched. I had not led so sheltered a life that I did not know what generally occurred on one's wedding night. Could I allow this cold-voiced stranger to take me in such a way, no matter how handsome I had originally thought him? But I must. It was what I had agreed to, after all…to be his wife, and one day to bear his children. It was what every ruler required of his consort, so the line might be continued to the next generation.

"…anything else?" the Hierarch was inquiring, and I jumped slightly.

"Your Majesty?" I asked in reply, for I had been so preoccupied I quite missed the first part of his question.

"I was merely inquiring whether you wanted anything else of this course, or whether the servant might take your plate."

"Oh…I am quite finished. Thank you."

The smallest wave of his hand, and the serving girl hurried forth and removed my plate, then set a new, smaller one in its place. I supposed I should have been expecting there to be another course, as our feasts back in Sirlende generally had at least four or five. What startled me, though, was that the servants brought out what was clearly intended to be dessert, some kind of flat cake drizzled with honey, and fruit, the concoction topped with chopped greenish nuts and more honey.

The Hierarch must have noticed my surprise, for he said, "We do not sit at table for hours the way you do in Sirlende. One course for all the main dishes, and one for dessert. It may take some getting used to."

"No, that is very well, Your Majesty. I must confess that sitting and waiting for all those courses to be brought in and then taken away could become rather tedious."

This time he appeared to approve of what I had said, for he nodded, and a corner of his mouth lifted slightly. "I am glad to hear that. I did not want you to think us provincial or less...sophisticated...because of that difference."

"Not at all," I said stoutly. Would I have told him the truth if I had not felt that way? I did not know. I only knew that, even in our short acquaintance, I did not want to do or say anything that displeased him, and such behavior was most unlike me. Not, of course, that mine was a disagreeable disposition, but neither had I ever lacked the spirit to stand up for myself when necessary. Perhaps it was merely a wish to avoid any further friction between us on this, our wedding night.

Wedding night....

I forced myself to attend to the desserts the servant girl had brought me, and the Hierarch did the same with what had been set before him. Even making myself eat slowly, and savoring every bite, it seemed I was done far sooner than I had hoped. I had thought to draw out our time at the feast, to postpone the inevitable. Foolish of me, I knew. I could not stop what was coming at the end of this night, no matter what I did.

And, sure enough, the servants came forth once again, this time to remove our empty dessert plates. They did not refill our goblets, which told me we truly had come to the end of the feast. I had drunk sparingly, and now I wished I had not been so careful. Perhaps it would have been better for me to be tipsy and lightheaded, and not so fearful of what was to happen next.

The Hierarch got to his feet, then extended a hand to me. I took it and rose from my seat, noting dimly as I did so that everyone in the hall had stood as well, that they not remain sitting in the presence of their ruler. "It is time, my lady."

I could but nod.

Still holding my hand in his warm, strong fingers, he led me down from the dais and through the watching throng. At least I was able to hold my head high as I passed among them and then out through one of the doors, which led us to yet another colonnade. The night air was warm against my skin, redolent of some sweet, spicy bloom I could not identify.

We passed through a garden planted with low hedges and shrubs, where yet another fountain splashed under the light of the two moons, Taleron nearly full and, high overhead, Calendir a faint crescent just peeking over the roof of the domed building we now approached. Behind me I could hear the crunch of gravel and the low murmur of voices as those attending the feast followed us to our destination.

It was a lofty building that stood on its own, unlike the rest of the palace, whose wings all seemed to be connected by covered walkways and corridors. Tall, slender trees stood sentinel at the entrance, and the doors were standing open, so I could see all within was illuminated by more oil lamps, glowing like jewels with their glass housings of blue and red and green and gold.

"This is the temple of our God," the Hierarch said quietly, his voice pitched low for my ears alone. "I promise you, my lady, that nothing fearsome awaits you. Here, our customs are not so very different from yours. I will prompt you for your responses, and you will make your replies."

I nodded, then said, "Your Majesty, one question." For it was something that had been preying on my mind ever since I had learned that tonight would also be my wedding night.

To my relief, he did not look impatient, or annoyed. "Only one?"

"Yes, just the one," I replied, and smiled despite everything. "Why is it that Ambassador Sel-Trelazar did not tell me of all this? Surely it would have been helpful for me to know in advance what to expect."

"Because it is not our way to speak of such things to outsiders, and to utter the words of our rites outside the borders of our land. You are here now, and will soon be bound to me, and so now at last I may speak. But the ambassador was not at liberty to do so."

I knew I must be content with that, even if I did not completely understand. "Thank you, my lord," I told him.

To my surprise, he turned the hand he held so my palm faced upward, then bent and kissed the sensitive flesh there. A not-unwelcome shiver passed through me, and I found myself gazing up into his face, searching his expression for some indication of what he might be thinking. Not very much luck there, unfortunately, for he obviously had suffered the same training as I, to keep his emotions safely hidden from the observations of others. But at least his touch on my hand was reassuring, and whatever had spurred his coolness back in the banquet hall seemed to have gone for now.

"It is time to go in," he said then. "I will not ask if you are ready, for of course you do not know what to expect, but at least you can say that you will come with me now."

"I will," I replied, even as that shivery sensation of not-quite anticipation passed over me. "And I am ready, my lord. This is what I traveled a thousand miles to do."

The light returned to his eyes, or perhaps it was only a reflection from the gleaming moon overhead. "So it is, my princess. Let us go inside, then."

His fingers tightened around mine, and he led me inside, where the illumination from all those lamps flickered over the mosaics, these ones gleaming not just with red and blue and green, but gold and copper and silver as well. A great altar of carved marble was set against the far wall, and on it sat more oil lamps, only these were made of what seemed to be gold. The air was filled with an intoxicating scent, one I had never smelled before, at once spicy and musky, so thick it seemed to make my head swim.

What I noticed at once, however, despite my current lightheaded state, was that there were no statues, no fig-ures of their god, to be seen anywhere. It was not thus in our own temple of Minauth, where the likeness of the god presided over all our ceremonies. And I recalled that, even as the Keshiaari people would not speak the name of their god, neither would they create any image of him, for to do such a thing was considered a great blasphemy.

From a hidden chamber behind the altar, three priests clad in long red robes appeared. Wrappings of gold cloth hid their faces, so I had no idea whether they were young or old. Dark eyes gleamed in the reflected light of the oil lamps.

"Approach," the one in the middle said in the Keshiaari tongue.

Up until that moment, the Hierarch and I had conversed in my own language—to put me more at ease, I was sure—but I knew I could not expect such an accommodation from the priests in their own temple. Nervous as I was, I thought I could still manage, as long as their utterances did not grow too complex.

Hand still holding mine, the Hierarch brought me to the altar. Behind us, the large open space began to fill with people, although I guessed barely half of those who had attended the feast could fit into the temple. I wondered how they had determined who would enter and who would stay outside. That decision had to have been based on their rank somehow, although precisely how that worked in a land of a hundred princes and no barons or dukes, I had no idea.

And then I told myself that certainly I had more important things to occupy me at that moment.

"Who gives this woman to His Most High Majesty, to be his helpmate, to be the mother of his children, so that the holy line of Kel-Alisaad may not disappear from the earth?"

To my surprise, I saw Ambassador Sel-Trelazar emerge from the crowd. He raised a palm to his forehead, then bowed and said, "I do, acting on behalf of her brother, His Majesty Torric Deveras, Emperor of Sirlende."

"And do you have the *marqat?*"

That last word defeated me, as I could not recall hearing it before. But as Sel-Trelazar came to the altar and laid a heavy piece of parchment upon it, I realized it must have been some kind of marriage contract that my brother had signed before I departed for Keshiaar. This did not surprise me overmuch, as the dispensation of a crown princess was by necessity accompanied by a good deal more paperwork than the joining of a factory worker and a flower-seller.

One of the other priests handed the high priest—for I had begun to call him such in my mind, even though I did not know his true title—a long black quill, which he in turn extended toward me. "You will sign now, showing that you enter into this union through your own free will."

I took the pen from him, and, after a brief encouraging nod from the Hierarch, I bent over the parchment and signed my name directly above the place where I now saw my brother's familiar heavy signature. Then the Hierarch took up the quill and signed as well, in the beautiful slanting script of his homeland, an alphabet I still had yet to completely master. Speaking that tongue had proved to be far easier than writing it.

"The union is now recognized by God. Speak the words of the final binding," the high priest intoned.

The Hierarch reached out and took both my hands in his, holding them so they were face up, while his palms rested lightly against mine. "I take you now, Lyarris Deveras, to be my wife in the eyes of God, to protect and succor you, and be your helpmate until I am one with God. So be it." He inclined his head toward me then, eyes intent on mine.

It seemed I was now required to speak the same words. I gathered my breath and concentrated on recalling not just the Keshiaari words he had just uttered, but the correct pronunciation as well. It would never do to falter here, to sully this most important of moments. "I take you now, Beshalim Kel-Alisaad, to be my husband in the eyes of God, to protect and succor you, and be your helpmate until I am one with God. So be it."

From the way he gazed upon me and smiled ever so slightly, it appeared I had acquitted myself well enough. I realized then this was the first time I had said his name aloud.

Would he kiss me? That was how such a ceremony ended in Sirlende, but I was a thousand miles from home, and I did not know what to expect. But then he bent and pressed his mouth first to one of my palms, then the other. When he was done, he raised his own hands so the palms faced skyward, and I followed suit, feeling his warm skin against my lips, and breathing in the faint spicy scent of his skin, not dissimilar from the incense that filled the air around us.

And at last he leaned down and touched my mouth with his, gently, with such a light brush of lip against lip that I might have imagined it. But no, the heat that went through me at even such a whisper of a touch was enough to tell me that kiss had been very real…and that I wanted more, wanted him to pull me into his arms so we might press against one another, taste the sweetness of one another's mouths.

Such a notion was madness, of course, for I would never engage in that kind of behavior in such a public place. Had he felt it, though, felt the desire flicker along my veins like a spark catching a nest of kindling? And had he experienced that desire as well?

From his reaction, I would have to say not. He straightened, standing tall and proud, and turned away from me to the crowd of onlookers, who had remained silent all this time.

"I give you my new consort, Lyarris Kel-Alisaad!"

Still they did not cheer, but almost as one pressed their hands together and bowed. The silence seemed to pound against my ears, as such a moment back in Sirlende would have been attended by a great deal of clapping and crying aloud of well-wishes. Since my husband did not seem discomfited by his subjects' lack of a vocal response, I decided this must be the custom here. Truth be told, I was still feeling the after-effects of that kiss, a tingling on my lips, a warm thrumming in my breast, and so perhaps I was not thinking clearly.

"Come," he said, taking me by the hand and leading me out of the temple, out into the warm night, where the two moons smiled down upon us, and the scents of night-blooming flowers seemed to follow us wherever we went. Also following us were some twenty of the crimson-robed guards, but I attempted to pretend they were not there. My footsteps had not been so dogged back home, and while I did not like the custom, I understood it. A ruler must be protected at all times, even within the sanctuary of his own palace grounds.

I did not know the building at all yet, and so as we walked down one colonnade and entered the palace, then ascended a great marble stairway, nothing looked familiar to me. It was not until we traversed a long corridor that terminated in a pair of pale wood doors carved with stylized leaves and flowers and birds that I realized the Hierarch had brought me to my own suite.

"But—" I began, then stopped myself. Surely I could not be so bold as to ask why my new husband had brought me to my chambers rather than his.

"But?" he repeated, only this time in Sirlendian. "These are your rooms, are they not?"

Mutely, I nodded.

His brows drew together. "Is it that you do not care for them? I doubt anything can be done at this late hour, but tomorrow—"

"Oh, no," I broke in. "My suite is everything I could have hoped for, and more. It is only…." And I let the words trail off into silence, for I found I did not have the courage to give voice to my concerns.

"Only?"

He did not want me. That was plain enough, for what other reason could there be for a man to abandon his wife on their wedding night? Never would I utter such thoughts, however. I possessed more pride than that.

Since he stood there, frowning slightly, clearly expecting an answer, I hastened to say, "Only—I am surprised that this is the end of the evening. Back in Sirlende, when my brother the Emperor married his bride, we danced until dawn."

A flicker of understanding passed over the Hierarch's face. "Ah, of course. Perhaps I should have warned you. We do not dance here in Keshiaar. That is, we have dancers who perform for us, at certain ceremonies and celebrations, but dancing as you have it in Sirlende, with men and women together—" He broke off, and shook his head. "It is not done."

"Oh," I said, for that was the only syllable I could muster. No dancing? I foresaw a number of grim evenings stretching out before me, with not even the simple pleasures of a ball to distract me from the realization that I had bound myself in a loveless marriage. A certain tightness seized my throat, one I knew would lead to tears if I did not take hold of myself now. I breathed in, and continued, "I understand, my lord. Thank you for explaining these matters to me." I was all too aware of the watching eyes of the guards, even though they had stopped several paces away, as if to give us a false sense of privacy.

"It is nothing. I should have said something earlier. But now, my lady, as it is late, I will leave you here so that you may rest."

"Yes, it is very late," I agreed, glad to seize upon that excuse to remove myself from his presence. "I will bid you good night now."

"Good night," he echoed, and I reached out to push open the door.

No sooner had I touched it than Miram opened it from the inside, bowing almost double at the sight of her Hierarch.

Without saying a word, I moved past her and into the antechamber, and after another bow, she closed the door behind me. Her dark eyes were curious, but she only bowed to me as well, and said, "Your Majesty."

No longer "Your Highness." I had the title, even if I had only a husband in name.

And with that thought it all became too much. I hurried on into the bedchamber and hurled the doors shut behind me, then threw myself on the bed and wept, sobbing for the love I had foolishly thrown away, and the world I had given up.

All was ruin, for the Hierarch desired only my connections. He did not want me.

CHAPTER SIX

What my attendants—both the women I had brought with me, and those provided by the Hierarch—thought of my breakdown of the night before, I had no idea, as they were far too well-trained to ever comment on the behavior of their betters. I could not precisely say that the world looked any more promising the next morning, for I still felt very low. However, I did know that sitting in my chambers and weeping over my lot would do me no good, and so I told myself I had best put my disappointment aside and come to terms with my new life, even if it was not the life I had envisioned.

And what precisely had I envisioned? I did not know for certain, save that I had hoped the Hierarch and I might find some harmony in our shared interests of learning and books. That clearly had been a silly dream, for if I had discovered only one thing in my short time here, it was that a woman's mind held very little value in Keshiaar.

It came to me then that most likely an outsider would see nothing amiss in my current situation, for even in Sirlende it was the custom for the Emperor and his consort to have separate suites. Indeed, Ashara had caused quite the little scandal when she declared that she wanted no rooms of her own, and would happily share my brother's chambers. My mother had declared it to be a clear indication of Ashara's inferior breeding, and the gossips had quite the time with my sister-in-law's declaration, until some other peccadillo claimed their attention. No, if I had not cried myself to sleep the night before, there would have been no indication that all was not precisely as I had expected it to be.

I doubted that Miram was a gossip, as she seemed far too reserved and cold for such behavior, and I did not know the other girls well enough to say for sure whether they had loose tongues. If my secret got out, then so be it. And what was I guilty of, really, save wishing to be a true wife to the Hierarch?

As that thought crossed my mind, I realized he had never invited me to call him by his name. I might be his wife, but apparently he intended to deny me even that intimacy.

The tears threatened again, and I forced them away as I went to the window and gazed out at the gardens, the bright blooms seeming to wilt under the force of that alien sun. Oh, if only it wasn't so horribly hot! It was not yet noon, and already my room felt stifling. The heat was a presence of its own, a weight that seemed to press against my head and chest. It felt as if I could not think clearly in those oppressive conditions. But there would be no relief, not for months and months, until the rains came in the winter.

"Majesty," said one of the Keshiaari girls, whose name I did not know, as she approached me where I stood at the window. She extended to me a silver goblet with garnets encrusted in the base.

I gazed at it in wonder, for I could tell it must be cool; moisture gleamed along the engraved surface. Reaching out, I took the goblet from her, felt the welcome chill of it against my overheated flesh. I sipped, and realized it was only water, but water with real ice floating in it. How in the world could they manage such a thing, when all around was so terribly hot and dry?

My puzzlement must have shown in my face, for she bowed and said, "Majesty, a day's run from here is a high mountain, Mount Teldashir. Snow and ice linger there until midsummer. Runners fetch the ice and bring it here, packed in straw so it will not melt. His Most High Majesty feared you might be feeling the heat, and so he asked that this ice water be brought to you."

A warmth that had nothing to do with the heat of the day flooded through me. Surely if he were truly indifferent, he would not have thought of my discomfort and sought to provide some means to assuage it.

I smiled at the girl and said, "Please send word that I am most grateful...." It seemed unkind of me not to ask her name, and so I said, "What do you call yourself?"

Her dark eyes widened. It seemed clear enough that she hadn't thought I would care about such a thing. "I am Lila, Your Majesty."

"Thank you, Lila. Please make sure that His Most High Majesty knows how grateful I am for his thoughtfulness."

She bowed again, then backed away and went out into the sitting room. Of course she would not be the one to directly pass on that message—she would most likely give it to Miram, who would deliver it to whoever acted as seneschal here, and then that august personage would finally present it to the Hierarch.

No. To Besh. I would call him that in my mind, even if he had not given me leave to do so in person.

I hoped then that he would never learn of my tears on our wedding night. How foolish of me to jump to the worst possible conclusion, when it was far more reasonable to think that he had allowed me to sleep alone so I might grow accustomed to the notion of being his wife. After all, we would have many years to share together, and forcing everything on me in that one night would have been rather shortsighted.

Then again, having seen him and conversed with him, felt his lips touch mine, I was not so averse to the idea of performing my wifely duties as I might have been even a day earlier. He could have had no way of knowing that, however. No, Besh would have only seen a woman in a new and foreign land, being asked to share the bed of someone who was next to a stranger to her. And because he was perceptive and intelligent, he had chosen to give me time to grow accustomed to the idea, so that we might come together in mutual desire one day in the future.

It was with that pleasant thought in mind that I gazed out the window again, taking measured sips of the iced water so it might last long enough to provide relief for a goodly amount of time, but not so long that all the ice should melt before I was done. As I did so, I noticed a building on the far side of the complex, somewhat set away from the palace proper, with a great golden domed roof and no windows that I could see. Puzzled, I watched it for some time, noting that it seemed to be still and quiet, with no one coming and going from it.

After finishing my water, I made my way to the sitting room, where Lila sat near one of the windows there and embroidered an intricate design of leaves and flowers onto a band of pale gold silk, using golden thread. I had no doubt the lovely piece would eventually make its way onto a new garment for me, for truly, what did all these attendants have to do with their time when they were not preparing me for a feast or some other public event? Again I wondered at having eight women assigned to me. Perhaps sometime in the future I could persuade Besh that I really did not need so many in my personal service.

In the meantime, though, I knew I would have to endure their presence, unwelcome as it might be. Lila seemed like a sweet girl, and so I would not ask her to be reassigned, but the other two young women seemed to take their cues from Miram, and were wary and quiet. Even upon my brief acquaintance with them, I could not say I enjoyed having them around.

Luckily, though, they were not in evidence at the moment, although I thought I caught the quiet murmur of their voices from the bath chamber, where perhaps they were cleaning. I approached Lila, and she started, then bolted to her feet. "Your Majesty," she said at once.

"Everything is fine, Lila," I told her. "Your embroidery is very beautiful."

She bowed, stammering, "Th-thank you, Your Majesty."

"I was wondering, though—what is that domed building on the far side of the compound? It seems very grand, and yet I saw no one going in or out."

"Oh, that, Your Majesty, is His Most High Majesty's observatory."

I did not understand the Keshiaari word, and so asked, "His what?"

"His…place where he goes to look at the stars." Her dark eyes were quiet, speculative, as if she were just realizing that my command of the language was not yet perfect. "With his…looking glass, I think you would call it, Your Majesty. A metal tube with pieces of glass. I do not know much more about it, I fear."

She looked a bit worried as she said that last, as if I would take her to task for her ignorance. Quite the opposite, for she had just provided me with a very valuable piece of information.

At least I would have something to discuss with Besh at dinner that evening.

It was a much smaller affair than the grand feast of the night before, this meal held in a more intimate chamber with perhaps thirty of his most favored family members and subjects in attendance. I must confess that I could not keep track of all their names, especially with so many princes and princesses and not a single duke or baroness or earl, although I did at least recognize Azeer Tel-Karinoor, the visanis, or chancellor. But there was no mention of a mother, or siblings, during all those introductions, and I wondered if Besh lacked any immediate family. Surely if he had any, I would have met them the day before, when we were wed. How terrible for him to go through that great trial with his former wife with not even a brother or sister to provide support!

He, however, gave no indication of being troubled by such a lack, and his expression was serene enough as I took my place next to him at the table. Here there was no dais, but the two of us still sat alone and separate at a long table while the other guests were seated at a series of low, round tables, men on one side of the room, women on the other. As before, they remained standing until Besh and I took our own chairs, but otherwise the feeling was far less formal. In one corner, a young man sat playing a stringed instrument I did not recognize, producing soft, delicate notes in a minor key.

I waited until we had been served and the wine poured before saying in the Keshiaari tongue, "I saw your observatory today, my lord. It is just visible from my sitting room window." As I spoke, I was careful with my pronunciation of the unfamiliar word, and I saw his amber eyes take on a surprised glint.

"Yes, I suppose you would be able to see it," he replied in the same language. "Are you interested in the stars, my lady?"

"As to that, I have not had much opportunity, Your Majesty. Iselfex is situated on a river much given to clouds and fog and mist, and so we do not have very many clear nights. But here I suppose it is a very different story."

"Very different," he agreed. "To be sure, during the winter rains I find my viewing somewhat obstructed. But that is only for a few months, and the rest of the time I am able to continue with my observations."

"And what are these observations?" I inquired. It was not an idle question; I was fascinated that he should be so interested in the stars that he would have a special building constructed just so he could watch them. And although I did not know him well yet, I could tell this was one of his passions, something that occupied a good deal of his energy.

"Oh, there are so very many that I cannot list them all now, but I track the positions of the stars, watch for their movements and conjunctions, and watch as well the moons in their orbits, and how they shift with the seasons." As he spoke, his tone warmed, and lost something of its formal quality.

Ah, here was where we could meet on common ground. For while I did not know much of the stars' movements and such, I did know the legends associated with them in my homeland. "That all sounds so very interesting," I said. "And the three stars that shine so brightly in the summer sky, and are now rising above the horizon? In Sirlende, we call them the Sisters, and speak of the legend where they were mortal girls once, of such great beauty that a long-ago Empress envied them, and had one of her magicians banish them to the heavens. But even in that she was defeated, as they continued to shine in the night sky, brighter and more beautiful than the most perfect diamonds."

Besh tilted his head to one side, regarding me with interest. I tried not to flush under that steady gaze, and told myself it was not precisely admiration, but rather a certain attentiveness, now that we were discussing something he clearly cared about. "I have heard something of that legend, and find it fascinating, for we call them the Sisters as well, although our story is that they were traveling to a shrine in the desert, and were overtaken by a great storm, one whose winds were so strong that the three girls were sent flying up into the heavens, where they remain to this day."

"It seems those poor sisters were not particularly lucky, no matter which legend you believe," I remarked, and Besh gave me a rueful smile, saying,

"Well, at least it is only a legend. Those are not the souls of lost women shining in the night sky."

"And what are they, then? Lights the gods—that God," I added, correcting myself, for I did not wish him to think me disrespectful of his beliefs, "has hung in the sky?" That was what I had been taught, that all around us, on both the earth and in the heavens, had been wrought by the gods… or perhaps the God of Keshiaar. Truthfully, we in Sirlende were rather a secular sort, and while we paid lip service to the legends of the gods who had supposedly created everything around us, no one I knew was particularly devout. At any rate, in my mind, I'd always thought of stars as lanterns set very far away, which was why they looked so small.

Shaking his head slightly, Besh sipped at his wine before he replied. Then he said, "I have no doubt that God created the stars, just as He created the world around us and the sun in the sky and the two moons that illuminate our night, but they are not lights in the way you might think of them, and instead are rather like our sun, being huge orbs of hot gas, but so far away that they appear as only pinpricks in the darkness."

My mind could barely process this notion, as both the concepts he was describing and the words he was using to explain them were quite unfamiliar to me. I hesitated, then asked, "And you know all this by looking at the stars from your observatory?"

That question elicited a chuckle. I quite liked the sound of it, for his laugh was low and throaty. "Not all, my lady. My people have been studying the stars for a thousand years. But I will admit that in the last generation or so the tools to make those observations have been greatly improved."

"It all sounds quite marvelous," I said honestly, for, as my brother liked to say, I had yet to meet a field of study that did not result in me burying my nose in a book until I felt I was sufficiently acquainted with a topic that I could converse on the subject without appearing ignorant.

"I am glad you find it interesting. In fact," Besh added, as he regarded me with a sharpened gaze, "perhaps you would like to see how some of it works firsthand? I could show you the observatory tonight, after we have finished our meal."

It was all I could do to prevent myself from clapping my hands together like a small child promised a particularly special treat. "That would be lovely, my lord. I think I would very much enjoy that."

He smiled and nodded, and we returned to our neglected food after that. It was much the same as the night before, only this time we had been provided with a sort of nutty-tasting flatbread with which to wrap up the highly seasoned meat. Although unfamiliar, it tasted very good, and I found myself eating with a light heart, glad that I had discovered a way to ingratiate myself with my new husband.

Then I glanced up, and saw the chancellor, Azeer Tel-Karinoor, watching me with narrowed eyes and a pinched set to his already thin lips. As soon as he met my gaze, however, he glanced away. For a second or two I continued to regard him in puzzlement, wondering why he should have been wearing such a look of disapproval on his face. Had I committed some breach of protocol? I could not think of what it might be, as Besh and I had merely been conversing in quiet tones, our voices pitched low enough that I doubted we could have been overheard. And in that moment I told myself I must be imagining hostility where there was none, and to pay it no more mind.

After all, I had far more pleasant things to occupy my thoughts, now that I had an assignation planned with my husband.

The observatory was, like all the buildings I had yet seen on the palace grounds, meticulously finished down to the smallest detail. Once again there were floors of patterned marble, this time in the shapes of stylized stars and moons and suns, and the walls were painted with frescoes that seemed to depict the various legends associated with the heavenly bodies. Oil lamps in brass sconces flickered along the walls. In the midst of all this were a great many complex instruments I could barely begin to describe, some with sheets of paper lying next to them covered in what looked like strings of numbers and symbols. The numbers at least I recognized, as Sirlende had adopted the far more convenient Keshiaari notations centuries before.

Besh passed by all those instruments, however, going instead to what looked like a long tube of silvery metal, perhaps tin, sitting upon a great framework with cunning little wheels so that it might be moved about the chamber as needed. As with all things in Keshiaar, the tin tube was not left plain, but engraved with complex designs, and the fittings were of chased brass.

"Is it a spy glass?" I asked somewhat hesitantly. I had seen Captain Talaver use such a thing on the ship, but this instrument was much larger, so large a single man could not have held it comfortably.

"Similar in principle, but a telescope can see things that are much farther away. Come, and I will show you."

I approached the…telescope…and noted that it had a piece of glass set into the narrower end. "How does it work?"

"Put your eye up to the glass. Here," and he came behind me, took me by the arms, and guided me gently into position.

His fingers felt very warm through the thin silk of my tunic. And oh, what a delicious sensation, to have him so close to me, his body almost touching mine as he made sure

I was standing in the correct spot. I hardly dared to breathe, for I feared one accidental movement would have me brushing against him in a most intimate fashion, and that would cause him to startle and move away.

"Very good," he said, his voice sounding so close that it sent another shiver through me. "Now stay there while I extinguish the lights."

To my disappointment, he stepped away and made a circuit of the chamber, blowing out the oil lamps one by one. By then it was full dark, and so when the last lamp was snuffed, the interior of the observatory became so black that I doubted I could see my hand in front of my face. I waited, and heard his footsteps returning to me.

"Can you see in the dark, like a cat?" I inquired.

Another of those delicious-sounding chuckles. "No, my lady. It is only that I have spent many a dark night in here, and I know the positions of the furniture and instruments so well that no doubt I could move amongst them blindfolded if necessary. But now, put your eye to the glass, and tell me what you see."

In silence I did as he bade me, leaning my head forward so my eyelashes almost brushed against the chased brass housing for the lens. I blinked, and suddenly I saw—a reddish-orange sphere, mottled here and there with lighter streaks of pale gold. And around the sphere I thought I could make out faint bands, or rings.

"What is it?" I asked, my voice shaky. "Is it a star?"

"No, Lyarris. It is a world like ours, but many thousands upon thousands of leagues away."

"'A world like ours'?" I repeated, puzzled, although I was also thrilled to have heard him say my name. How lovely and exotic it sounded in that delicious accent of his. "How can there be more than one world?"

"We believe there are many, although so far we have only charted six. That one is closest to us, and is called Balasir."

Mind churning with this new information, I stared through the glass eyepiece once more. The tiny sphere seemed to shimmer as I looked at it, but I guessed this had something to do with the glass through which I looked, and not the actual movement of that faraway world. Finally I asked, "Do people live there, too?"

"That we do not know, my lady, but our thought is that they probably do not—or if they do, they must be very different from us. You can see from the color that there are no oceans on that world, no water at all. Nothing can survive without water."

No, I thought, *for even here in dry, dusty Keshiaar there are rivers, and ice on the high mountaintops, and springs hidden in the depths of the desert.* "It is still very beautiful, though," I told him.

I felt rather than saw him nod, for it was very dark in there. "I am glad you think so. There are many beauties in the night sky, and Balasir is just one of them."

"I would like to see more," I said impulsively.

"And so you shall. But for now, though, it grows late, and I should return you to your quarters."

I wanted to protest that I was not weary at all, but I held my tongue. Besh had promised that he would show me more of these heretofore unknown splendors in the sky, and I must content myself with that. It was perfect, really, for here in the observatory we were as alone as we could ever be, since the guards had taken up their positions at the entrance to the building, letting us enter unaccompanied. Returning here night after night would only give Besh and me more opportunities to be alone with one another, which must aid in breaking down the barriers between us.

So I nodded, feeling him step away from me, then heard the soft but heavy tread of his booted feet on the marble floor. A few heartbeats later, a tiny flame flared as he lit a match and touched it to the wick of the nearest lamp. He did not appear concerned with lighting any of the others, as that single lamp gave us enough illumination to find our way to the exit.

We emerged into the warm night air, and once again he guided me back to my quarters. Now that I knew he did not intend to accompany me inside, I was somewhat more in possession of myself. I was able to say calmly, "Thank you again for showing me your observatory, my lord. You have made my world so very much larger, in only a single evening."

Those extraordinary amber-brown eyes seemed to light up, and he replied, "It pleases me very well to hear this from you, Lyarris."

Again a thrill went through me at the sound of my name on his lips. "I am glad of it, my lord."

"And it also pleases me that you have a quick and inquisitive mind, one that is not afraid to learn new things. I cannot say the same for—"

But then he clamped his lips shut, and the glow in his eyes quite died away. I could not be sure, but I sensed that perhaps he had begun to speak of his late wife, and then had stopped himself. So, had she not been a lover of learning? Or perhaps she had been jealous of the time he spent away from her in his observatory, and so sought comfort in the arms of another?

I would never ask him those questions, of course. Even if that was truly what had happened, I could not find much sympathy in my heart for this Hezia, for surely she must have known that the ruler of a vast and powerful empire had many claims on his time. Was she so petty as to begrudge him a few hours indulging in a pastime that clearly meant a great deal to him?

Hastening to fill the strained silence, I said, "Oh, that mind is something my brother often teased me about, saying if I did not pull my nose out of a book from time to time, I would develop a dreadful squint, and who would want a princess with a squint?"

Besh chuckled then, although it sounded strained, lacking the easy, throaty quality I had noted earlier in the evening. "No, my lady, you most definitely do not have a squint. Your eyes are…quite beautiful."

A tremor went through me as our gazes locked. Could he see into those eyes of mine, see how much I wanted this delicate beginning between us to grow into something stronger, more intimate?

But then he looked away, saying, "And it is late, so I shall take my leave of you. Good night, my lady."

"Good night, my lord," I replied formally, adopting his tone. Somehow I knew I must take his lead in this, for if I pressed the issue, he might find a reason to back away, to erect yet another barrier between us.

He bowed to me and moved off, flanked by his guards. Once again Miram opened the door for me, and I went to my lonely bed.

CHAPTER SEVEN

It seemed I had not frightened him off, for the next night Besh took me back to his observatory, this time to show me the contours and odd, craggy landscapes of our world's attendant moons. The night after that it was al-Adin, a tiny pale world that evoked images of ice and snow to me, although of course I could see nothing of it save mottled areas of darker gray against its overall chalky surface.

And so it went, each time with him having something new and wondrous to reveal to me. During each of these meetings, I was careful to show my enthusiasm, but I also made sure that I remained polite and circumspect. There were moments when I wished I had the sort of forward temperament Ashara's good friend Gabrinne possessed. I had no doubt that good lady, if put in my position, would have found a way to fling her arms around Besh and kiss him soundly, and tell him that his diffidence was silly, for were we not husband and wife?

I, however, did not have that sort of courage, or daring. All I could do was show Besh that I was very different from the wayward Hezia, and that I only wanted to be a good wife to him. Doing so by sharing his interests seemed the safest route. The rest would come in time…or so I prayed, for every passing moment I spent with him, I found myself longing for him more—the sound of his voice, the light in those beautiful eyes of his, the brief touches of those long, sensitive fingers against mine.

It did seem my strategy was working, for a ten-day after our wedding, Besh informed me that there would be a great conjunction in the skies above the desert, and that he planned an expedition to view it properly, as apparently the lights from Tir el-Alisaad would disturb his observations.

"And I would like you to come with me, if you do not mind rough living for a few days," he said as we walked back from the observatory that night.

"I do not mind at all," I said at once. Truthfully, I would have agreed to sleep on the ground, if it meant some time away from the stifling palace and the eyes which seemed to be on me at all times. I had tried to ignore them as best I could, for it was a simple fact of life that the consort of a great ruler cannot call her life her own, but I could not deny that a change of scenery would be very welcome.

"Excellent. We will be setting out three days from now, so that we may reach the oasis of Tir-Kamar in time. You may bring two attendants, but I do not think our party can accommodate any more than that, as we will be traveling swiftly."

I wanted to laugh, to say that I'd happily make do with only one attendant. However, as I had not yet broached the subject of my unwieldy personal staff, I merely nodded and said I thought I could manage.

Indeed, his invitation put me in such good spirits that I sat down to write a long-overdue letter to my brother. As I knew it would most likely be read by more than one pair of eyes before it reached Torric, I did not give the real truth of my situation, but set down such things as would not raise anyone's suspicions.

Dearest Torric,

I hope this letter finds you well, and Ashara, too. I daresay she must be close to childbed by now, and perhaps by the time you write back to me, I will already have a nephew or niece. As for myself, I am doing very well, and enjoying my new home a great deal. His Most High Majesty is the most considerate of husbands, and it is beautiful here, far more beautiful than I could have imagined. Yes, it is quite hot, but I am finding that as time goes on, I do not notice it as much, which I suppose is the way these things generally work.

The Hierarch is teaching me about the stars, and has an observatory where he goes to view the heavens. It is all quite fascinating, and something I had never had a chance to explore back home. So that is yet another blessing this marriage has brought me. In fact, we shall be traveling to the desert soon to make some important observations, and I shall have the opportunity to see more of this land I now call home.

I miss you and Ashara and everyone else, but I am happy. I have made the right choice.

    Your loving sister,
    Lyarris Kel-Alisaad

Whether he would be able to see past the various exaggerations and prevarications in that missive, I did not know, but certainly there was nothing in it that could be deemed exceptional, and so I thought it should not rouse any suspicions. And, at the very least, it would tell my brother that I was alive and well enough, things he might not have known for certain. Then again, even though he did not speak of such matters openly, I guessed he had spies of some sort in Keshiaar, and so perhaps he already knew more than I thought he did. Ah, well, that could be, but my letter would serve as a counterpoint to their own observations, and Torric could make of it what he liked.

The expedition threw the palace into turmoil, as such things usually did, but three days hence we were heading out into the heat and the white, scorching sunlight, moving almost due east, away from the coast. I brought Lila and one of the other Keshiaari maids, Marsali, as Miram had said she thought the journey would be too much for any of the serving women I had brought with me from Sirlende. Her tone seemed to indicate she thought the journey would be too much for me as well, but since my presence on the expedition had the Hierarch's blessing, there was not much she could do about it.

To be sure, I worried about the heat somewhat as well. Ever since I had come to Keshiaar, I had taken a brief walk in the gardens early in the morning before it was barely light, then huddled in the palace during the rest of the day, and had not ventured forth until the sun was low on the horizon. But I would not let my fear keep me confined, especially when my staying back at the palace would surely disappoint Besh. I wanted to show him that I could survive the worst of whatever his harsh homeland might throw my way.

When we did finally ride forth, early in the morning, I found the conditions better than I had feared. Yes, the sun was not fully up yet, but even as it rose and the heat of the day soared with it, I realized that the brisk canter of the horses we rode kept our own breeze flowing over us, helping to cool us somewhat. My mount was of the pure Keshiaari breed, fleet of foot, more delicate than the horses of Sirlende, but bred to survive the desert nonetheless.

Out here was a different kind of sea, one of sand everywhere, an unending dun-colored plain that seemed to stretch in all directions. Behind us trailed a great smoke-like plume, from the dust kicked up by our horses' hooves. The party was small by royal standards; we numbered fifty altogether, enough to ensure the safety of His Most High Majesty, but not so great a contingent that we could not ride hard, and fast.

Back home I had enjoyed riding, even if I had had no stomach for the hunts that were such a part of court life. Here, despite the heat, it felt good to be on horseback again, especially to be riding such a beautiful animal. Her name was

Selkar, and she seemed to be enjoying herself immensely as we pounded across the Keshiaari wastes, her pale coat shining in the merciless sun.

Even those wastes were not entirely empty; that first night we made camp in an incongruous island of life in the middle of that unending sea of sand, a place where freshwater springs bubbled up from deep underground, and tall slender trees Besh called palms grew there as well, drinking deeply of the precious water. The guards pitched a series of tents in that unexpected haven, and we passed the night under the stars, the hot winds finally cooling to a tolerable level so that we might sleep in peace.

So went the next day, and then on the third day, we approached another one of those areas of green, which Besh said was called an oasis, only this one was as large as the first two combined. Once again the guards pitched our tents, and we waited for the sun to be quite down so we could get a clear look at the stars.

The ruddy glow seemed to linger on the horizon for a long while. The group of us eating in the royal tent was quite small, for Besh had only brought with him a young man named Nezhaam, apparently his best and oldest friend, and also a cousin of some sort, and an older man called Alim, who was my husband's former tutor. I had listened to them banter the previous two nights, and knew that Nezhaam had come along mainly for the sheer adventure of the outing, while Alim was the one who had first instilled a love of the stars in his former pupil, and who still provided counsel when needed.

Lila and Marsali and I were the only women in the company, and of course they took their meals separately from the royal party. At first it had felt odd to sit down on the clever folding chairs of heavy canvas and wood, and eat and drink with no mention of having to stay separate from the men, but I enjoyed it, once I got past the novelty. Being with them in such an informal setting gave me a much better opportunity to see my husband relaxed and in his element, away from the rigid etiquette of court.

I drank some of my water, and listened to Besh and Nezhaam trading barbs. "You would not know Balasir from Kalawar, Nezhaam, so do not try to convince me that you are here out of any scholarly fervor. No, I will hazard a guess that it is more a wish to avoid your mother's matchmaking efforts. Truly, I must applaud you for managing to stay unattached for so long."

Nezhaam, a handsome young man a year or two younger than my husband, and therefore far past an age to be married, put a hand to his breast and exclaimed, "Majesty, you wound me! I assure you, I am motivated by a keen interest in science!"

"And not being married off to Jesair Sel-Malantar's cross-eyed daughter, I think," Besh put in.

"Can you blame me? I cannot imagine spending the rest of my life with someone like that. I should not know where to look."

"Azara Sel-Malantar is a very worthy young woman," Alim put in severely. "It is not her fault that her eyes are crossed."

"I never said it was, but that does not mean I wish to spend my time on this earth looking at them." Nezhaam swallowed the remainder of the wine in his cup and added, "I would much rather be lucky like you, Besh, and be blessed with a wife of surpassing beauty. Tell me, Your Majesty, do you have any sisters back home?"

I could feel my cheeks flush, but as the night was quite dark, with neither of the moons risen yet, I did not think any of them could see me blush. Lightly I replied, "No, my lord, I fear I do not. It was only my brother and myself. You will have to find a wife among your own people, I am afraid."

"Dashed again," Nezhaam said, although he appeared in the light of the flickering torches to be anything but dashed.

Besh shook his head. "I think it best that we all attempt to get a few hours of sleep. The conjunction occurs an hour and a half before dawn."

"I am shivering with anticipation," Nezhaam quipped.

"You should be," Alim interjected. "Such an alignment in the heavens will not occur again for another two hundred years."

"But, as you two keep pointing out, it is just a group of planets creating a singular configuration. At least the astrologers back at court would make sure to say it meant I would be inheriting a great fortune, or blessed with great luck at the gaming tables, or something similarly useful."

"Yes, they are quite talented at telling people what they wish to hear," Besh retorted. "Off to bed with you. The guards will burn an hour candle, so they know the precise moment to wake us." He turned from his friend to face me. "I hope it will not be too much of a hardship for you, my lady, to be awakened thus in the middle of the night."

I smiled, hoping to reassure him. "Not at all, my lord. I would not want to miss such a sight, even if it meant losing an entire night's sleep."

"You have a stout heart, my wife." He got to his feet and extended a hand to me, so as to help me from my chair. I took it, glad of the feel of his warm fingers wrapped around mine. But as soon as I was on my feet, he released my hand, saying, "The guards will wake you at the appointed time."

"Very good, my lord," I replied, my tone calm, showing no sign of the disappointment I felt at his letting go of me so quickly. I nodded at both Nezhaam and Alim, and they bowed in return. Then I slipped out of the tent, going the few feet to the next pavilion, which had been designated as my own.

Lila and Marsali were there, both of them yawning, as they had dutifully attempted to stay awake until I returned. Since I would only be getting up again in a few hours, I chose to remain in the thin linen shirt and billowy trousers I wore beneath my silken tunic, and had Lila pull my hair into a loose braid. After I had cleaned my face and teeth—and murmured a quick thank-you for the supply of fresh water the oasis provided for such tasks—I lay down on my cot and pulled the thin linen covering over me, more because I felt odd sleeping with nothing on top of me than because I really needed another layer of warmth.

Just as I had the previous two nights, I fell asleep more quickly than I had expected, most likely because of the hard day of riding I had put in. My body was exhausted, even if my mind was not. It was a deep, dreamless sleep, one I allowed to consume me, until somewhere at the edges of my consciousness I heard the low rumble of a male voice, followed by Lila's light hand on my arm.

"My lady," she said, and my eyes opened then, to a darkness broken only by a single lantern sitting on a camp table a few feet away. "It is time."

"Thank you, Lila," I replied, glad that I at least was the sort to wake up quickly, no matter what the hour might be.

She bowed and handed me a cup of water, so I might rinse my mouth, and then she took it away and helped me back into my tunic. Marsali stood by with a hairbrush, removing the braid and then smoothing my hair before pulling it back with a golden clasp. By then I could hear Besh and Alim and Nezhaam moving about outside, so I thanked my two maidservants for assisting me before stepping out of the pavilion and going to join the men.

The campfires had been banked down, and so we were in utter darkness, save for a few lanterns located here and there throughout our encampment. Overhead the stars blazed forth, more brilliant than I had yet seen them, even brighter than they appeared when viewed at Besh's observatory.

The three men bowed as I approached, and I gravely bowed in return. Custom satisfied, Besh said, "Some of the men are setting up the telescope and other instruments now. It is just a little beyond the encampment—come, let me show you."

He took my hand and led me forth, guiding me across the sandy ground, Nezhaam and Alim a pace or two behind us. Nezhaam yawned several times, and I wondered if he was regretting the wine he had drunk with dinner. Most likely not; he did not seem like the type of man to regret much of anything that brought him pleasure.

We did not go far, most likely less than a hundred yards. But it put enough distance between us and the camp that even the light from those sparsely scattered lanterns could not be seen. The night remained moonless, the stars glimmering uncontested in the black velvet of the sky.

The telescope Besh had brought on the expedition was far smaller than the one kept permanently in the observatory, but it was still large enough to require a sturdy stand, one that had been placed on a slight rise, along with a sextant and a small table set up with a book where I presumed Besh and Alim would make their notations.

As we approached, the men who had been making adjustments to the telescope's stand bowed and backed away. Alim went at once to the sextant, moved it slightly, squinted up at the sky, and then shifted it a bare fraction of an inch. Nezhaam stayed back, scratching his head and yawning, and I guessed that I would not have to worry overmuch about him wanting to share the telescope.

I followed Besh up the rise where the instrument had been placed. We stopped a foot or so away from it, and he let go of my hand now that we were on more or less stable ground. "Look up," he said quietly.

At first I had wondered why we did not go to the telescope immediately. As I followed his direction and tilted my
face upward so I could observe the vast, starry sky above us,
I realized why he wanted me to look upon it with the naked
eye. The telescope was a marvelous thing, to be sure, but it
narrowed one's line of sight, removed some of the context
of what one was viewing. Standing here, with the unending
sweep of the desert all around us and the immense expanse
of the dark skies above, I felt as if I were floating somewhere
between heaven and earth, suspended in a single point of
eternity.

"There," he went on, pointing almost directly overhead.
"Do you see them?"

I did, for they were almost impossible to miss—four
bright stars making an almost perfect square. "How can they
do that?"

The starlight was so bright that I could see his teeth flash
as he smiled. "Everything in the heavens is constantly moving. It just happens that at this particular instant in time,
those worlds have lined up in such a way that it appears to
us, from where we are standing, that they are creating the
grand square. If we were somewhere else—say, observing
them from the surface of Balasir—then they would appear in
a very different configuration."

He stood very close to me, and I wished then that we
were alone, that we were the only two people in a thousand
miles. Perhaps then I would have had the courage to reach
out to him, to pull him against me. As it was, with Alim only

a few feet away, and Nezhaam standing just a little farther off, I of course would never attempt such a thing.

I did not quite trust myself to speak, but merely nodded.

"They are moving into final alignment," Alim said, glancing up from the sextant.

"No time to waste, then," Besh replied, and gestured for me to move closer to the telescope. "Let me look first, to make sure it is properly centered. Then you will be able to see for yourself."

Murmuring, "of course, my lord," I watched as he peered through the eyepiece, made a minute adjustment, then looked into it once again.

"Magnificent."

Yes, you are, I thought, watching the starlight fall on his gleaming black hair, illuminating the fine, strong nose and beautifully sculpted mouth and jaw. But somehow I doubted that was what he meant.

"Come, Lyarris," he said. "They have made their conjunction."

He stepped away from the telescope so I might approach. By then I had grown accustomed enough to using the instrument that it felt natural to look through the eyepiece, then pause as my vision adjusted to the view I was seeing.

Once they were magnified thus, I could see that each of the tiny worlds forming the square was slightly different in hue. They glowed in shades of red and yellow and orange and soft, milky blue. How strange, for when seen with the naked eye, they all appeared a cool, serene white. And they looked close enough for me to reach out and touch, although I knew they had to be uncounted leagues away.

I could have stood there and gazed upon them for hours, but I knew it would not be fair to Besh to monopolize the telescope when he had traveled so far to witness this wonder. So I stepped aside, saying, "They are beautiful."

His gaze lingered on my face. "Yes…." he replied, then appeared to gather himself and turned to the telescope.

Once again the wish passed through my thoughts that we could be alone here. Perhaps if it were only the two of us, he would leave aside the telescope for a moment, then gather me in his arms. But no, that was merely a foolish fancy. He had been solicitous, yes, but I had seen no true desire in his eyes. Having observed it in Thani, I thought I must surely recognize it in Besh.

Give it time, I told myself, and tilted my head to gaze up at the heavens once more. The stars shone down, cool and tranquil. They had many thousands of years to trace their separate paths, and I did not. Still, I had been Besh's wife for barely a fortnight. I could not expect everything to happen as I willed it, simply because I was impatient. And somehow I knew if he sensed that impatience, he would only become that much more distant.

He did step away from the telescope, but only to write down some notations in the book set out for that purpose. As I watched, Nezhaam approached me and murmured, "So you really do humor him in this obsession of his."

I lifted my brows, replying in an equally subdued tone, "I would not call it 'humoring' him, as I find all of it quite fascinating. My only regret is that I did not begin to learn of the stars and the planets and the science ruling them until I came here to Keshiaar."

"Then God is very great, for not only has he sent my friend the most beautiful princess in the world, but one as scholarly and bookish as he. Truly you will have great joy in each other."

"Are you teasing me, my lord?"

He made the familiar gesture of pressing his hand to his chest in mock dismay. "I am offended, Your Majesty, that you would think me anything but sincere."

I couldn't help chuckling at that remark, delivered in wounded tones as it was, and Besh looked up from the telescope to glance over at us.

"Nezhaam, stop provoking her."

"How do you know it wasn't the other way around?"

"Because I know you." Having delivered his statement, Besh bent toward the telescope once again.

Not bothering to defend himself, Nezhaam grinned. "It is true. It is very hard to hide things from someone who has known you since you were born."

"Were you raised in the palace?" I asked, for I thought now, while Besh was occupied with taking his observations, might be a good time to pry some information out of his long-time friend.

"No. We are cousins, but then, almost every prince in this land is his cousin in some fashion or another. But my house is in the Tanamir District, very close to the palace, and since our fathers were great good friends, I spent much time there, and the Hierarch and I became friends as well, even though his—" Nezhaam broke off abruptly then, as if suddenly realizing he was about to divulge more information than he had intended. A small pause, and he added, "At any rate, we have been around each other most of our lives, although there was a span where he wanted very little to do with someone two years younger. Luckily, he realized how foolish that was."

"Of course," I agreed with a smile, even as I wished he had not stopped himself so quickly. Somehow I thought that whatever Nezhaam had almost revealed would help to cast some light on why Besh was so very reserved. He had been wounded, that much I knew. Even so, I felt there was more, some secret everyone was taking considerable pains to keep from me. Perhaps it should not have bothered me so, as I knew every court had its secrets. But there were secrets and secrets....

Nezhaam had seemed to watch me as I looked on my husband. Perhaps my thoughts were more obvious than I had intended, for the prince said, "I do not think you need to trouble yourself, my lady. I know that he would never have asked you to come along on this expedition if he did not take joy in your company. That you share his enthusiasm for these things is surely a gift he could never have imagined receiving."

"Thank you, Nezhaam," I replied quietly, hoping he could hear the gratitude in my voice. If Besh's oldest friend saw the matter thus, then surely I must accept his insights. After all, he knew his cousin far better than I did.

He bowed. "You are most welcome, my lady." A yawn seemed to split his face then, and he gave a rueful shake of the head. "While I understand the need to be up at such unholy hours for these sorts of things, I cannot help but think it can't be all that healthy." Turning away from me, he raised his voice slightly and called out, "Ay, there, Besh! How much more fiddling are you going to be doing with that thing?"

Besh did not reply at once, but remained bent over the telescope. After a few seconds passed, he gathered up his pen and made a few more notations. Only then did he straighten, one hand going to the small of his back, as if he were at last feeling some discomfort from the awkward position. "Not very much. The planets are beginning to move apart again. But I think it will be at least another quarter-hour."

That answer did not seem to please Nezhaam, for he shook his head. "If that is the case, then I believe I will retire for what is left of the evening."

"If that is what you wish." Besh glanced over at me. "Would you like Nezhaam to walk you back to your pavilion, my lady?"

That was the last thing I wanted. No, I wished to stay here with my husband until he finished making his notations, for then he would be the one escorting me to my tent. I did not have any great expectation of the evening ending differently from any other evening I had spent with him. On the other hand, nothing would most certainly happen if I did not at least give him the opportunity.

"No, my lord," I said. "The stars are so beautiful, I would like to stay out a little longer."

"Mad, the both of you," Nezhaam remarked. His dark eyes had a certain glint that told me he had guessed at my true reasons for wanting to remain where I was, but he only added, "I will retire then, and if you wish to stay up until the sunrise, I suppose that is your choice. A very good night, my lady"—he bowed to me — "and to you, my lord."

Besh made a waving motion with his free hand, but that was his only reply, as he was occupied with making another adjustment to the telescope. Apparently not offended in the slightest, Nezhaam bowed to me once again and made his way back to the encampment.

Truthfully, in that moment I was beginning to feel weary, but I would not allow that to keep me from remaining where I was. And, even without the telescope, the night sky was very beautiful, the stars clustered so thickly across heaven's zenith that they made a bright band against that velvety darkness.

At long last, though, Besh stepped away from the telescope one final time, made a few more notations in his book, and then glanced over at Alim, who had been working with his sextant and his own notes the entire time. "That seems to be all," Besh said. "Are you done as well?"

"Almost," Alim replied. "Please, my lord, do not trouble yourself to wait, if you are finished."

A nod, and Besh closed his book of notations and shoved it under his left arm, then descended the small rise where the telescope had been placed so he might approach me. Inwardly I rejoiced, for without Alim walking back with us, I thought perhaps there would be a better chance of something—anything—happening between Besh and myself.

"I hope the late hour has not wearied you overmuch, my lady," he said, as we headed toward the encampment. Behind us, I caught movement out of the corner of my eye, and realized it was one of the guards stepping forth to pack up the telescope and bring it back to the encampment.

"Not at all." Not precisely the truth, but a few hours of lost sleep seemed a small price to pay for the wonders I had witnessed. "It was beautiful."

"And lucky we were to see it, for such a conjunction will not occur again in our lifetimes."

In that moment, my slipper caught on a rock, and I stumbled. At once Besh's hand was on my arm, steadying me, and I thought I would never be so happy as to feel those strong fingers at my elbow, the welcome pressure of his touch.

"Are you all right?"

"Yes," I replied, hoping I did not sound too breathless, and that my expression did not betray me.

His lips parted, as if he were about to say something else, but then the darkness seemed to come alive, and around us was the thunder of horses coming in from the open desert, pounding toward us.

"Guards!" Besh cried as he thrust me behind him, then drew the long dagger he wore in a jeweled scabbard hanging from his belt.

There were shouts from the encampment, and the dull thud of booted feet against hard-packed sand. From seemingly nowhere appeared a rider garbed in black, astride a black horse, and he bore down on us through the darkness. Besh's dagger flashed in the starlight, and the horse let out a screeching whinny and wheeled off, stumbling as dark blood began to flow down one of its legs.

Arrows whistled overhead, finding their targets with an accuracy I would not have expected, given the black night in which they were launched. Another rider came pounding toward us, and Besh pushed me to the ground, standing over me, shielding me with his body. I did not see how he could possibly be so lucky as to drive off a second horse, armed as he was only with the long dagger with its curved blade. But another arrow sliced through the air, driving clean through the rider's throat, and he fell, blood splashing over his dark garments.

This all happened in less than the span of a minute. Then the guards of Besh's household were all around us, shielding their ruler and his consort with their bodies, and within another minute or two, the attackers were killed or driven back into the desert.

At once he turned to me, helping me from the ground. "Are you all right, my lady? Have you taken any hurt?"

Wordlessly I shook my head, even as I clung to his hand. Certainly I had never been witness to such violence before, never seen a man killed.

He seemed to sense this, for he drew me against him, putting a protective arm around my shoulders before he shot a stern glance at the captain of his guards. "Accompany me and my lady wife back to the pavilions, but have five of your men stay here to search the bodies. And make sure someone goes to make sure Alim has suffered no hurt."

The man bowed. "At once, Most High Majesty. A thousand apologies for allowing such an attack to take place—"

"It did not succeed, which is the important thing." Even in the darkness I could see Besh's expression harden. "But I want to know who is responsible for this."

"Of course, Most High Majesty." A few curt orders, and several of the guards hurried off into the darkness, while the rest of the company escorted Besh and me back to the heart of the encampment where our pavilions stood. Neither of them seemed to have suffered much hurt—and neither had Nezhaam, who hastened to meet us.

"My friends, you are well?" he cried out.

"Quite well," Besh replied, and added grimly, "No thanks to the cowards who attacked us in the darkness."

"Was it—"

"But my lady wife is quite shocked and tired," he went on, cutting off Nezhaam before he had a chance to say anything else. "Let me see that she is safely returned to her pavilion."

"Of course, my lord," Nezhaam said, sounding uncharacteristically formal.

Still with his arm around my shoulders, Besh guided me to my pavilion, where Lila and Marsali awaited us, their frightened dark eyes revealing how much the attack had upset them. Then he did begin to let go of me, but I held on to his arm, loath to lose the reassurance of his touch.

"Please, my lord, can I not stay with you in your pavilion?" I asked, hating the tremor in my voice but lacking the strength to control it. "I will not feel safe here alone."

"You will be quite safe," he said reasonably. "For there will be ten guards to watch over you, and I will be only a few yards away."

"But—"

To my surprise, he bent and pressed his lips to my forehead, let them rest there for a few seconds before saying, "My lady, the attackers have been defeated. It would not be seemly for you to share my pavilion. No harm will come to you—I swear it."

I wanted to argue, but I guessed he would not look favorably on any further protests. And he was right; it would not be appropriate for me to sleep in his tent, not in this mixed company. No, I would have to gather myself, and remember that I was the consort of the Hierarch, and not a weak woman. "Of course, my lord. I understand."

An expression of relief passed over his features. He took my hand and lifted it to his mouth, gave it a gentle kiss before releasing it once again. "Thank you, my lady. Now, I pray you, rest as best you can, for we will be riding early so that we may return to Tir el-Alisaad as quickly as possible."

I nodded, and retired to my pavilion as he walked away, Nezhaam joining him, the two of them appearing to fall into a hushed but heated discussion. How I wished I could hear what they were saying! But I could not, so I allowed Lila and Marsali to flutter worriedly about me, then help prepare me for bed, although I somehow doubted I would get much sleep that night.

For even as I lay on my cot and closed my eyes, I could not forget that odd, clipped exchange between my husband and Nezhaam, as if they had a very good idea who might have attacked the encampment.

But who on earth would have the temerity to assault the Hierarch of Keshiaar?

CHAPTER EIGHT

We did ride quickly, and hard, reaching the eastern gates of the capital city before not quite three days had passed. By then I was no closer to knowing the identity of our attackers than I was the night of their assault, but I had the feeling that Besh and Nezhaam and Alim did, or at least had made a few informed guesses. Certainly they were tight-lipped and grim. Gone were the easy conversations like the ones we'd shared after dinner on the journey out to the great oasis, and that made the return trip feel much longer, even though it was actually half a day shorter.

Certainly I was relieved to see the white walls of Tir el-Alisaad rise up before us, shimmering in the heat waves coming off the desert sands. I'd enjoyed a measure of freedom on the journey that I did not have when immured in the palace, but not having to continually look over one's shoulder did have its merits.

That relief was short-lived, however, for after Besh and I had made our goodbyes and a smaller group of the guards had guided Marsali, Lila, and me back to my suite, I made a most unwelcome discovery.

"But where are my maids?" I demanded of Miram when I saw only the one other of the Keshiaari maids, the woman I had left behind, hurrying forth to assist Lila and Marsali with unpacking my things.

Miram's face was expressionless. "They were sent home, Your Majesty."

"Sent...home?" I said, my tone blank with confusion. Certainly I was very tired. Perhaps I had not heard her properly. "How is that possible? Under whose orders? For certainly I did not request such a thing."

Just the barest tightening of her thin lips before she said, "They complained of the heat, of missing their homeland. I asked the seneschal what to do, and he went to the chancellor, as this was not a simple domestic matter, but one involving the Hiereine's household. Then the chancellor decided they should be sent back to Sirlende, as a ship was just about to sail there, bearing a load of spices. Have no fears, Your Majesty. We will replace them with Keshiaari women—"

"No," I cut in. What the true story was behind this, I couldn't begin to guess. However, since just a few weeks earlier I had been wondering how on earth I would keep eight women occupied with looking after me, I saw no reason to have Miram bring in more strangers. Four servants were quite enough to manage my apartments and my person. Lila I liked, and Marsali, although reserved, seemed thoroughly unobjectionable. I would not risk having anyone else assigned to my service, for I might not be so lucky with one of them. "I do not see the need to have any replacements sent to me. You four will manage well enough, I think."

And I let the matter go there, although in my mind that was certainly not the end of it. I would not trouble Besh with my silly domestic affairs, as he had a great many more serious matters to occupy his attention, foremost being the search for whomever had hired the men who attacked us in the desert. Most likely the same questions were occupying the chancellor as well, but since it was his direct order that had sent my countrywomen back to Sirlende, I did not scruple at questioning him further on the matter.

He could not delay me forever, but he did make me wait until the following afternoon before agreeing to an audience. Not in my chambers, of course; the only man allowed there was my husband, and he did not seem terribly eager to exercise that right.

But Azeer Tel-Karinoor met with me in the outer, public chamber of the suite of rooms reserved as his offices. Miram attended me, as I could not be left alone with any man not my husband, although I heartily wished that I could have had this conversation without her listening in.

I waited as the chancellor's manservant brought us cool, sweet tea tasting of mint, and fine light cakes to go with it. After sipping the tea and taking a dainty bite of one cake, I decided that custom had been met, and it was time to go to the heart of the matter.

"Chancellor, I do wish you had consulted me before sending my servants back to Sirlende."

He leaned back in his chair and steepled his fingers under his chin, dark eyes watching me carefully, but with no real expression. "A thousand apologies, Your Majesty, but it was clear they were not happy with their situation. And because a ship was available to take them home, I thought it best to see them safely on their way."

How very convenient, I thought, t*hat such a ship should be here precisely when I was away from the palace for an extended period.* I picked up my tea glass in its elegant pierced bronze holder and took a sip. "I see your point, Chancellor. All the same, I must ask that such matters be brought before me before any decision is made. Yes, there was a ship ready to sail for Sirlende, but many such ships ply their trade between the two realms, and I do not see how waiting a few days could have made any difference."

Save that I might have returned before the next one sailed, and put a stop to the whole thing.

"Of course, Your Majesty. I understand your concerns. His Most High Majesty gives me a good deal of autonomy to manage such matters as I see fit, and so I assumed that you would also allow me the same kind of liberty."

"I have no doubt that in most things such a policy is wise, but as these were my personal servants, the decision should also have been mine."

Azeer pressed his hands together and bowed slightly. "I understand, Your Majesty. It will not happen again."

Of course it wouldn't, for I had no more servants left that he could dismiss in such a way. But I also knew that to continue to argue the matter would make very little difference. Those women were gone, on their way back to Sirlende, and now I was very much alone here, surrounded by people whose motivations I did not clearly understand. True, Lila seemed friendly enough, but she was only a servant girl. She certainly had no power, and she could never be my friend, even if I had attempted to make such an overture, for I was the consort of the Hierarch.

As there was little else I could say, I replied, "Thank you for understanding, Chancellor. I know you are a busy man, and so I will take no more of your time."

"My time is yours to command, Your Majesty."

Correct words, the response custom demanded. I knew he did not believe them, not really. Fair enough.

Neither did I.

Although I promised myself I would not bring up the matter to Besh, he did learn of it somehow. A few days after we had returned to the capital, he murmured to me as we were leaving dinner, "My lady, I have recently heard how your servants were sent away from here. I must apologize on behalf of my chancellor, for I would never have approved such a thing if I had known of it in advance."

"I thank you for your concern," I told him, "but there is nothing any of us can do about it now. Besides," I added, essaying a laugh, even though the handling of the situation still rankled, "I had meant to say something to you on the subject, to tell you that eight attendants was really unnecessary. So perhaps your chancellor read my thoughts somehow and did as I wished, even though I had never mentioned it."

Besh did not appear amused. Mouth unsmiling, he replied, "Even so, it was ill done. If any of your servants were to be sent away, it should have been some of the Keshiaari women. I did not want you to feel alone here, with no one of your homeland to keep you company."

I would not admit that I had been thinking something very similar. It warmed me, though, that he was showing such concern for me. "My lord, how can I feel alone, when I have you for a husband?"

It was precisely the wrong thing to say; I saw it as soon as the words left my lips, for his jaw tensed, and he glanced away from me, frowning up at the dark heavens above. "The skies tonight are not clear enough to bother with the observatory. I will take you back to your apartments."

My heart seemed to shrivel in my breast, but I somehow managed to keep a note of polite concern in my tone as I asked, "Oh, do you think so? It was quite clear when we went in for dinner."

"Look now."

I did as he asked and saw that the heavens were covered by a thin blanket of clouds, just enough to blur and obscure the stars and the one moon that had risen, making it a pale smudge of light off to the east. "That is unfortunate. I did not think you had much in the way of clouds here until the rainy season."

"We do...sometimes. But they will not bring rain."

And that appeared to be all he wanted to say on the subject, for after that he led me to my apartments, bade me a rather brusque good night, and was gone.

As there was nothing else for me to do, I went into my suite, allowed myself to be undressed, and fell into my solitary bed.

The days passed after that, blending into one another, until they became weeks, and then months. I took up my writing again, as there was little else for me to do, and in finding something to occupy my time, I attempted to learn something of Keshiaar's tales and legends from Lila. After being startled at first that I would care about such matters, she would tell me what she could—as long as Miram and the other two maidservants were not around to overhear. I supposed that since she was the youngest, she felt they all had some right to govern her actions, even though of course my voice should overrule all of them.

But I did not wish to cause her any trouble, and so I always waited until Marsali and Alina were scrubbing the bath chamber, or occupied in some other task, before I would ask Lila to draw her chair and her embroidery close to the table where I sat with my papers. Then I would write, hearing her speak of enchanted caves of gold and magic lamps and carpets that flew and all manner of wonders. I did not ask if someone else had set down these tales, as what I did now I did for myself to occupy my mind, even if it could not fill the emptiness of my heart.

For truly, as the endless blistering summer finally gave way to the shorter days of autumn, I had begun to despair that I could ever do or say anything to touch Besh's heart. Ever since the attack, his councillors and captains of the guard had been consumed with discovering the miscreants behind the vile assault on their Hierarch. For some time I'd begun to think Besh did have an idea as to the identity of the guilty party or parties, but when the days and weeks wore on and no arrests were made, I thought perhaps I had been mistaken. Still, it seemed strange that no progress had been made, even with the crown's vast resources massed to hunt down the perpetrators.

Besh used that preoccupation to hold me at arm's length, and although he did not bar me from the observatory altogether, he did manage to find one excuse after another as to why star viewing was not suitable every night. We did go to make those observations three or four times in a month, just enough that I could not claim he had forbidden me the activity altogether. I knew better than to question his motives; I guessed well enough what they might be. We had begun to grow too close, and he had not wished to allow me any further intimacy.

Perhaps if I had been made of sterner stuff, I would have confronted him, told him outright that if he truly wished to continue the line of Kel-Alisaad, then perhaps he should not be doing quite such a good job of avoiding me. But I did not wish to force such an encounter. He would only retreat that much further into his shell, and I would be left worse off than I was now. All I could do was hope that perhaps one day he would realize I was not Hezia, and that I would never betray him.

It was a morning in late Octevre, the heat finally abating somewhat, when I sat with Lila in my chambers, writing down a story of a horse made of ebony that could fly to the sun. Marsali and Alina were off attending to the washing, while Miram had excused herself to oversee the selection of silks and linens for a new set of bedclothes. Very seldom was I left so alone, and as I enjoyed Lila's company, the time was passing more quickly than it normally would.

Then the door to my suite was flung open, and I heard a childish giggle just before the door was slammed shut again. Startled, I looked up from my writing table to see a young girl of perhaps five or six come running into the room. Upon glimpsing Lila and myself, the girl came to a skidding halt, hand going to her mouth.

"Someone lives here!" she squeaked.

"Yes," I said gently, wondering who she might be. The palace was vast, with apartments provided for some of the most favored courtiers and their families, and so I thought this child must belong to one of them, and perhaps had escaped her nanny. "I have lived here for many months now, but I have never seen you before. What is your name?"

"Nadira," she said, staring at me with wide amber eyes.

Amber eyes....

I had only seen one person here in Keshiaar with eyes that color.

Was it possible? Had Hezia born Besh a daughter? There had been much mention of there being no heir, but here in Keshiaar—as it was back home in Sirlende—a girl child could not inherit the throne.

No, surely he would not have kept such a thing from his own wife. We were not intimate, and he hid much from me, but surely he would have told me he had a child.

Lila was looking on, aghast, but then quickly bent back down over her embroidery once she saw my gaze travel in her direction. Seeing her expression, I doubted very much whether she would willingly volunteer any information as to the girl's identity.

So I went to this Nadira, then knelt before her so our eyes were nearly level. "I am Lyarris. I am the Hiereine of this land. Do you know what that means?"

She nodded, regarding me with those eerily familiar eyes. "It means you are married to my father."

It was as if someone had delivered a powerful blow to my stomach. Somehow I couldn't seem to draw in a breath, could only stare into the little girl's guileless features, delicate and pretty, with heavy black lashes framing her extraordinary eyes, and her mouth a pretty rosebud pout.

"Did he—did he tell you that?"

A shake of her head, disarrayed black locks tumbling over her shoulders. "No, Nurse told me Father had a new wife."

"And you—you did not mind?"

Nadira's head tilted slightly to one side. "Father had to get a new wife because my mother was a whore."

Once again it felt as if the breath had been slapped from me. Who on earth could be saying such things to an innocent little girl? Her nurse? "Nadira, your mother made a terrible mistake."

"No, she was a whore, and they killed her because of it."

Good gods, had no one thought to shelter the child from the reality of what her mother had done? "Nadira, who has said these things to you?"

Her shoulders went up, just a fraction, and she replied simply, "Everyone."

In that moment I heard a frantic knocking at the door, and Lila set down her embroidery and hastened to answer it, clearly glad of the distraction. As soon as she opened the door, a heavy-set woman garbed in black hastened in, recriminations and apologies tumbling over themselves, as if she did not know which she should be saying first.

"Ah, Your Majesty, a thousand apologies for this intrusion! Nadira, you naughty girl, you know you were never supposed to come to this wing of the palace! Your Majesty, she is now at the age where she can outrun me, and I—"

I raised a hand. "It is quite all right. No harm done. In fact, I am very pleased to make Nadira's acquaintance."

The woman, who I assumed must be the nurse, went pale then, as if she had just realized truly how unfortunate it was that I had seen the child at all. "That is—that is most gracious of you, Your Majesty. But I will take Nadira back to her rooms, and we will trouble you no further." She advanced toward us, bowed in my direction, and then seized Nadira by the arm, hauling her back toward the door.

Perhaps I should have made some attempt to stop her, but I was feeling so unbalanced by the entire encounter that I could only watch wordlessly as the nurse, moving quite quickly for a person of her bulk, pulled Nadira through the entryway and then shut the door behind them.

For the longest moment I stood there silently, as Lila watched me with wide dark eyes, seeming to wonder what my next words would be. Did she think I would berate her for being in on the secret? For clearly she had known of Nadira's existence.

But no, I would not take Lila to task for such a thing. She was only a servant; if she had been told to keep her mouth shut, then I could not fault her for that.

Besh, on the other hand....

It was the first time I had ever requested an audience with him, had not been content to wait for our brief interactions at dinner or directly afterward. I did not know if it was because of this that he accepted my request, but I would not question his reasons for doing so.

His suite was, of course, magnificent—more than a suite, really, but an entire wing of the palace, with an audience chamber, a library, offices and bath chambers and bedchambers and much more, opening off a central corridor. At least he saw me in his library, a far more intimate space than some of the others, and one I liked immediately, with its tall bookcases of carved warm-hued wood and the beautiful sconces of dark wrought bronze and alabaster. Then again, the presence of books, the very scent of the leather bindings and the aged paper, had always comforted me.

After his manservant had shut the door behind me, Besh stood off to one side of his desk, arms crossed. A slight frown pulled at his brow. "What is it, my lady?"

It was odd seeing him in even the filtered daylight that passed through the latticework which covered the windows. Always we met by lamplight and starlight and moonlight, as if the light of the sun was too real, too harsh to be allowed to beat down upon us.

For the past few hours I had been debating the best way to go about this. I realized, though, that no polite words, no carefully couched phrases, would make any difference. "I have met Nadira," I said simply.

A long silence as he watched me, face blank. Something flickered in those eyes, that glinting amber so like his daughter's. "Ah," he said at last.

Anger flicked through me then, anger that he could be so cool about it, could show so little reaction. "That is all you have to say? You have hidden your child from me! To what purpose, may I ask? Did you think I did not have the constitution to be a stepmother? What possible good could it do, my lord, to conceal the existence of your only daughter from your wife?"

The black lashes dropped, concealing his eyes. I heard the barest sigh escape his lips. "It is because I do not think she is my daughter."

It was the last thing I had expected him to say. I stared at him, perplexed, then finally ventured, "But—but I have seen her. She has your eyes, my lord! I have never seen another person in this land with eyes that shade. So how can you deny that you are her father?"

He said nothing for the longest moment, his own amber eyes still downcast. Then he glanced back up at me, gaze narrowed. "My brother also has eyes this color."

It went through me then, the realization of what Hezia had done to him. Not only had she been unfaithful, but she had broken her marriage vows with Besh's own brother. Perhaps she had thought to pass off the child as Besh's, or perhaps she truly did not know who the father was. "I see," I said at last, when the silence was so terrible that it needed to be broken before it grew any worse.

"Do you?" The anger in his voice was so palpable that I flinched; it cracked through the still, warm air like a whip. "Do you know what it is like to have the woman you love dishonor you with your own flesh and blood, to see him laugh as he tells you that she chose the better man?"

Oh, how my heart ached for Besh then, and how I wished things were different between us, so I might go to him and take him in my arms and give him what comfort I could, and tell him that no, Hezia had most definitely not chosen the better man. But as I knew Besh would not countenance such actions, I could only shake my head and murmur, "No, my lord, I cannot begin to understand what that is like."

"Then do not presume to tell me you see when you so clearly do not."

The voice might have belonged to a stranger, cold and foreign. Then again, Besh was the next thing to a stranger to me, was he not? This latest revelation only proved how little I did know of him, of his past.

"My apologies, my lord." In that moment I wished I could run from the room, flee so I would not have to meet his eyes. But I had been born a princess and was now a queen; I would not allow myself such weakness. "It was not my desire to cause you pain. It was just so…very unexpected, seeing the child, seeing her resemblance to you."

A shadow seemed to pass over his face, and all at once the anger appeared to drain away, leaving behind only a great weariness. "I can understand that, for I have experienced it myself. Sometimes she looks so very much like me, but my brother and I were very much alike, so…." The words died away, even as he shook his head. "I wish, Lyarris—I wish I could claim her as mine. But I cannot be sure that she is, and so I cannot acknowledge her, cannot do anything save make sure she is taken care of and lacks for nothing."

Nothing save her father's love, I thought, but I did not utter the words aloud. That was something I had been lucky in, for my father had been as considerate and kind as my mother was sharp-tongued and cold. Every once in a great while the uncharitable thought had crossed my mind that the gods had done no one any great favors for taking my father young and yet leaving my mother behind to plague us all.

But poor Nadira did not have even a distant, critical mother. Only her nurse, who seemed to be little more than a jailer for the little girl.

So many thoughts raced through my mind then. I knew that Hezia had been executed a little more than a year ago, and so Nadira could not have been more than five at the very most. Surely that meant the affair must have been carried on for some time before it was discovered. I could not ask Besh for the details, of course; I had already dredged up enough painful memories.

I asked instead, "And what will become of her?"

Besh moved away from me, went to his desk, and moved a book from one pile to another. Without looking at me, he said, "Even if she is only my brother's bastard, she still has royal blood in her veins. She will be raised properly, and then married to a younger son who will overlook the taint of her birth in order to be allied with the house of Kel-Alisaad."

It was not that much different from what her fate would have been as a legitimate daughter. How much choice did any of us royal women have? Well, I had chosen Besh, I supposed…not that I had had much joy in that choice.

"And your brother?" I asked the question quietly, not expecting an answer. But something in me wanted to know, despite the possible consequences of making such an inquiry.

For a few long seconds, Besh said nothing. Then he raised his head and met my gaze, an ironic smile tugging at his full lips. "Ah, well, what is one more broken secret between us? It is forbidden for a commoner to spill the blood of any of the royal house, even when they have transgressed so horribly, and so the executioner was rendered powerless. The only punishment I could mete out was banishment. So my brother was taken to the border of Purth and sent forth with only what he could carry. He went, and has not been heard from since."

To someone else, someone with no experience of such matters, this might have sounded plausible enough. But I had been raised in the royal court of Sirlende, and I knew no ruler would allow such a threat to wander freely without some sort of surveillance. "And you truly have no idea where he is?" I asked, my tone so neutral he could not possibly misjudge my meaning.

He rubbed his chin, fingers brushing against the faint late-day shadow of his beard there. "Those eyes of yours see much, my lady. Yes, of course I know where he is, what he has been doing. Quite the charmer, my brother. He has located a baron's widow, some years older than himself, and has made himself…indispensable…to her. I am not surprised, as he always had the facility of landing on his feet, rather like a cat."

"Oh," I said flatly, for in the back of my mind I had begun to think that this brother must have been the one behind the attack on our encampment so many months ago. However, I did not quite see how, if he had been ensconced in this widow's castle all that time, so many leagues from his homeland.

"Yes, it would have been easy to blame him for the assassination attempt," Besh said, startling me with how quickly he picked up on my thoughts. "And believe me, it is an avenue we have thoroughly explored. But my councillors and I have not found one piece of evidence to support such a conclusion, and so we have moved on to other areas of investigation."

Which I knew had been unsuccessful so far, but I did not bother to comment on the subject. Surely Besh must be feeling frustrated enough without me weighing in on the matter. So I only told him, "I am glad to hear he was not responsible. That would have been even more difficult, I should think."

"Actually, I think not," he said, his voice hardening. "For such open treason is the one transgression that would have allowed me to strike his accursed head from his neck. But alas, in that one matter, it appears he is innocent."

What possible reply could I make to that statement? I stared at him, one hand going to my throat, as if unconsciously feeling the blow of the executioner's sword against my own flesh.

Besh did not miss the gesture. The sardonic smile returned to his lips as he said, "But now that I have satisfied your curiosity on the matter of Nadira, I fear I must ask you to take your leave. I have many more appointments to keep today."

I did not question him on that point. One might think that a king or emperor is given to idleness, as he has so many people to do his bidding for him, but in the end, if he is any kind of ruler at all, he must be involved in so many decisions affecting the welfare of his land…negotiating trade agreements, mediating squabbles between his nobles, consulting with his advisors as to the best placement of resources, construction projects, collection of taxes, and so many more. I had seen first my father, and then my brother, embroiled in such minutiae, and so I thought Besh spoke only the simple truth.

Or perhaps he merely wanted to be rid of me. Either alternative was plausible enough.

"Of course, my husband," I replied, and pressed my hands together and bowed from the waist. "Thank you for seeing me…and for your honesty."

"You are very welcome," he said, but the words sounded indifferent at best. No, he was not pleased with me for dredging up a painful past, and now only wanted to move on to something else so he could forget again.

I nodded and went out, chin high, even as my thoughts darted this way and that. Yes, he had given me some of the answers I had sought, but in doing so had only raised more.

And I knew I dared not approach him in such a way again.

CHAPTER NINE

I saw no more of Nadira after that, and knew the poor child must be watched more closely than ever before. As there seemed to be nothing I could do to remedy the situation— after all, I did not even know where in the palace the child was housed—I attempted to put her from my thoughts. Unfortunately, I had little success on that front, for my mind kept picking at the problem. I tried to tell myself that yes, there was every possibility she was not Besh's child, and so there was not any real connection between the little girl and myself. Such cold practicality did not suit me very well, though, and I worried about her, wondered if there was anything I could do to make her lot in life a little more pleasant.

And if it turned out that she actually was Besh's child? Did I not then have some responsibility toward her, as the daughter of my husband? Perhaps I did, but as no one seemed inclined to allow me any further access to her, there seemed to be very little I could do to remedy the situation.

In the last week of Octevre an ambassador, one Sir Marten Morlander, a man I had met in passing but did not know well, came from Sirlende, bearing letters from my family, including a jubilant one from Torric, telling me of the birth of his son Allyn, as well as small gifts, things that I might miss, such as blackberry confit and the sweet, sticky toffees the palace confectioners excelled at making. I could see Sir Morten studying me, attempting to gauge how I fared, and so I put on my most serene public face, and assured him that I was enjoying myself here very much. Besh greeted him gravely, fed him well, and pored over the signed trade agreements the man had brought with him. Apparently he found nothing objectionable in them, saying all was well, and that he was most pleased by the air of cooperation that now existed between Sirlende and Keshiaar. It was almost as if he wanted to make sure the man would have no reason to overstay his visit. To be sure, by mid-Novedre, the sea lanes would be all but closed, as the currents became rough and dangerous, and I doubted Sir Marten wanted to be trapped in Keshiaar for the entire season, even if the weather here was at its most pleasant during the winter months. After a stay of some ten days, he took his retinue with him and departed, and I was left once again to my own devices, missing more than ever the familiar faces and accents of home.

My thoughts, I fear, were more than a little dreary after he left, although the blessed rains had finally come to

Keshiaar, and for the first time in months I did not feel as if I were stifling. I would not say it was precisely cold, not like back home, when frost would be painting all the windows in Iselfex, and, if we were lucky, snow would turn the spires and towers of the capital city into icy wonders from a fairytale. But it was cool enough that I put on heavier tunics, these made of silken brocade and even velvet, and I donned closed slippers instead of the sandals I had worn all through the summer and fall.

Gray were the days, and the nights murky. Besh made no mention of the observatory, and I knew better than to ask. It would have been futile to attempt to watch the stars when they were obscured by clouds. He seemed restless, though, as if annoyed he had been denied even that outlet. I wished I could comfort him, could be there for him, but of course he showed no sign of wishing to take solace in my arms.

Perhaps he did so with others, but if that were the case, I heard no whisper of it. Not that tight-lipped Miram would have ever revealed such a thing to me, and the women who served under her followed her lead. And although I had become somewhat familiar with many of the women who dined with us, those wives of Keshiaar's innumerable princes, I could not say any of them were friendly. Polite, yes, but there was no warmth. True, I did see Nezhaam from time to time at these gatherings, but as he was seated with the rest of the men, all he could offer was a smile and an encouraging nod from time to time. At any rate, he was Besh's friend, not mine. I had been here for the greater part of seven months, and yet I was still an outsider.

A stranger.

In one thing I did get my way. I could not have brought my library with me, numbering as it did many hundreds of volumes, but only chose some thirty books that I knew I could not live without. But Besh had a vast collection of his own, and as by then I had gained some mastery of the written version of the Keshiaari language, I asked that I might borrow those of his books which interested me, if such a thing would not discommode him too greatly.

He bowed to me and said, "Of course, my lady. I should have thought of it ere this. You may take whatever pleases you."

That reply thrilled me greatly—until I went to fetch the first batch of books, accompanied by Miram, and found my husband nowhere in evidence. I had thought that perhaps we might encounter one another in his library, but it seemed he had received word of my coming, and made sure to be occupied elsewhere. Never would I show my disappointment in front of my chatelaine, so I surveyed the titles with as unruffled a demeanor as I could manage, then selected some ten volumes. That would be enough to keep me occupied for a few days, and when I went to replace them, perhaps he would be in his chambers then.

Alas, he was not, but the books did help somewhat to ease the passing of the endless, dreary days.

Midwinter came and went, with little of the feasting and celebrations I was accustomed to. Here in Keshiaar the great festivals came at the turn of the year, not at the solstice, and although I was glad to know the season would not be completely barren of holiday observances, still the difference bothered me, as if serving to underscore how very far from home I was, and how truly alone. In that moment, I wished the ambassador had been stranded here, if only so I would have one face and voice that made me feel at home. But he was gone, and I had very little to offer me comfort.

Through it all, I tried to harden my heart against Besh. I did. If he did not want me, then better that I should not want him, either. Unfortunately, my body and heart were at war with my mind, and every evening I would go back to my chambers, ears filled with the rich sound of his voice, limbs trembling from even the faintest touch of his hand on mine. It was as if I had been afflicted with some illness that had no cure. Or perhaps there was a cure, but one that seemed to be denied me.

On New Year's, my routine was changed slightly, as Miram had asked leave to spend the holiday with her family in the city. Of course I could not deny her, and truly, it made little difference whether I had four women or three attending me. So I sent her away, bidding her to enjoy herself, then let Marsali and Alina and Lila dress me for the feast.

I could not take much joy in the beautiful deep blue velvet tunic trimmed in bands of gold embroidery and studs of turquoise, for I saw no wakening admiration in Besh's eyes when I came to take my customary seat next to him. And although I had spent the last seven months in prevarication, pretending to enjoy the shows of dancers in their filmy veils and spangled skirts, in truth it only frustrated me to watch them. Oh, what I would not give to lose myself in the spinning movements of a *verdralle*, or laugh with my partner through the lively romps of Grey Mare. Alas, even these simple pleasures were denied me, and so I could only keep the ever-present false smile affixed to my mouth, telling myself inwardly that I did not miss all those things nearly as much as I thought I did.

It was quite late when Besh brought me back to my suite. At least he still always accorded me that minor courtesy. The day would come, no doubt, when he would weary of even this small charade, and would have his guards accompany me to my chambers so he might not have to waste any more of his time.

Now, though, he was here, although being with him had begun to be mainly a torment. Being denied any sort of a relationship with him was bad enough, but having to be around him, to pretend that nothing was amiss, to have him so close and know I could not reach out to him—ah, that was the very worst of it.

"It was a lovely celebration," I told him, and forced a smile.

He did not offer me a smile of his own. Instead, I saw the amber eyes narrow slightly, as if he were considering me. "Are you quite well, my lady?"

"I?" I returned, and managed a small laugh. "To be sure, I do not know what you mean, my lord. I am in excellent health."

His expression remained sober. "That is not what I meant."

Oh, gods. What could I say? If I told him a little of me died inside every time he left me here alone, that I wanted only to be his wife in more than name, what then? It was clear that he did not love me, and so such utterances would only increase his discomfort. All I could do was lie a little more, and hope he would not press the issue.

I lifted my shoulders, saying as guilelessly as I could, "Ah, well, I suppose I am the smallest bit homesick. Our celebrations are so very different there, and it is a time to be with one's family, so I cannot lie and say I do not miss them. I have a nephew I have never seen, and I wonder what he must look like, although Ashara writes to say that he favors his father. But still...." I let the words trail away, and shrugged again. "It is of no great import. But you did ask."

"Truly, I do understand. You have managed so well here, far away from everything you know, that sometimes I forget how difficult it all must have been for you."

Oh, no, do not be sympathetic! I thought then. *For that will surely undo me.*

"Somewhat difficult," I agreed, adding quickly, "but truly, I have had the best of care here, and I do not want you to think that I am complaining."

"I do not think that at all." He glanced away from me, staring down at the broad gold ring on his right hand. I wore its mate; the Keshiaari people, although they loved adornment otherwise, did not believe in marring the surface of their wedding bands with stones or engraving. Gaze still fixed on the ring he wore, he continued, "It is only natural to miss one's family at these times. Indeed, I would worry if you felt otherwise."

"That is very generous of you, my lord."

"Is it?" Finally he turned his eyes on me once more, and I forced myself to stand steadily beneath that piercing stare, to not look away, nor allow myself to be lost in those shimmering depths of amber and gold and subtle, glinting copper. "I fear I have not been generous with you at all."

"My lord?"

He blinked, dark lashes sweeping over his eyes, and the contact was broken. "It is nothing." To my surprise, he reached out and took my hand, then turned it over, one finger tracing the line which signifies life. How warm was his touch, how strong his fingers. I scarcely dared to breathe as he touched me, my heart pounding so loudly that surely he must hear it.

In that moment I realized he had drunk more than he usually did at such feasts, and was perhaps not entirely himself. *Good,* I thought, *for perhaps that will allow him to break past the cursed reticence which has held him back all these months....*

My hand was lifted, and he pressed it against his mouth. A rush of heat went over me, my blood seeming to sing in my veins. *Yes, oh, please, yes....*

But then he let go of my hand, saying heavily, "It is late, my lady. A very good New Year's to you."

Before I could protest, before I could do anything to stop him, he had moved away from me and was walking, with just the barest trace of unsteadiness, down the corridor back toward the stairs. His guards fell in around him, just as they always did, and he was gone.

For a second or two I could only stand there, staring at the space where he had stood less than a moment before. I raised my hand, then pressed it to my mouth, hoping I would still feel some of the warmth he had left there. But no, it had disappeared, just as he had.

Fighting back tears, I went into my chambers. My women came to me, and I held myself still and cool, vowing that they should see nothing of my upset. They removed my jewels and put them away, then divested me of my fine garments. At length I was ready for bed, and I laid myself down there, alone again as always.

It was not, perhaps, the most auspicious way to begin a new year.

Miram returned late the next morning. It seemed her visit with her family had reinvigorated her, for she was full of energy, sending Lila and Marsali and Alina into quite the frenzy, declaring that my chambers needed a good scrubbing.

"More than that," she declared, hands on her hips as she surveyed the sitting room. "This rug surely hasn't been beaten in the last month. Take it out to the courtyard, and don't come back until you've spent at least an hour on it."

The three maids exchanged weary glances, but of course they would never gainsay her. Instead, they moved the furniture about, getting the various pieces out of the way, then rolled up the rug and carried it out of the chamber, staggering a little under its weight.

I listened to this latest edict of Miram's with some bemusement, as I could have sworn my maids had undertaken this same procedure only a fortnight earlier. Like the maidservants, however, I was loath to make any protests. During my tenure here, I had learned that it was best to allow Miram to have her way when it came to domestic affairs.

So I only sat down on the divan, currently placed under one of the windows, and began to reach for the book I had discarded when this latest tumult began.

Miram crossed the bare floor where the rug had previously lain, then paused a few feet away from me, her hands on her hips. "My lady, I do not think it a good idea for you to be reading right now. Those girls will not be distracted forever."

This was such an un-Miram-like remark that I did, in fact, stop what I was doing and look over at her. Her dark eyes were twinkling. Had Miram's eyes ever twinkled? I did not think so—at least, not that I could recall. "Miram?" I said, my tone questioning. "Are you quite well?"

"Oh, I am quite well, my lady." Another twinkle in those dark eyes. "However, I cannot say that I am feeling exactly *myself.*"

And as I gazed at her, perplexed, her face and body seemed to shimmer, to shift, features altering subtly, hair and eyes still dark, but the chin more rounded and softer, the mouth quirked in amusement, the nose smaller, almost pert. All this happened within the space of a few seconds, and then a woman who most definitely was not Miram gazed at me.

The odd thing was, she looked strangely familiar. Blinking, I realized there was only one woman in the world I knew of who possessed this sort of talent.

"Surely—surely it cannot be—but you are Therissa Larrin, are you not?" I stammered.

"Ah, so you do remember me," she replied with an approving smile.

How could I have forgotten the only wielder of magic I had ever seen? True, I had never met her formally, had only seen her the night of the grand ball when her ruse in providing Ashara with a magically created wardrobe had been discovered, but that was certainly a memorable night, and I did not easily forget a face.

"But—but what are you doing here?" I decided I would leave aside her use of magic for now. Such things were not precisely forbidden in Keshiaar as they were in Sirlende, and besides, even if they were, I knew there was no malice in Therissa Larrin. What she had done for Ashara, she had done out of love for her niece, and surely I could never condemn someone who had acted from such motivations.

Her eyes widened. "Why, I have come here for you, my lady. Ashara spoke of you highly, even on your brief acquaintance, and when I heard you had come here to the court of Keshiaar, rather than staying safely in Sirlende and marrying your duke—"

"Truly, was it the subject of so much gossip?" I asked with some bitterness, for I had not thought Thani's and my relationship merited any discussion back in the days before Therissa was banished from Sirlende.

"Word does get around, my lady." Her mouth pursed, and she went on, speaking briskly, "But that is neither here nor there. For you are here now, and I can only shake my head at what a mess you've made of things."

"I?" I repeated, not sure whether to be mystified or angry. In truth, I did not have much of a temper, as I had seen enough of one in my mother to know it was not a very attractive quality in anyone, let alone a queen. "And how, pray, have I made a mess of things?"

"Well, it is no great secret that you have been here for months and months, and yet you are still not truly a wife to the Hierarch."

My heart gave a single painful thump, and I repressed a gasp. Was the nature of our relationship such common knowledge? "I fear that is not something I wish to discuss with you."

Her expression softened, and to my surprise she came forward and knelt on the floor next to me, then reached out and patted my hand. "I am not saying that it is not a difficult enterprise, for dear Besh has retreated into himself like a snail into his shell, and prying him out is not a task for the faint of heart."

"It—it isn't?" I asked, mind reeling a little at the sound of her saying his name so familiarly. Even I had not had the courage to address him thus. Yes, I spoke his name in my thoughts, but I had never said it aloud.

"No. And I'm also not saying that he doesn't have his reasons for being this way, for the gods only know having an unfaithful spouse is bad enough, but to have that spouse disgracing you with your own brother?" She threw up her hands and glanced skyward, as if asking for divine clarification as to how anyone could commit such iniquitous acts. "But even with all that, this strategy of yours, of maintaining your distance, of dancing around him as if he might break— no, that will not do at all."

"And have you so very much experience in such things?" I inquired dryly. "For I see no ring on your finger, Mistress Larrin, and so I wonder how it is that you are an expert in managing a husband."

To my surprise, her eyes only twinkled, and she pushed herself to her feet with a laugh, brushing at the skirts of her flowing tunic. "A husband, no, but I do know a thing or two about men."

It took a second or two for that remark to penetrate my brain, for me to realize what she was saying. Blood rose to my cheeks, even as I replied, "I am not sure that is something I would be proud of, Mistress Larrin."

"Oh, pish," she said with an airy wave of her hand. "I knew early on that a conventional life would never be mine, and so I resolved to enjoy myself. And men can be quite wonderful, you know, if you choose the right one. Or ones, as the case may be. At any rate, it is because of a man that I am here—one I think you know. Ambassador Sel-Trelazar?"

"The ambassador!" I exclaimed. Truly, I had been missing him these last few months, for after spending much of the summer here, he had taken ship back to Sirlende, bringing with him letters and gifts from me—fine wines for Torric, jewels of citrine and amber for Ashara, a cunning little gold teething ring for the nephew who had not yet been born at that point. Not that his mission was entirely frivolous; he had also taken with him official documents from the Hierarch, amendments to trade agreements, that sort of thing. "But— he was bound for Sirlende, and you have been forever barred from our homeland. So how is it you saw him?"

"As to that, rough winds necessitated that they land in Tarenmar, in South Eredor, to make repairs. I had been staying there, determining where I should go next, and wondering if perhaps I should remain in that city, as it is a more pleasant place to overwinter than most. It was a happy circumstance that the ambassador and I saw one another in the street. Since he was bound over there for a few days, we… renewed our acquaintance."

I did not bother to press her for the particulars of that relationship, as it seemed clear enough to me. And why should it matter? Her magic had made it so that she could never have a normal life, with a family and children, and as his necessitated a great deal of travel, he most likely had never married, either. Why should they not seek comfort in one another? I liked the ambassador very much, and from what I had seen of her, I liked Therissa as well. Truly, they made a more amiable couple than many I had met.

Since I only nodded, and made no other reply, she pressed on, saying, "He told me of how you had come to Keshiaar. I had heard the rumors, of course, for in South Eredor they are worried what this new alliance between the two great empires will do to the smaller lands crushed in between, but I had not paid it much mind." Her mouth thinned somewhat, and she continued, "I fear I did not think very well of your brother when I heard the news, for of course I thought he must have forced you into the match."

"He did no such thing," I said with some indignation. "It was my decision, and mine alone."

"And that is what Malik told me, when we met in Tarenmar and shared several meals together. He spoke of your beauty and wisdom and grace…and your sadness, my lady."

"My what?" Had it been that obvious? And here I thought I was doing at least a passable job of concealing my troubled heart.

"Malik is a perceptive man. That is, I think, part of what makes him a good ambassador. Yes, he must carry out his lord's agenda, but he is willing to look into the hearts of others, to perceive their hopes and dreams and fears. If the world were a different place, I could see myself being very happy with him. But it is not, and so we have our fleeting moments, and then part again." Her tone grew wistful as she said this last, but then she seemed to shake her head, as if forcing her mind back to the task at hand. "He told me he thought you were not happy, that you seemed to enjoy your lord's company, but that you had not grown close as he had hoped you would. I did not know you, of course, but you were kind to my Ashara, and so it troubled me that you had not found the same happiness she did in her marriage."

This was all true, and so I did not bother to dispute it. I stood, then went to the window and looked out on the sodden gardens. It had rained again this day, just as it had the past two, as if the clouds were attempting to compress a year's worth of rain into a few short months. Finally I said, "Mistress Larrin, while I appreciate your concern, I do not see what you can do to help." A wry smile forced itself onto my lips, and I added, "Unless, of course, you propose to take on my form and seduce my husband."

Her hand went to her mouth. Odd, as she did not seem to be the type of woman who was easily shocked. "Gods, no, my lady! I would never do such a thing, and I do not think you would allow me, even if I were. No, I have come here to be a companion, and perhaps a confidant—something I think you are woefully lacking."

I thought then of the maidservants who had been sent away. Would any of them have become a comfort to me as the long months of exile from Sirlende passed? I did not know. But I could not dispute Therissa's point, not when I had thought much the same thing myself on several occasions. "It is true, I could use a sympathetic ear." Frowning, I turned from the window. "But what of the real Miram? What have you done with her?"

"Nothing ill, my lady, I assure you." The twinkle was back in Therissa's eyes. "Miram is a servant of the palace, but even she is not above greed. So when a friend of mine approached her as she was coming back here to take up her duties, saying he was a long-lost relative, and that he had been seeking her for many months so she might have her inheritance—well, let us just say she was eager enough to believe his story, take the money, and leave Tir el-Alisaad as quickly as possible."

"And did she not ask any of her other relatives—whose home she had just visited, by the way—if they knew of this man?"

"And risk having them lay claim to the money she just received? You have had everything you wanted in this world, so I think you cannot know precisely the lengths to which greed will drive some people."

I almost said that I did not have everything I wanted in this world. After all, I did not have Besh. But certainly I had never wanted for anything material, had never given much thought to the vast wealth at my disposal. Because of that, I could not know what it might feel like to have riches suddenly thrust upon me, especially after a life of servitude.

"Where did you get the money to pay her off?" I inquired. "I must find some way to reimburse you."

"Not at all," Therissa said at once. "Your brother gave me a very handsome settlement when he banished me, you know, and I spent very little of it, seeing as I stayed with friends while I was in Tarenmar. So, indirectly, that money has already come from you...or at least your family."

Something in this logic bothered me, but as I could not quite put my finger on what it was, I decided to let it go for the moment. Truthfully, though I might be the Hiereine of Keshiaar, I did not have much access to the wealth my husband controlled. Anything I wanted could be bought and brought to me, but I had less ready cash on hand than an ordinary housewife going shopping in the bazaar.

"Very well," I said. "We may revisit that point sometime in the future, but in the meantime, I will only thank you for your generosity. So, you are here, and Miram safely distracted and out of the way. What do you propose I do next? For unless you count love spells in your arsenal, I do not see what you can do to make my husband love me."

Her eyes widened, and she made an odd little movement toward me, as if she wished she could come and give me an encouraging embrace the way she might have with Ashara, only to realize that I was not her niece, and such forward behavior would not be encouraged. "Oh, my dear," she said quietly, "it is what you can do to make your husband love you. It is really not all that difficult, you know. You are very beautiful, but besides that, you and Besh are both so similar in so many ways. He is a man of learning, and I know you love your books. You will just have to show him that he has nothing to fear in giving you his heart, for you are nothing like the woman who broke it before."

"But if he will not allow me to spend any time with him, I do not see how I can make that happen," I argued. It was not that I wished her scheme to fail, only that I had spent so many weary months battering myself against the walls Besh had built around himself, and I no longer had any idea how to wear them down.

Her gaze shifted from me to the mess of papers on my desk. "What is all that?"

"Oh, it is but a little pastime of mine, something to while away the weary hours. Back in Sirlende I had undertaken to write down as many tales and legends as I could collect, and I have begun to do the same thing here. I confess I do not know what I intend to do with all of them, but—" I broke off as the twinkle returned to Therissa's eyes, and she hastened over to the desk to look at the writings there. "What are you thinking, Mistress Larrin?"

"Why, my lady, I think you have your solution right here." Her hand hovered over one of the papers, and she glanced over her shoulder at me. "May I?"

"Of course," I said, beginning to understand what she had in mind. "But as His Majesty has never evinced any great interest in local tales and legends—"

"Oh, never mind that," she said, picking up the paper and appearing to scan its contents. "For I do believe that deep down he wishes to be with you, but has no real excuse for doing so."

"Save that I am his wife," I replied dryly.

"But he cannot use that as a reason, for he is doing his very best to avoid being your husband. However, a few nights ago I plied one of the servers with a goodly amount of spiced wine, and took her place while she was sleeping it off—"

"Mistress Larrin!" I broke in, shocked.

She only laughed. "'Twas the best night of that poor woman's life, I have no doubt. At any rate, what I am trying to tell you is that I saw how the Hierarch looked at you, my lady, when he thought your attention was elsewhere. That was not the gaze of an indifferent man, let me assure you."

Oh, how I hoped that what she was saying was true! For that meant I did have some chance of swaying Besh to me, of making him mine at last. Still, I was wary. Hope could be such a very treacherous thing. "And so you propose that if I find some way to speak to him of these tales and legends, to spend more time with him—"

"Then he will realize what he has been denying himself all these months, and will abandon this foolish reticence of his once and for all." Perhaps I frowned, for she hastened to add, "Not, my lady, that it is foolish for a man to wish to protect himself after he has been dealt such a grievous hurt. But surely seven months is quite enough time in your presence for him to realize you are nothing like the woman who inflicted that hurt. So a little…nudge…would not be amiss."

A nudge. That was one way of looking at it. Then again, how much did I really have to lose? At worst he would rebuff my overtures, and we would be back where we were now. Surely it was worth making the attempt, if it meant that perhaps I might finally have a way of piercing the apparently impenetrable armor he had built around himself.

"Very well," I said at last. "Perhaps it is time for a little… nudge."

CHAPTER TEN

The next evening I was nearly as nervous as I had been upon meeting my husband for the first time. Understandable, I supposed, as I hoped that what I was about to attempt would reestablish our footing with one another, would allow us to start over.

So, as he was escorting me back to my chambers after dinner…and when I knew we were very close to the corridor that led to his own suite…I said, with apparent carelessness, "Did you know, my lord, that in the far north of Farendon there is a lord who also happens to be a dragon?"

His eyebrows lifted. "A what?"

"A dragon," I replied. "A great, fierce winged serpent which breathes fire."

"I know what a dragon is," Besh returned, although I detected no irritation in his tone. Then his head tilted slightly, and he inquired, "But how is it that one came to be a lord?"

We had arrived at the junction where we could turn off to his private wing of the palace. "As to that, there are conflicting stories, but…." I hesitated, then lifted my shoulders. "Perhaps we could go to your library, so I might tell the tale?"

He paused then, eyes perhaps narrowing slightly as he regarded me. I could only hope that my expression was serene and guileless, so he could catch no hint of the desperation which made my heart seem to beat all too quickly, and my fingers to tremble. Luckily, the skirt of the long tunic I wore was quite full, and I concealed my hands within its folds, praying he would not notice my unease.

Then he gave the smallest lift of his shoulders before replying, "If you wish, my lady. This way." He offered me his arm, and I took it, willing my foolish and weak flesh to be calm and steady, so it would not betray me. Perhaps it was feeling the strength of his arm beneath mine that allowed my hand to rest lightly on his with no hint of a tremor, or perhaps I finally had gained enough mastery of myself to keep my limbs from shaking. Whichever it was, I walked serenely enough at his side down the long corridor, with its patterned marble floors and sweet-smelling oil burning in lamps of alabaster and bronze, until we reached his chambers. Two of the guards hastened forward to open the huge doors of pierced wood, nearly twice the height of a man, and the rest of them filed in behind us, taking up their positions in the antechamber as we continued to the library.

Once we were there, I did feel slightly more at ease, most likely because the presence of books always calmed me. As evenings went in Keshiaar, it was rather chilly, and so a brazier flickered in one corner, away from the bookshelves that lined all the other walls.

In addition to the chair behind the desk, there were several more scattered about the space. To my relief, Besh pulled out one of those for me, saying, "please sit, my lady," before taking another for himself. I had feared he might sit behind the desk, using it as a way to keep me at a distance, but it seemed those fears had been for naught.

"And so there is truly a lord in Farendon who is a dragon?" he inquired. "However did you hear of such a thing?"

So it seemed he was willing to humor me for now. Good. I knew I must seem interested enough to keep him engaged, but not so over-eager that he would suspect any motive lay behind my wishing to be here, other than to share my tales with him. "Well, my lord, I have long made a habit of collecting the stories I hear and writing them down, and so people know to come to me with their fantastical tales."

"They would come to you?" Besh inquired, head tilting slightly as he regarded me. "I had no idea the Crown Princess of Sirlende was so...available."

A flush touched my cheeks, and I replied in an off-hand way, "Oh, they had to request an audience, of course, unless it was something I heard from one of the servants. They are quite a wealth of information, if one allows oneself to acknowledge that they are far more than merely servants, but people with their own thoughts and hopes and dreams."

Most men in his position would have been taken aback by such a statement—even my own brother was not immune to the isolating effects of his title—but Besh seemed to consider my words carefully, expression thoughtful. "That is true enough, I suppose, although I must confess it is the first time I have ever heard a woman—or anyone—with such lofty status admit such a thing." He straightened in his chair and rested his hands on his knees, then said, "So it was one of the servants who told you this?"

I shook my head. "No, my lord. It was a young nobleman from Farendon, who had come as part of a diplomatic party on behalf of his king, to bring gifts to my brother in advance of his wedding to a princess of that land." As I told Besh this, though, I felt a twinge of sadness for that poor girl, dead so young, and wondered how different all our lives would be if she had married Torric as planned. For then of course he would never have met Ashara, and so I would have known nothing of her aunt—Mistress Larrin most likely would not have lifted a finger to help me in my current situation, as I would only be to her a princess of the land that had cast her out so many years before.

"And so this young man thought to impress you with wild tales from his homeland?"

The curl of Besh's lip as he asked this question told me he guessed very well what the nobleman's true objective had been, which was to flirt with the Crown Princess of Sirlende and per-haps gain her favor. I, too, had guessed his motives, and only smiled and asked him about Farendon, as of course I had never been there. And that was when the young nobleman—good-ness, what had his name been?—told me about the dragon.

"Perhaps that was his intention, but as he was only the younger son of a baron, he had no hope of pressing his suit with me."

At that Besh actually chuckled. "Ah, well, men do like to dream."

And what is it you dream of, Besh, as you sleep here alone? Of course I could not give voice to that thought, and so I went on, "But he was rather charming, and of course I began to listen very intently when he told me that in the far, far north of his land, just outside a small town called Lirinsholme, there is a castle called Black's Keep, and in that castle lives a lord named Theran Blackmoor."

"That does not sound like a very dragonish name to me."

"Well, he was not a dragon when he was given that name."

"Ah, so he became a dragon?" Besh's eyes gleamed with curiosity, and he leaned forward slightly, attention fixed on my face.

Oh, gods, this may be working! I nodded, replying, "That is what the young nobleman told me. He did admit that some claimed this Lord Blackmoor had been born a dragon, a curse from the gods because of some transgression committed by his parents, although no one was able to say precisely what that transgression might have been. But then the young man went on to say that most believed his lordship had been cursed in some way many, many years ago, when magic was still freely practiced, before the great mage wars."

I paused then, for of course I knew that magic had not disappeared entirely from the world, although its practitioners must needs hide their gifts to avoid persecution and possibly even death. In Sirlende, that was the penalty for using magic, and I had heard they were nearly as strict in Farendon. Which, if they once had mages so powerful they could curse a man into dragon form and have him live for hundreds of years afterward, I supposed was understandable. Keshiaar had escaped the ravages of those terrible wars, and so magic was still practiced here—or so I had heard. Not in a way so any one person could gain an advantage over another, but I had gathered from overhearing several whispered conversations between Marsali and Alina that no one thought twice about consulting a soothsayer at the bazaar, or asking for a potion to relieve one's aching joints…or attract a husband.

Hmm. Perhaps that was something I should consider. For if this plan that Mistress Larrin had concocted failed, then I could always send Lila to the bazaar to purchase a love potion to open my husband's unwilling heart….

"So many years, and yet this lord still lives?" Besh asked, and now his tone was plainly skeptical.

Well, I had learned that my husband thought of himself as a man of learning, of science, and so I supposed he would raise an eyebrow at the notion of a mortal man not only cursed into a dragon's form, but also gifted with what appeared to be unending life. "That is what the young nobleman told me."

"And had he ever seen this dragon?"

"Oh, no, of course not. The dragon lord does not leave his castle very often."

"I suppose that is wise, if one does not wish to be stared at."

I lifted my chin and inquired, somewhat archly, "Are you mocking me, my lord?"

"Of course not." But a quirk at the corner of his mouth told me otherwise.

"At any rate, the dragon stays inside his castle most of the time, unless he is angry. Then he has been seen flying above the town of Lirinsholme, and all its citizens hide inside, and hope he does not rain down fire upon them with his fearsome breath."

"And what does one do to invoke the dragon's wrath?"

"The young nobleman did not say, I fear." Actually, he had mentioned that long, long ago, a king of Farendon did attempt to vanquish the dragon, so the town of Lirinsholme might be free of its curse, and had been met with fire and death in retaliation. "It may have something to do with the Brides—" And here I broke off, and feigned a yawn, as if I had only then realized how late the hour actually was.

"The Brides?" Besh asked, ignoring my yawn.

"I am so sorry, my lord, but I am very weary. Could we continue tomorrow night?"

For a second or two he paused. Then he gave a reluctant nod and said, "Of course, my lady. It is important that you get your sleep. We will speak again tomorrow after dinner."

My heart leapt within my breast, but I only summoned what I hoped was a faint, tired little smile. "Thank you, my lord. I must confess that this unending rain has made me more fatigued than usual." This was a complete fabrication, as I was finding the cool, grey days a welcome relief from the blazing heat that reigned in Keshiaar three seasons out of the year.

But Besh did not seem to question the proffered excuse, and only rose from his chair, then offered me his hand. I took it gratefully, and he led me from the library out to the antechamber, where the guards fell in around us. From there he safely delivered me to my own suite. The customary bow and a polite "good night," and he was gone again.

We had parted in such a fashion so many nights before this one. Now, though, I felt my blood seem to sing and dance in my veins, for Besh had agreed to see me alone again, and that could only be a promising sign. And as "Miram" approached me, her dark eyes full of questions, I could only smile and nod, for the other three maids were present, and we could not share any confidences until we had the opportunity to be alone.

But Mistress Larrin, in her guise as the chief of my maids, seemed to understand, for she sent me a returning nod before bidding the other women to see to my wardrobe, while she lifted the heavy headdress from my hair and pulled the bracelets from my arms and the necklace from about my throat. My jewels were so extensive that I had a tall chest with many wide, flat drawers to hold them all, and "Miram" took away the pieces I had worn this evening and stowed them carefully in their proper places.

Odd that I trusted her so implicitly to handle them; after all, they were worth a great deal, and she was in a perfect position to take what she wanted and sell it to the sort of people who dealt in such goods. However, while I could not say I knew Therissa Larrin well, I did know that Ashara loved and trusted her, and so her intentions could only be noble. She had come here to help me, and nothing more.

And it seemed that her assistance was providing results even more quickly than I dared hope. When I was finally ready for bed and my maids had withdrawn to the outer rooms, I lay down and closed my eyes, smiling as I fell into welcome sleep.

The next evening we entertained several princes from the far south of Keshiaar, and Besh seemed so involved in his conversation with them, about the gold mines there, and the need for better roads to them, that I feared he would forget our assignation altogether, or at least postpone it. But although he had broken with tradition by inviting them to sit at our table and converse with us, at the end of the meal he excused himself, saying he had a previous engagement.

So we walked through the corridors once again until we reached his apartments, and once again the guards took up their posts outside the door to the library as we seated ourselves within. It seemed that Besh had prepared himself in advance for tonight's appointment, as a decanter of dark wine awaited us, along with two cups of gold studded with turquoise.

In that moment I was glad I had drunk sparingly at dinner, knowing that I needed to keep my wits about me. Even so, I would have to be cautious.

"Some wine?" Besh asked, and I said,

"Yes, thank you."

He poured some into each goblet—not a good deal, not even filling them halfway. So perhaps this was more about hospitality than wishing to make me intoxicated. More's the pity.

I had just taken my first sip of the wine when he prompted, "So...yesterday evening you mentioned the dragon lord having Brides? What on earth does a dragon want with a wife?"

Good question, my lord. I must wonder whether you have asked yourself very nearly the same thing. But I made sure my expression was one of polite interest as I replied, "The young nobleman who told me the story didn't know, for I asked him that as well. All he knew was that from time to time, usually every five years or so, although sometimes it could be much longer or much shorter, a red flag would be hoisted above the dragon lord's castle, and that was the signal that a new Bride must be selected from the girls of Lirinsholme."

"And how does that happen?" Besh asked, smiling faintly. I could tell he still didn't quite believe the tale. To be sure, I wasn't sure I believed it myself, either, although the young nobleman from Farendon had insisted that every word of it was true. "Does the dragon come down and choose the comeliest young woman for himself?"

"That would make it more like a fairy story, I think, but that is not what actually happens. All the names of the young women of the correct age are put in"—I paused, for in that moment I could not recall that exact detail. A basket? A hat? Oh, well, I supposed that one small subtlety wasn't terribly important—"a small container, and one of the town elders pulls the name out."

"I'm sure that's terribly unbiased," Besh remarked. "For of course they would never think to employ some gambit that would ensure no one of their own families would ever be chosen."

"As to that, I cannot say. It did not occur to me to ask such a thing, but one would think that a being as powerful as a dragon might have some way of finding out that such tactics had been employed. I am not sure I would take such a risk."

"No, of course you would not, for you are an honorable woman."

I hoped I did not flush too much at his praise. Oh, how starved I was for even the smallest compliment from him, even if it was simply calling me "honorable." Then again, I had been raised at court, and so I knew that in many cases, finding those with honor was a more difficult task than one might think. Perhaps praising my honor was not quite as pale a compliment as I had first thought it.

"Well," I began, waving what I hoped was an airy hand, "that is not something the young nobleman divulged."

"And so?" Besh inquired. "What happens to the Brides after they go to the dragon lord?"

"No one knows," I said simply.

"What do you mean, no one knows?"

"I mean that the young nobleman told me the young women would go to Black's Keep on the very day their names were selected, but" —I made sure to pause for effect— "no one ever sees them again. They disappear completely from the world."

At that Besh raised his eyebrows and settled back in his chair before placing his wine goblet on the desktop. "And no one has tried to investigate what has happened to them?"

Ah, Besh, trying to attack the problem logically. That works quite well for calculating the angles of a planetary conjunction,

but is probably not the best approach for a situation such as this.
"But you see, there's a dragon," I pointed out.

"There is the *myth* of a dragon," he replied, tone mild enough that it didn't precisely sound as if he was correcting me. "That doesn't necessarily mean there really is a dragon. Something quite different could be happening to those young women."

"Such as?"

When I asked that question, he actually looked rather uncomfortable, as if he could think of several quite unsavory things that might be occurring with those young women, none of them involving a dragon. But because he clearly had no wish to wander into such topics with me, he lifted his shoulders and reached for his wine. "I am not sure precisely. However, I feel that there are many more logical explanations for their disappearances than a dragon lord who was either cursed into that form or had the misfortune to be born that way."

I widened my eyes at him, asking, "My lord, are you mocking me?"

"No, of course not." His amber eyes took on a sly glint. "You are only relating what was told to you. However, I may be mocking that young nobleman from Farendon."

"And have you no fantastical stories here in Keshiaar that nonetheless people take as the truth?"

"A few, but—"

"Well, then." Once again I feigned a yawn, then said, "But I fear I am too weary to debate you on this topic. We will let the dragon lord go for now. And I just recalled something a merchant told me once of the wolf-men of North Eredor, but if you have no interest in such stories—"

"I did not say that," Besh cut in. "Who are these wolf-men?"

"Their name for themselves is the *corraghar*, or so the merchant said." I stopped once more, a real yawn overcoming me in that moment. "I am sorry, my lord, but it is very late. Perhaps I can tell you more of that tomorrow."

He paused, gazing at me, and I held myself very still. In that moment I feared he had guessed at my game, and these two stolen evenings were all I would have with him. But then he inclined his head, expression one only of concern, as he said, "Of course, my lady. I would never wish to deprive you of your sleep. Let me take you back to your chambers, and we will speak of these wolf-men tomorrow night after dinner."

I smiled and thanked him, but inwardly I was exulting. Thank goodness I had collected so many stories over the years. Surely I could keep spinning them out long enough for him to realize how much he enjoyed my company, and that I truly was meant to be his wife in all ways possible.

That thought buoyed me as he returned me to my chambers and bade me a good evening. I fell asleep that night with yet another smile on my face, envisioning a long string of such evenings stretching out before me, all with Besh more interested, more engaged, until at last he would take me in his arms and proclaim his love for me, tell me that he should never have ignored me for so long.

It was a pleasant fantasy. I could only hope that it might one day come true.

The next day Therissa, in her guise as Miram, once again manufactured an errand to get all of the other maids out of my chambers, this time dispatching them to the storerooms in search of fabrics for a new set of underthings for me. Most likely this was a task Miram had undertaken herself in the past, deeming it too important for the under-maids to manage, but, as usual, they did not think to protest, only ducking their heads and scurrying from my chambers, whispering amongst themselves. Even if it was an unusual request, I thought they probably enjoyed the prospect of poking through the stores of fabric kept in the palace, and would no doubt stay away as long as they possibly could.

Which, of course, had been Therissa's intention all along.

"Well," she said, once we were safely alone, "how are things faring?"

"Better than I could have hoped, because we have now spent two evenings alone together with no protest from him, and we shall see each other again tonight after dinner." I had been primping in front of the mirror, trying the effect of an ensemble of diamonds in silver with my white and silver costume. Or perhaps something that would show up more against it, such as the emeralds? Now I laid the emeralds down and turned toward Therissa, gratified to see her beaming in a way that Miram most assuredly never had.

"Oh, that is wonderful news, my lady," Therissa said.

I smiled, but told her, "Therissa, as we are co-conspirators in this, please call me Lyarris. There is no reason to stand on ceremony when it is only the two of us."

That seemed to surprise her, for her dark eyes widened, even as she protested, "Oh, no, my lady, I do not think I could be so familiar as that. You are very generous, but—"

"What is so familiar about it? Really, we are related, as you are my sister-in-law's aunt. In my family, we did not go around calling one another 'my lord' and 'my lady'—even though I sometimes had the distinct impression that my mother might have preferred it that way." This argument seemed logical enough to me, although I was sure many might have thought my reasoning not quite correct. But my entire life had been one of rules and decorum and etiquette, and now, when I had only one person I could count as my friend, I did not want that person clinging to what I thought was a rather foolish custom.

Therissa's lips curled up at my comment. "Well, I will do my best, Lyarris, but do not scold me if I slip up from time to time and still call you 'my lady.'"

"I promise that I shall never scold you," I replied. "And truly, this plan does seem to be working quite well. I have to take care and not stare at Besh with what my brother used to refer to as 'goggle eyes,' but I must confess that as Besh and I are talking with one another, I become so focused on what we're discussing that I can almost forget my infatuation."

A slight chuckle had escaped Therissa at my "goggle eyes" remark, but her expression grew severe at the end of my little speech. "I would not call what you have for your husband an 'infatuation,' my…Lyarris. You have come to care for him very much, I think, and are well past infatuation. Or am I misreading the situation?"

"No, you are not," I said, attempting not to sigh. "Sometimes it's like a horrible, empty ache right here." And I laid my hand against my breast, feeling the slow, calm beating of my heart beneath my palm. "I have done my best to ignore it, but sometimes that is very difficult."

"I can well imagine. But that ache will lessen the more time you spend with him, and once he wakes up and realizes that he has been hurting both himself and you by trying to hold you at arm's length, then things will be ever so much better."

"I will have to pray that you are right." I turned from her then, and held up both the diamonds and the emeralds. "Which would you choose?"

"The diamonds, I think, for they sparkle more, and that will make it more difficult for the Hierarch to keep his eyes off you."

That sounded like excellent advice to me, and so I clasped the diamond collar around my throat, even as Therissa hastened over to my dressing table to fetch the headdress and lay it gently on my hair. Yes, the contrast between the white gems and my dark hair was very good, and I smiled and nodded, then thanked her for her advice.

It was the least I could do, after all, for it was her counsel that was helping me to win my husband's heart.

CHAPTER ELEVEN

I was glad of my primping, for that night's feast was a larger one than usual, given to honor Nezhaam's father, who I gathered had been a great friend of the previous Hierarch and was still among Besh's circle of trusted advisors. However, I worried that my husband would be so preoccupied with ensuring the guest of honor was properly entertained that he would quite forget my promise to speak to him of North Eredor's "wolf-men" this evening.

As it turned out, my fears were not realized, for although the gathering did extend farther into the night than some of our earlier, more staid get-togethers, at length the guests departed, and Besh turned to me and said, "Now, these men of the north?"

"Wolf-men," I corrected him. "But yes, I can speak to you of them, if you wish."

In reply, he offered me his arm, and I took it gladly, feeling the strength of the muscles beneath mine, the warmth of his flesh through the thin silk that covered the lower half of my arm. Did he relish the touch of flesh against flesh as I did, or was he steeling himself against it, attempting to tell himself that the contact truly meant nothing more than it would if he had offered such a courtesy to another lady of the court?

I told myself to let it alone, that for now it was enough we touched at all. At least as we walked through the palace and those around us bowed when we passed, Besh and I gave the semblance of a happy couple. Perhaps one day soon that semblance would become a reality.

As before, we took our respective seats, but when he went to pour me some wine, I demurred. "If you have some cold water, that would do very well," I told him. "I fear I had rather more wine with dinner than I intended, and I do not want to become so muzzy-headed that I forget something of what I am trying to tell you."

"Wise as always, dear wife," he said, the words thrilling me, even though I knew he had not intended anything exceptional by saying them. The servants had left a silver pitcher of cold water behind as well, and he poured some into one of the goblets that had been set out, then handed it to me.

I took it from him, letting my fingers brush against his as I did so. This was something of a test, for it seemed rather a more intimate touch than simply taking my arm to lead me here. He did not pull away, and I fancied that perhaps he let his fingers rest against mine for a second or so longer than was strictly necessary.

A thrill passed through me, my blood seeming to heat from within, although I did my best to keep my expression calm and pleasant, to not allow him to see his effect on me. I could have been mistaken in my judgment of his character, but over the months I had had ample opportunity to survey his behavior, his reactions to actions of my own, and being forward was not the way to manage this. Rather like a spider in her web, I would have to lure him toward me. Not that I intended him any harm—no, rather the opposite. But he, like the oblivious fly, needed to be unaware of the machinations I had to perform to bring him close to me.

Then he drew away, settling into his own chair. I drank some of the water he had given me, for in truth I was thirsty, and I knew we might be talking for some time. The amber eyes were fixed on me, waiting for me to begin.

I wanted to lose myself in those eyes, in those shimmering layers of bronze and topaz and warm brown, but I knew if I stared for too long, he would most certainly sense something was amiss. So I sipped at my water once more before lowering the goblet and holding it loosely between my two clasped hands.

"This is something I had from a merchant out of North Eredor, a man who—"

"And did your brother the Emperor encourage you to speak with such men?" Besh inquired, his tone more amused than anything else. The gods only knew what sort of opinion he must have formed of the imperial court, based on these stories of mine.

"Oh, no—that is, of course he did not encourage it, precisely, but then, he was also very busy with the running of the empire, something you must know of as well, I would imagine." I turned the goblet in my hands, feeling the smooth silver against my palms, the chill of the iced water within. "And it was our custom to have what we call an open audience once a month, where the people of the realm might bring their concerns or questions to their Emperor."

"He made himself so available?" Surprise was evident in Besh's tone, and he leaned forward slightly, his gaze never leaving my face.

All I could do was hope that no flush touched my cheeks under that intent stare. "Yes, my lord husband, he did. He thought it wise to hear what the people had to say, and to consider it as carefully as any advice he might receive from the great lords who were his councillors. For they were denizens of our land just as much as any lords and ladies, and so their ideas and opinions had just as much worth."

During my little speech Besh had been listening carefully, brows drawing together as he appeared to ponder what I had said. "That is very…clear-thinking…of him."

"Is it?" I lifted my goblet of water to my lips and drank, then went on, "Perhaps. It is something our father instituted during his reign, and so Torric made sure to continue it, although I always got the impression that some of his advisors would have been all too glad to abandon the practice."

"That does not surprise me," Besh said. "I can only imagine the uproar if I were to try something similar here."

His tone was not precisely wry…if anything, it sounded disappointed, as if he wished he could have expected more of his advisors. I did not know what I should say, for I had lived such a cloistered life here that I had not enjoyed the freedom to see how he interacted with his own councillors. We saw each other at dinner, and on those rare occasions when he deigned to invite me to his observatory, and that was, unfortunately, the extent of our relationship.

But even with that, I thought I understood. For all its power and strength, Keshiaar somehow seemed to be looking back, hanging on to the days of its glory, instead of reaching out for the future the way my brother was. Now, some of those innovations I could have done without, such as the factories whose smoke and steam made the air around Iselfex hazy even on an otherwise clear day, but one felt remarkably freer there. Even I, as a princess whose days had been bounded on every side by custom and protocol, had the liberty to leave the palace—accompanied by guards and attendants, of course—and ride in the countryside, or go to the theater, or have a picnic on a fine spring day.

Here, I had done none of those things, and I somehow doubted I ever would. It was not expected of the Hiereine. I was supposed to sit at my husband's side during feasts and look beautiful, and do little else other than that. And bear his children, of course, but I had not been allowed to fulfill even that particular duty…although not from a lack of wishing on my part.

"It would be difficult, yes," I said. "But not impossible. You are the Hierarch, after all. Is your word not law? Would your advisors not be compelled to do as you asked, should you ask it?"

"One would think so, but…." He let the words fade away into the still air. "Such things are not as easy to put in motion as you would think."

It was on my lips to protest further, but I quelled that impulse. He knew this land and its people far better than I. Besides, we had not come here to talk politics.

"I would suppose not," I told him. "In any case, I had seen the merchant on an open audience day, and I thought it would be a good thing to speak with him, if such a thing were possible. North Eredor and Sirlende suffer an uneasy peace, for, as you probably know, those in the north do not accept what we have set as the boundaries of our realm, and are forever attempting to take back what lands they may. Because of this, we do not have as many travelers from that land as we do from South Eredor, with whom we enjoy good relations."

"And so you sought out this merchant? He must have been surprised at such attentions."

"Indeed he was. I had one of my ladies-in-waiting approach him as he was about to leave the audience chamber, then tell him that the Crown Princess wished to have discourse with him in one of the small salons."

A smile played about Besh's lips, and I had to tear my eyes away. In that moment I recalled what those lips had felt like, laid against mine as he gave me the wedding kiss, and I wanted to feel their touch once again, the heat of his mouth on my flesh. Warmth flooded my cheeks, and I went on hurriedly,

"It was all very proper, I assure you."

"My dear wife, I did not think otherwise."

At least he would think my blush had come from even the hint that I might have intended anything less than honorable with the merchant. Not that he wasn't actually quite a fine figure of a man, tall and black-haired and blue-eyed, and probably no more than a few years past thirty. But I felt it best not to pass along that particular information.

"Two of my ladies-in-waiting were with me, and my maid Arlyn," I said, in somewhat severe tones, and Besh's smile only widened. "As you might guess, the merchant was rather confused by my request to speak with him, but when I told him one of my occupations was collecting tales from the various lands of the continent, he was only too eager to tell me what he could."

"Of that I have little doubt, for what man would not want to spend a few hours in the company of a beautiful woman?"

My cheeks burned even more, if such a thing were possible. I did not know what to make of such a compliment. Oh, how I wished to believe that it was an indication of his further softening toward me. Surely if he thought I was beautiful, he must want me. Or was my perceived beauty an impediment? After all, the treacherous Hezia had been very beautiful....

Not looking directly at him, I replied as lightly as I could, "As to that, we also provided cakes and wine, and so perhaps that had something to do with his eagerness as well. At any rate, he told me of these wolf-men, the *corraghar*, who live in the hill country of the northernmost part of his land."

"And are they truly part wolf?" The amusement in Besh's tone was so subtle that I couldn't take offense at it. Not quite, anyway.

"That is not precisely what the merchant told. Rather, they hold the wolves sacred, call them their brothers, go safely among them when a normal man would surely be rent in pieces by a wild pack. He said sometimes they would go hunting with the wolves."

"Hunting what? Men?"

"Oh, no," I replied. "That is, perhaps that does occur on certain dreadful occasions, but the merchant spoke of deer and elk. The *corraghar* are very reclusive, although in later years they have become somewhat more mixed with the rest of the society in North Eredor, as the current Mark's father is said to have been one of the *corraghar*. Thani—that is, the Duke of Marric's Rest—his sister is married to the Mark, and he described his eyes once."

I recalled that conversation, where we had hidden ourselves way in an alcove at one of the unending galas held at the palace. Thani had spoken of his family, had talked of how much he missed all of them, with his sister so far away in North Eredor, and the rest of his relations still back in the south. It was during that conversation that I had begun to fall in love with him, for it was the first time he had allowed me to see something of the man behind his public face.

But I knew I should not be thinking of Thani, not while I was here sitting across from my husband, so close that our knees were almost touching. No, Sorthannic Sedassa should have been the furthest thing from my mind.

How much Besh had known about the relationship between the Duke of Marric's Rest and myself, I was not sure, but he had to have at least been aware that we fancied ourselves engaged, and that I had broken off the engagement to come here.

For the longest moment my husband said nothing, while the silence weighed heavily between us. Was he wondering how truly intimate Thani and I had been, and whether I was now regretting my choice?

I could not ask such things, of course. No, I could only sit there and pray that he would speak soon, for I did not know what to say to him. Everything that rose to my lips felt dreadfully wrong.

Fate saved me then, for there sounded a knock at the door to the library.

"Come," Besh said shortly, a brief flicker of annoyance passing over his face before he smoothed it away.

The door opened, and one of the guards stood there, bowing at the waist. "Most High Majesty, a thousand apologies for the intrusion. But the *visanis* is waiting without, and he says he has urgent news he must discuss with you."

One of Besh's eyebrows lifted, but he said only, "Show him in."

I could not help wondering what news could be so urgent that it brought my husband's chancellor here at such an hour of the night, but I supposed we would find out soon enough. The guard went away, returning a scant minute later with Azeer Tel-Karinoor on his heels.

By some unspoken request, the guard slipped back out to the corridor, leaving the chancellor to stare down at my husband and myself. There was something in Azeer's expression that told me he was none too pleased to find me here closeted with the Hierarch, but of course he could not outwardly express his displeasure.

Instead, he bowed from the waist, hands pressed together before him, gaze fixed on Besh. "Most High Majesty, I have news...news which I believe should be given to you in private."

Meaning, I supposed, without me present, for certainly we were private enough here, cloistered in the Hierarch's library.

Besh must have thought more or less the same thing, as he said at once, "I have no secrets from my lady wife. Speak."

No secrets? Well, I had managed to discover several that he would have rather kept hidden, but I did not know if he had any others. Perhaps not.

Lips thinning, Tel-Karinoor said, "Most High Majesty, through the grace of God, we have captured the one we believe was behind the attack on your most noble self. He is now in the dungeons, awaiting questioning."

At these words, Besh stood. Unsure as to what I should do, I remained in my seat, apparently forgotten.

"You are certain?" he asked, gaze fixed on his chancellor.

"As I said, Most High Majesty, he will be questioned soon, and then we will have the answers we seek. However, the evidence pointing to him is strong...very strong. I have no doubt that when all the truths of the matter are revealed, we will know for certain—and he will know the bite of the executioner's sword."

Because I had been watching him closely, I saw how Besh winced just a little at the mention of that dreadful blade. No doubt he was not welcoming the reminder of how his own wife had lost her life.

But because he was the Hierarch, he could not acknowledge that pain, could only say, "That is excellent news, *visanis*. Do keep me apprised of any further developments."

"As you wish, Most High Majesty," Tel-Karinoor replied. His jaw seemed to stiffen, and I felt rather than saw his gaze shift toward me briefly before returning to Besh. Perhaps he blamed my presence for my husband's subdued reaction to the news that the would-be assassin had been apprehended. "I will go to the dungeons now to oversee the interrogation."

"Very good, Tel-Karinoor."

And that was the end of the interview, for after another bow toward both of us, the *visanis* exited the chamber, heading, presumably, for the dungeons, wherever they might be. From the bits and pieces I had picked up, listening to the maids talk amongst themselves when they thought I was occupied with a book or with my writing, there was a veritable maze of storerooms below the palace, and perhaps below one wing or another the dungeons lay as well, although I rather doubted they would be here, beneath the Hierarch's own apartments.

"Well," Besh said, then paused, gazing down at me. "I apologize for the disruption, but I fear now it is quite late.

We shall have to speak of these wolf-men of the north at a later date."

I noticed he did not say "tomorrow." Perhaps he thought he would be occupied, now that the transgressor had been caught. I did not know for sure, and I could not think of a way to ask without revealing to him how important these nightly discussions were to me. All I could do was rise from my seat and say, as calmly as I could, "Of course, my lord. Whenever the opportunity presents itself."

At least he did offer his arm, made no attempt to fob me off on the guards so he would not have to waste precious time taking me back to my own chambers. We walked quietly, without speaking, and I wondered what he was thinking of. Was he wondering who the would-be assassin was, and why he would have taken such a terrible risk? Great men always had their enemies, it was true, although I had seen nothing in Besh's words or deeds that would lead me to believe he was the kind of man to engender the hatred necessary to make an assassination attempt. Indeed, he was always even-tempered, thoughtful, not easily swayed to a decision without pondering it for some time beforehand.

When I considered these parts of his nature, I thought him to be a very good measure of a ruler, the sort any realm would be lucky to have as its sovereign. Perhaps my own feelings toward him influenced my opinion, but I didn't believe so. Truly, I would be lying if I did not admit to myself that in some hidden corner of my soul, I was angry with him for not allowing me to be his true wife, for letting his terrible experience with Hezia color all his dealings with me. Despite that buried resentment, which was purely personal, I could see nothing about him that would make him a target.

Save that he was the Hierarch, and therefore seen as something more than a man, instead a figure, a symbol. Perhaps in the mind of an assassin, killing a symbol did not carry the same weight as killing a man.

"You are very quiet," Besh said, and I realized that we had gone all the way to the entrance to my chambers without exchanging a single word.

"Oh!" I replied, rather discomfited. How on earth had I allowed myself to be so lost in my thoughts as to remain silent that entire span of time? "I suppose I have merely been thinking of the news the *visanis* has brought. It must be a tremendous relief to you."

"Yes," he said at once, and yet I thought I noted a slight hesitation in his manner. "We will see this man and whatever allies he has brought to justice, and then we may go on as we were before."

No, not that, I thought, *for I do not wish to go on as we were before. I want things to change between us, so you can finally see me for myself, and not as an echo of the woman who wronged you.*

But I said only, "Yes, that will be very good."

Besh paused then, gaze fixed on my face. I could only hope that I looked serene and untroubled, secure in the knowledge that the guilty parties had been apprehended, and that the undercurrent of unease which had run through the court for the past half-year and more would finally lessen.

He said, "Be well, my wife," and bent and kissed me on the forehead.

Again I felt a rush of heat along every limb, even from that one mild, chaste kiss. But I had been so deprived of any sign of affection from him that any touch at all was equal to the most passionate of embraces. I drew in a breath, willing myself to stay calm. "And you, my husband," I said quietly.

A faint movement of one hand, as if he had been about to reach out and touch my face, caress my hair. Then he stilled. "I will see you tomorrow night, then."

And that was all. He bowed to me before turning and leaving me there alone.

Ah, well. At least by then I was used to such things.

Even in my secluded chambers, we felt something of the buzz that had overtaken the palace at the news that the assassins' mastermind had been caught. Naturally, I was not allowed to precisely participate in the whispered conversations between my maids as they tidied my rooms and worked at their interminable needlework, but no one was there to keep me from eavesdropping. Thank goodness my knowledge of the Keshiaari tongue had only grown and deepened during my time here, and so it was not any great difficulty to follow their lightning-fast *sotto voce* exchanges.

Pretending to be engrossed in a book, I sat in my favorite chair by the window and heard Marsali whisper to Alina, "They say he is a giant of a man, and possessed by dark spirits, and that is what made him do it."

Alina's eyes widened, and she whispered back, "Do you think the spirits will come out when they cut off his head?"

"I do not know, but I suppose that is a risk they will have to take. After all, they cannot allow such a man to live."

Lila jumped in, saying, "But I heard from Alzham down in the kitchens that the villain is not possessed at all, but rather an evil magician from Purth, who came here to kill His Most High Majesty so the empire should be disrupted, and armies from Purth could then invade."

"Don't be silly," snapped Marsali, who was a few years older than Lila and therefore deemed herself infinitely more sensible. "For although that would be a very great tragedy, it is not that His Most High Majesty does not have an heir designated."

I wondered then who this heir was. Some cousin, I guessed, as of course Besh's brother had lost any chance he might have had of inheriting the throne.

"Besides," Marsali continued, "His Most High Majesty's advisors and generals would still be alive. Purth is not even one-fifth the size of Keshiaar, and they would lose before they even began."

Faced with such convincing arguments, the other two young women fell silent, staring at one another as if attempting to wrestle with the conundrum in their minds. In that moment Therissa, in her guise as Miram, came bustling in.

"Cease this chattering immediately," she commanded, and the three maids at once returned to their needlework, eyes studiously downcast. Across the room, Therissa's eyes met mine. I could see they were fairly dancing, which meant she must have some news to impart.

Once again I wished for a simple life, one where I was not tasked with having so many attendants. Truly, their presence made it so very difficult to have a private conversation. I would have to trust that Therissa could manage to remove them somehow, for I could think of nothing to task them with that would require all three of the young women to be gone at the same time.

Apparently she had been pondering the same question, for, after allowing the maids to work for another quarter-hour or so, during which time I attempted to read and did not do very well at it, Therissa clapped her hands together and said, "That will do for now. Go down to the storerooms, for the seneschal has informed me that the new silks Her Most High Majesty ordered for her draperies have arrived, and I want you to go and fetch them."

I could feel my eyes widen, although I forced myself not to look up from the book I held. There had been no such order—or at least, I had not placed it. As with all the other furnishings in my apartments, the azure-colored brocade curtains that framed the windows looked almost new. I had gotten the distinct impression that Besh had had these chambers redone from top to bottom in preparation for my arrival, and so of course there was no need to replace anything in them, let alone the draperies.

But I was not so foolish as to not recognize an opportunity to be alone with Therissa once she presented it, so I laid aside my book and said, "Yes, I had been hoping for some days now that the new material would have come in. I cannot think why it was delayed. Do as Miram instructs, and take care when bringing the fabric back here, as it will not do for it to become dusty."

At once all three of them got to their feet, setting down their embroidery and mending, and murmuring, "Yes, Your Majesty. At once, Your Majesty."

And then they were gone in a rustle of silk and a jingle of bangles, for of course the Hiereine's maidservants must be dressed well, if not as well as their mistress. The door shut behind them, and Therissa let out an exaggerated sigh of relief.

"And what I'm going to come up with next, Lyarris, I have no idea," she said frankly. "They all seem like sweet girls, but I am certain they will be the death of me. They are so very underfoot."

That seemed a very apt way of describing them, and I nodded. "Indeed. If I were back home in Iselfex, I could send them out beyond the palace to fetch me something from the market and know they would be gone for some time, but I have not that luxury here."

"No, it is a very confining existence, here in the Hierarch's palace," Therissa admitted. I must have looked stricken at those words, for she hurried on, "Not that it isn't a beautiful place, of course. I thought I'd gotten an eyeful when I was in your brother's palace, but here—"

I reflected perhaps that one reason for the Keshiaari crown palace being so beautiful was that so many of its residents were compelled to spend an inordinate amount of time within its walls. But I decided to let that pass for now, as Therissa clearly had much she wanted to tell me, and only a limited amount of time in which to tell it before my three maids returned.

"So, what have you learned?" I asked bluntly, and Therissa came back to the here and now, abandoning her comparison of the two palaces.

"Well, even Miram does not have the freedom to go where she wills in this place, but we both know that is no great impediment to me. There is a certain lieutenant of the guard who is a smallish man, not much greater than I in stature. He is quite easy for me to imitate, for I do not have to stretch myself to appear so much taller than I am. And I must admit it is rather fun, for I can tell he is quite puffed up with his own importance, and has the most peculiar gait." Here she stopped and jutted her chin out, then bent both arms at the elbow and took a few paces with them swinging back and forth, so I might see.

I muffled a laugh and said, "I can see why you might enjoy taking on his guise. I can only hope that his fellows take him a bit more seriously?"

"As to that, I am not quite sure. But because he is a lieutenant, they must at least play at deference, whatever their private thoughts might be. I took care to examine his movements, when he was on duty and off, and once I knew he was safely away, I went to the dungeons, pretending that I had forgotten some item or another."

"That must have been quite dangerous," I said, rather alarmed that she would take such a chance.

She waved a hand, saying, "Not at all, for of course none of the other guards had any reason to think he—or I—was anyone save who I was supposed to be. They are not much accustomed to magic here, at least not anything beyond small enchantments of personal items or love potions or seeing the future in some leaves at the bottom of a cup. And also, this lieutenant is not a man of such great importance that he would be the likely target of such a spell in the first place."

This sounded sensible enough, so I nodded and told her, "Very well, it sounds as if you have done your due diligence. And what did you see, when you wore the guise of this lieutenant?"

Her expression sobered, and she hesitated for a few seconds before she made her reply. "The prisoner, this would-be assassin, is a man of normal size and appearance, no matter what the rumors might say. As to his particular features, I fear I cannot comment on that, as he has been tortured so badly that I doubt even his own loved ones could recognize him."

"Tortured?" I repeated, staring up at her in dismay. Had Besh ordered this? I did not want to believe it of him, thought his too gentle a soul to call for such pain to be inflicted on another human being. Then again, the captive had attempted to murder him. Such a transgression might waken a heretofore unknown rage in a man. "If that is truly the case, there must have been a good reason for it," I added, but the defense sounded weak even to myself.

Apparently Therissa thought the same thing, for she said, "I am sure there are many in the palace who would agree with you, my lady, but I fear I am not one of them. I heard this man pleading for his life, saying he was innocent, and that he had only been taken because he had had the temerity to be heard speaking against some of the Hierarch's policies."

"That sounds like the sort of thing a man bargaining for his life might say." Even as I spoke the words, however, I felt doubt coiling within my breast. Surely someone with the courage—or recklessness, I supposed—to make an attempt on the Hierarch's life, especially one as coordinated as the attack at the oasis, would not bother to hide behind weak excuses, but would take credit for his actions. Or perhaps I was assigning too much bravery to this unknown man, who was strong enough when working in the shadows but only wanted to beg for his life now that he had been caught.

"Yes, Lyarris, I thought that at first," Therissa said gently. Perhaps she had guessed something of my thoughts, that I did not want to believe Besh was capable of ordering such pain to be inflicted on another human being. "But I heard him...and I have spent many years observing people. It is part of what I must do, to wield my magic effectively. And I know I could be wrong, but I do not think I am."

She drew in a breath, then added, "My dear, I am quite certain he is innocent."

CHAPTER TWELVE

All I could do was stare at her, gaze up into her worried dark eyes. She still wore Miram's face, for we had decided this was safer, in case any of the maids might return unexpectedly from one of their manufactured errands. But her expression, the faint pull of the eyebrows, the distressed pout of her mouth, were definitely Therissa's, and not that of my erstwhile chief maid.

"But…why?" I asked at last. "What is the point in torturing an innocent man?"

She gave me a look that was almost pitying. "Lyarris, you were raised in a royal household. I know that you are well aware of the depths to which some will go when playing their political games."

"If you are suggesting that Besh—" I began hotly, and she raised a hand.

"That is not what I am suggesting at all." She tugged at the sleeve of the filmy under-blouse she wore, pulling it a little farther down over her wrist, her gaze shifting away from me. "What I am suggesting is that there has been a great deal of pressure placed on certain members of the royal staff to find the would-be assassin. This hunt has been going on for some time now. It seemed as if the trail had gone cold. But now the man has been caught, and everyone in Keshiaar is rejoicing. I have no doubt that most will not want to look too closely to determine the truth of the situation."

"So who—" I began.

"Most likely that *visanis* of your husband's, Tel-Karinoor. I always had the impression from Malik—that is, Ambassador Sel-Trelazar—that he did not have any high opinion of the chancellor."

Her words caused a faint trickle of cold to find its way down my spine. I, too, had found myself not quite trusting him, although I could think of no real reason why. Save sending my maids away, but I still could not imagine why such an action would profit him. "And did he ever speak of his misgivings to the Hierarch?"

"Goodness, no!" she responded at once. "That would have been political suicide. True, Malik is from a very good family, younger brother of a prince, but even so, he knew when to keep his mouth shut. However, the subject did come up once or twice, when we were speaking of our homelands, and the people we knew."

"And what would be Tel-Karinoor's reason? Merely to advance himself in my husband's eyes? I had gotten the impression that his was the highest position in the court already, save for those in the royal household."

"That impression is correct. But the *visanis* is granted that title, not born to it. According to Malik, such things do not happen very often, but it is possible for a chancellor be relieved of his title. If the Hierarch had intimated in any way that he was not pleased with the progress in this case, then I think it not so unlikely that Tel-Karinoor would do whatever it took to secure his position—even if that included capturing an innocent man and torturing him to prove that the mystery had been solved and the realm was once again safe."

Thoughts churning, I got to my feet and went to the window, gazing out over the gardens below. Now, at the end of Fevrere, the rains had begun to dissipate, and a bright sunny sky shone down on the green grass. It was beautiful, but I could not be much cheered by that beauty, for I knew with the rains gone, the temperatures would begin to rise once again, propelling us once more into the endless heat and painful white light of spring and summer and autumn.

I did not know what to make of Therissa's pronouncement. As I had had only a few face-to-face dealings with him, I found I could not give myself a true measure of the visanis' integrity. We had gotten off on rather the wrong foot, he and I, and yet that could have been a simple misunderstanding. No doubt Besh would brush it off as such, if I attempted to use it as a reason for distrusting his chancellor. Oh, how I wished we were more open with one another, that I could simply go to him and tell him I thought perhaps Tel-Karinoor was not dealing with the situation in an honorable manner.

If I did gather the courage to do such a thing, I very much feared that Besh would not give my misgivings the attention they deserved. He would not, I thought, precisely laugh them off—he was too courteous to do such a thing to his wife—but he would attempt to convince me that I was manufacturing these worries from nothing. And of course I could not bring Therissa in to bear witness. Although Besh had heretofore been rather neutral on the subject of magic, I did not think he would much appreciate my sister-in-law's aunt taking on the guise of one his servants and using that position to roam the castle freely, gathering what intelligence she might.

In truth, the very thought of his reaction made me shudder slightly.

"So what should I do?" I asked at last, turning away from the window and nervously twisting the jeweled bangles on one wrist.

"I am not sure," Therissa said frankly. "This is a new situation for me as well. I do not think it best to say anything, for I am fairly sure His Most High Majesty would not want to believe what you were telling him. It is not easy to acknowledge that those around us are not entirely trustworthy."

That I could well believe. I tried to imagine my brother's reaction if someone were to come to him and say that Lord Keldryn, his own chancellor, had lied to him about a matter of such great importance. Pompous and blustering he might be, but Keldryn was a man of great personal integrity, and would gladly lay down his life in service to Sirlende. But... what if he were not? Would my brother listen to such accusations, or would he dismiss them out of hand, saying he had known the man in question his entire life and so could not believe him to be capable of such a thing?

I feared that was the situation in which I found myself now. More than ever I regretted that I was not in a position where Besh had confided in me, for perhaps then I would have had the courage to confront him on the topic of his visanis. If we had a relationship such as that which Ashara and my brother shared, then I knew I would not even hesitate. But they loved one another passionately, and had done so almost from the time they first met, whereas I…

…I had still only shared one true kiss with Besh, had not yet penetrated the wall he had built around his heart. We did not share everything, hide nothing from one another. Yes, he had declared to Tel-Karinoor that he kept no secrets from me, but I did not believe that, not truly. I thought there were still a great many things he kept hidden. Perhaps not to wound me or deceive me, but only because we were not so intimate that he felt he had any reason to share them with me.

Before I realized what was happening, a tear trickled down my cheek, followed by another. And then it was as if a veritable dam had burst, for I was standing there, weeping, kohl-inked tears dropping onto the priceless rug beneath my feet.

"Oh, my dear," Therissa said softly, taking a step toward me. She paused, as if not certain what she should do. Then she shook her head and closed the distance between us, taking me in her arms and murmuring soft, comforting sounds of the sort I supposed a mother might bestow upon her child… if I had had a mother who believed in offering her children such reassurances.

I knew protocol demanded that I push her away, for no one not a direct relative should have taken such a liberty with the Hiereine, but I found I could not. For so many months I had felt so alone, so unable to reach out to anyone and show any weakness. Besh had been kind to me, true, but although kindness was of course better than the reverse, I wanted more than that. I wanted his love. I wanted all of him, not just the empty courtesies of a man too well-bred to ill-treat a woman but who could offer nothing more.

How long I wept, I did not know, but at last the tears began to dry up on their own. Only then did I back away from Therissa…but I did so with a grateful smile, so she should know I was not rebuffing her. "Thank you," I said, lifting a hand to wipe away the last of the tears from my cheeks. At least now my fingers were not stained with kohl, which meant I must have sobbed it all away. Essaying a watery smile, I added, "I suppose I had better repair the damage before the girls return."

"A very good idea," Therissa replied. I could see she would not press the issue, would not make me explain the reason for my sorrow. Or perhaps she knew it well enough already.

So we went into my bedchamber, and the dressing table there, and she helped me reapply my cosmetics. Not much could be done for my reddened eyes, but after she had ringed them with kohl and added a bit more rouge to my cheeks, she deemed it would do well enough.

All this was accomplished with barely a minute to spare, for just as Therissa was setting down the brush she had used to apply the rouge, Lila and Marsali and Alina re-entered my apartments, carrying an enormous bolt of deep claret-colored silk so massive that it required all three of them to transport it into the sitting room, then maneuver it into position propped up against one wall.

"Whyever didn't you ask one of the guards or the manservants to help you with that?" I inquired, somewhat astonished that they'd managed to get it here without mishap. The bolt of fabric was half again as tall as they were.

They all exchanged a nervous glance, but then Marsali replied, "It was not nearly as bad as it looked, my lady. We did have the three of us to carry it, after all, and besides, we did not wish to take someone else from their own tasks to help us with ours."

"That was very well done, girls," Therissa put in, and they beamed and ducked their heads at this unexpected praise from the usually harsh "Miram." "We will undertake all the measurements tomorrow. I am sure Her Most High Majesty will not mind the bolt being there for a day more."

"No, of course not," I said immediately. Perhaps if I had been more exacting of them, I would have claimed that I could not bear to have that enormous length of fabric propped up against the sitting room wall for a day and a half. But then, it was not as if I were expecting company. Besh would accompany me to this apartment after dinner, true, but he had never once set foot across the threshold. I could have upholstered all the furniture in spotted cowhide and painted the walls purple, and he would never have known the difference. Repressing a sigh, I added, "Do rest, and take some water and some of those cakes Miram has set out. I do not expect you to return to work until you are fully recovered from your…ordeal."

Their eyes lit up at that, but even so they all sent a questioning glance in Therissa's direction, as if wishing to make sure such largesse would be allowed, even if granted by the Hiereine. "Miram" gave the slightest of nods, and at once they went and poured themselves water from the silver pitcher that sat on a side table, then helped themselves to one cake each. During all this they kept sending her sideways glances, as if worried that she would scold them for their idleness, even though she had been the one to invite it. But of course she said nothing, and instead left them to their brief respite, asking if I would be so good to come look at the fabric in the afternoon light.

"It has something of a brown undertone, my lady," she said, peering at it more closely and furrowing her brow in a good imitation of disapproval.

"I think it is lovely," I replied. While I understood the need to play along with her, I certainly wasn't going to say anything that sounded as if I did not want the new fabric after all. I was sure the very thought of having to cart it back down to the storerooms again would send my poor maids into a panic. "It is good that the divan and the chairs are covered in gold and ivory and tan, for they will go with just about anything. Indeed, I think this claret-colored silk will actually suit better than the blue. Of course, it means we will have to redo all the pillows as well, but I am sure my maids' needles are up to the task."

Therissa shot me an approving glance at these words, even as I heard something that almost sounded like a sigh coming from Lila's lips. She was at work with her needle most of the day, when she wasn't scrubbing, and no doubt the realization that I would require all new embroidered bolsters for the furniture did not appeal very much to her. Still, I knew I had to do what I must to keep her occupied, and if that also included sending her out for embroidery silks to match the new draperies....

And so Therissa and I plotted and planned, while the maids finished their makeshift meal before going back to their unending scrubbing and mending and embroidery. If Lila's gaze lingered a bit too long on my face, especially my still sore and aching eyes, well, there was little I could do about that. At least I could trust her not to gossip...at least, not very much.

As I feared, Besh seemed preoccupied, distant, during dinner that night. No, he did not completely ignore me, asked me commonplaces about my day, and even commented that now with the rains beginning to clear out, we might spend more time at the observatory.

I could not ignore this olive branch, and so I said with some gratitude, "That would be lovely. I have missed looking at the stars."

I did not add, "with you," but he might have heard those words echoing, unspoken, between us. He paused, then gave a nod before he told me, "I fear that I have much to discuss with my chancellor this night, business that was not finished before dinner. Please accept my apologies, for I cannot discuss more of your legends of the north with you this night. Perhaps tomorrow?"

Swallowing my disappointment, I said, "Of course, my lord husband. I understand that affairs of state must needs take precedence over our personal pleasures."

He seemed satisfied with my reply, inclining his head slightly before he returned to the food on his plate. What he and Tel-Karinoor had to discuss, Besh had not said, but I thought I could guess. That poor man held in the dungeon, the one who kept proclaiming his innocence, even though his protests fell on deaf ears. I found myself hoping that Besh would examine the facts of the matter and find the evidence wanting, but it was a faint hope. He, like everyone else, must wish to have this matter ended. It seemed unlikely that he would do much to question the counsel of his *visanis*.

My stomach churned, and I found it difficult to eat much more, although I took a few dutiful bites so as not to attract too much attention. Luckily, it was a small gathering, no more than fifty or so of us, so I knew nothing terribly elaborate was planned for entertainments and such that night. No, we would eat, and then retire to our various quarters.

For the first time since I had come to the palace, Besh turned to me at the end of the meal and said, "I must apologize to you again, lady wife, for I have not the time to spare to guide you to your chambers. The guards will see you there. I hope you understand."

"Of course I do, my lord," I replied, somehow getting the words out past the choking thickness in my throat. "I would not expect you to waste time on me when you have such pressing matters you must attend to."

At these words, his brows drew together, and he studied me for a few seconds, clearly attempting to see if I had meant them as a criticism. But since I kept my expression blank and calm, I did not think he noticed anything in my aspect that would indicate how truly upset I was.

This is how it begins, I thought, and knotted my fingers around the napkin in my lap.

"It is only a temporary situation, I assure you," he said.

"Of course, my lord."

His lips compressed, and I could see the tension in the fine lines of his jaw, but he said nothing else, only stood, offering me his hand. I took it, and after he bowed to me, by some unspoken signal, four of the guards approached. My escort.

"Good night," I told Besh, not waiting for his reply as I moved away from where he stood and allowed the guards to flank me. Well, it seemed they served some useful purpose, for with them surrounding me like that, they effectively blocked me from my husband's view. We left the dining hall, the echo of their footsteps on the inlaid marble floors seeming louder than usual as they guided back to my rooms. Yes, the Hierarch and I always had the same complement with us when he walked me to my apartments, but I had not paid them much attention when I had him to accompany me.

Now there were no goodbyes, only the guards bowing as one of them reached out and opened the door for me. I went inside, stony-faced, inwardly relieved that my maids were not in the main sitting room, only Therissa, wearing as always the guise of Miram. I wondered if she somehow was able to maintain the illusion as she slept, or if she had to allow herself some respite from constantly maintaining the spell. To tell the truth, I had very little idea as to how it all worked… only that it did.

"It did not go well?" she murmured in question as she came to pull the jeweled cuffs from my wrists, unclasp the necklace of gold and rubies from around my throat. Normally she did this in my bedchamber, where she could immediately put them away in the chest reserved for their storage, but I thought she could tell that I wished to be free of the heavy pieces. Now she carefully laid them on a side table before returning her attention to me.

"He had an urgent need to confer with his *visanis* after dinner, and so he sent me here accompanied by his guards," I replied in the same undertone. Once again I felt that ominous tightening of my throat, but I forced it back. I had wept enough that day already. "I cannot say I am feeling very hopeful."

Because we were not truly alone—the three maids were still awake, if not in this same room—she could not do as I thought she wished, which was to make some kind of consoling sound, or even reach out to give me a reassuring pat on the shoulder. Voice still quiet, she said, "It is only one night, my lady. I know it is difficult to be patient, but—"

"I weary of being patient!" I burst out, then immediately lowered my tone. "That is, I have been here for one month shy of a year. I have been patient and meek and good, and I cannot say that any of it has done me any favors. And now I sit here while I know Tel-Karinoor is feeding my husband lies about this man they have accused of the assassination attempt, and I can do nothing. Nothing. People look at me and think because I am the Hiereine, I am the most powerful woman in the land. But I have begun to think that the least beggar-girl in the streets has more control of her life than I do."

Therissa cast a worried glance in the direction of the chamber where the three maids had been waiting up, no doubt nodding over their embroidery, but I had heard nothing from within, Perhaps they were eavesdropping. In that moment I was so wretched, I could barely summon the energy to care.

Voice barely above a whisper, she said, "I know it is difficult. But until you know precisely what your husband plans to do, there is no need to get yourself so upset. Please, my lady, I think it best if you try to sleep. It has been a long day, one of worries and disappointments. I can't help but think that you might look on all this with a clearer eye tomorrow, after you have had a chance to rest."

These were sensible enough words, I supposed, and yet I chafed at her advice, that I should go quietly to bed and let the matter rest for now. But what else could I do? Bolt from my rooms, go running to Besh's chambers, assuming I could even locate them? I should not get two steps from my door, for I knew guards stood there day and night. My accommodations were far more luxurious, but I was just as much a prisoner here as the poor man held captive in a dungeon somewhere far below where I stood.

"Very well," I said to Therissa, knowing how utterly defeated I sounded. "I will go to bed, as there is nothing else I can do."

So I went to my large, empty bed, and lay there with my eyes wide open as I tracked the passage of the moonlight across the floor, an intricate traveling shadow following it, cast by the latticework that covered the windows. Odd that I should be so weary, and yet unable to sleep. I knew some people were plagued by wakefulness, could not enjoy the oblivion that comes with slumber, but before now I had never been one of them. Must I be tormented in that way as well, so that I might not even escape my cares for a few hours each night?

At last I crept out of bed and went to the window, carefully opening the latticed shutters. They squeaked faintly, and I paused, wondering if the sound had been enough to wake any of my maids where they slept in the next room. But I heard nothing, save the long, mournful cry of an owl from somewhere far overhead, and my breathing stilled somewhat.

The moon had tracked its way to the west, and was now about to disappear behind the spires and towers of the city. I leaned on the windowsill of carved stone, breathing in air that finally was cool, sweet with the scent of a night-blooming flower Besh had told me was called jasmine. And as I looked down, I realized that a narrow ledge was set beneath my window, a ledge that seemed to run the length of this wing of the palace, until it met an open balcony that was the terminus of a long corridor.

That ledge was just wide enough to stand on.

No. Even entertaining that thought for a few seconds was madness. I couldn't possibly be thinking of making my escape that way. And even if I did...for what?

To see Besh, I thought then. *To speak with him alone. Surely in these deep hours of the night, with no one around us, he might be more open to having a true conversation, instead of one couched in interminable politenesses.*

When I thought of it that way....

The ledge was perhaps a foot wide, if even that. Not that I would have to rely on it completely, as there were windows spaced at even intervals along the face of the building, windows with sills that I could hold on to as I inched my way over to the balcony. Once I was there, I would be safe enough. I could simply climb over the balustrade and make my way down the corridor, until I came to the hallway it intersected, and go on from there, moving ever closer to Besh's apartments.

No, that was absurd. Even if I somehow managed to evade all the guards stationed between here and there, he always had six more standing watch at the entrance to his wing of the palace. I would have to turn myself invisible to accomplish that.

Turn myself invisible....

Of course. Why hadn't I thought of it sooner? Surely if Therissa could enchant herself to look like someone else, or enchant my sister-in-law so it appeared she was wearing the richest of garments and jewels, when in reality she had on barely more than rags, then she must be able to do something that would make me, if not invisible, then unnoticeable.

Turn me into one of the guards, or my maids. No, perhaps that would not do so well, for if one of them went wandering around the palace in the dead of night, she would be stopped and immediately returned to her quarters here.

After drawing on my dressing gown and sliding my feet into a pair of sandals, I slipped out into the hallway and inched my way down to the chamber—cubbyhole, really, barely half the size of my bath chamber—where Therissa slept. No doubt Miram had been content enough with that cubby, for at least it was her own, a sign of her status that she did not have to sleep in the same chamber as the lesser maids.

I bent down and touched the enchantress on the shoulder, whispering, "Therissa."

She awoke at once, eyes flashing in the darkness. The fading moonlight was just bright enough that I could see she wore her own face, but as she blinked up at me, instantly her features shifted into those of Miram. Well, that answered one question. It was a calculated risk, for I thought she probably guessed the maids would knock before entering the place where she slept. Failure to follow the protocols would be grounds for dismissal, after all.

"What is the matter?" she whispered in return. "Is something wrong?"

"No—well, yes, I suppose it is, but I just realized that I have been foolish in not asking you this before. Is there any way for you to, I don't know, cast a spell so no one will see me? For I very much wish to speak to my husband now, in secret."

Her eyes widened. "Begging your pardon, my lady, but have you gone mad? Surely whatever you have to say to him can wait until morning. The risks—"

"I was not asking about the risks," I cut in. "I was asking whether you could do it."

For a long moment, she hesitated. Then she said, words coming slowly, as if she were thinking it through as she spoke, "It would not be the same thing I did for Ashara, or even what I have done here to disguise myself. Those spells are quite intricate, and require me to make an alteration that is accurate down to the way my eyes crinkle when I smile— not that Miram smiled very much—or, in Ashara's case, to imagine the way a gown falls and rustles and feels, and not merely how it looks." Again she paused, watching me with worried eyes, as if she wished she could think of some way to dissuade me but knew she could not. After all, she was Ashara's aunt, but I was the Hiereine of Keshiaar, and before that the Crown Princess of Sirlende. It was not her position to refuse me my request.

"So what is it, then?" I prompted, when it seemed she was loath to continue.

"It is more an illusion of darkness, of shadow. This will work well enough now, for although of course the corridors of the palace are not left in complete darkness, neither are they blazing with light." She sat up in her narrow bed, fingers tightening around the thin linen coverlet. "But as you do not wish to be a shadow being when you go to see your husband, I must know how long you think it will take you to reach His Most High Majesty's apartments, so I may cast the spell in such a way that it will have run its course by the time you get there."

Relieved that she did not seem inclined to offer any more arguments, I said, "No more than ten minutes. At least, that is how long it seems to take when we walk at a somewhat leisurely pace from there to here."

"All right, then. That should be easy enough." She drew in a breath and then let it out, staring at me for a long moment. "Are you sure, my lady? Absolutely sure? For of course you will not be able to offer any good explanation as to how you managed to walk all the way to your husband's apartments with no one noticing. His Most High Majesty is no fool. He is sure to ask questions."

"He may ask," I said blithely. "But I will only tell him that perhaps his guards are not quite so perceptive as he thinks."

"I do not like that," she replied at once. "For one thing, while you cannot be punished in any way for escaping your apartments, the guards do not have the sort of immunity. Do you wish to see them beaten or dismissed for something that is not their fault?"

I hadn't thought of that. Bother. For while I chafed to be away from here, to speak with Besh alone, I most certainly did not want to cause trouble for any of the guards. I did not know them, even the ones who watched outside my chambers, for they were too well-trained to do anything save murmur "Most High Majesty" as they let me in and out of these apartments. But that was no excuse for carelessly allowing them to receive whatever punishment might be meted out when it was discovered that I had slipped past them.

But perhaps if I combined Therissa's spell with my earlier plan of going out the window....

I explained as much to her, and her eyes widened even more, if that were possible. With a shake of her head, she protested, "My lady, that is a far greater madness than trying to somehow evade your guards. What if you should fall?"

"What if I did?" I asked with a lift of my shoulders. "My family will mourn, and I suppose Besh would get himself another wife at some point. You cannot say that he would weep too heavily over my death."

"I will say it," she replied immediately. "You are not thinking clearly. Forgive me for telling you so bluntly, but it is only the truth. He does care, no matter what you might think."

No, I was not thinking clearly. In that she was correct, but I was determined on my current course of action. As long as I could manage it without any undue punishment falling on the guards' heads, I did not think she had the right to try to stop me.

Something in my aspect must have told her my mind was made up, for she let out a long sigh, then said, "So what is your plan?"

"You will cast your spell, and then I will go out by my window and move along the ledge to the balcony at the end of the main corridor. It is only some hundred paces or so. Then I'll make my way to Besh's apartments. I will distract the guards somehow, and then get in past them. But if he asks, I will say I came in through a window, just as I escaped from here."

She listened to all this with an increasingly troubled expression. "There are so many things that could go wrong—"

"And I am willing to take that risk."

Apparently she had given up on making any further arguments. "Very well, Lyarris. But please—be as careful as you can. It is not that you have any experience climbing ledges."

"No," I replied, "but as a child I used to walk along the stairway railings at the palace. Torric and I would egg each other on, until we were caught and punished by being confined to our rooms for three days in a row. True, it was his idea, but I did once have quite a good sense of balance."

This didn't seem to comfort her much, but at length she gave a reluctant nod, saying, "I will cast the spell now—but I will make it last for twenty minutes, not ten, for I think that it will take you a good deal more time to inch along a ledge than it would to walk sedately down a corridor."

"That is probably wise," I agreed. "And if it has not worn off by the time I get to Besh's apartments, I will simply wait until it does."

Since she apparently thought there was nothing else to say, Therissa drew in a breath, then murmured a few words I could not quite make out, save that they sounded like no language I had ever heard. I had asked Ashara once if she felt the spell taking shape around her, had somehow sensed the magic, and she had replied that she had not. Only when she looked down and saw the alteration in her appearance did she realize that a spell had been cast.

It was not quite like that for me. I could not say exactly what it was—perhaps like the faintest touch of an unseen breeze, or the odd prickling one can feel on one's skin when a lightning bolt strikes nearby. But I could tell magic was being worked, and even though I had invited it, still my blood seemed to run a little colder in my veins at that realization.

I looked down and saw…nothing. No, that was not right. Yes, there was no sign of the crimson silk of my dressing gown, or the light linen of the sleeping chemise I wore under it, but I noted a blurry darkness something in the shape of a woman's body. In the shadows of the darkened palace, it would probably never be noticed.

"Gods," I breathed, and Therissa's lips compressed.

"There is your spell. I must beseech you to think sensibly and retire to your chambers so that it may wear off with no one the wiser, but I fear that is not what is going to happen next."

I began to shake my head, then realized she probably could not see the gesture. "No, dear Therissa. I will go to my chambers, but only so I might escape through the window. I will be quite safe—you'll see."

She did not reply, only glanced away from me, her expression troubled. Not wanting to waste time on any more words, I left her tiny sleeping quarters and padded down the corridor to my own bedchamber, where I went at once to the window. After opening the shutters as wide as I could, I hoisted myself up to the sill, then dropped lightly down onto the ledge.

CHAPTER THIRTEEN

The night breeze seemed to come to greet me, sweet and cool. I clung to the windowsill for a moment, getting my bearings, trying to re-familiarize myself with the sensation of balancing on a narrow strip not quite a foot wide. I had been very good at this sort of thing, once upon a time, but that had been almost fifteen years ago.

I inched out with one foot, then another, realizing this was going to be more difficult than I thought, simply because I couldn't really see my own feet, just an odd, wavery dark blur. Hesitating, I wondered if I should abandon my mad plan and do as Therissa had said: return to my bed and wait for the spell to wear off. But that would be admitting defeat before I even got started. Besides, I realized that beyond the windowsill there was still a raised line of decorative tile, something I could use to cling to. No, it wasn't nearly as wide as the ledge upon which I stood, but it was something.

So I began to inch my way along, fingers clinging to the tile, the rough edge of the raised surface biting into my flesh. Not that I minded terribly, as at least it reassured me that I still had a good grip on it. Since I faced the building, I could see nothing of what was beneath my feet. Just as well, I supposed. If I could really see what I was doing, I might truly lose my nerve.

How long that took, I wasn't sure, although the entire time I was conscious that the spell would not last forever. I could not rush, though, for that would only increase my chances of falling. Five minutes—or an eternity—later, my outstretched hand fell upon the smooth balustrade that enclosed the balcony which was my destination, and I let out a little sigh of relief. I had survived the first part of my journey.

With arms that shook slightly, I pulled myself up and over the balustrade, then dropped onto the reassuringly solid floor of the balcony. Then it was time to concentrate as I moved as lightly as I could down into the adjoining corridor, always keeping an eye out for any guards on patrol, while at the same time reminding myself of the route to the wing Besh occupied. Left around a corner here, then straight on until I reached the staircase, then down the steps and left again until I came to the long hall with the palms in their stone urns spaced at equal intervals. Follow that to the end, then emerge into the colonnade that faced the gardens, then left once more....

It was a nerve-wracking process, one made all the more so because every so often I would come across a pair of guards making their nightly rounds. To be sure, they looked rather bored—or it seemed that way in the uncertain light of the few oil lamps that illuminated the hallways—but even so I found myself flattening against the wall as they passed, hardly daring to breathe, then waiting until they were out of earshot so I could resume my ghostly journey. At last, though, I came around a corner and saw the large carved doors that served as the entrance to my husband's apartments.

As I'd feared, six guards stood there, all grasping long-handled poles topped with curved blades. These guards did not look bored at all. Their dark eyes were bright even at this hour of the night, glittering in the shadow of the helmets they wore.

In the back of my mind, I had hoped they would not be so alert, and that I might somehow be able to sneak past them and gain entry without having to come up with a suitable distraction. This, however, was clearly not going to happen, and so I hesitated, looking about to see what I might possibly be able to do that would draw them away from the entrance to the suite and allow me to open the door and slip in.

Around the corner were more of the heavy potted plants, and although I disliked being the cause of any destruction, I could not see anything else that might allow me to make the sort of noise that would cause the guards to come running. Gritting my teeth, I grasped the edges of the stone planter— it was nearly as high as my waist—and pushed. It rocked slightly, but it was clear that I needed to make even more of an effort. So I drew in a breath, then shoved with all my might.

The planter toppled over with a resounding crash, and I jumped, startled, before I realized I had no time to lose. Already I heard the sound of heavy boots running in my direction. Flattening along the wall, I moved like the shadow I was, back toward the double doors of Besh's apartments. As I did so, five of the guards bolted past me, headed toward the planter I had just overturned.

A whispered curse escaped my lips. I had hoped that all of them would go, but I supposed it was too much to ask that they wouldn't leave at least one man to maintain his guard over the Hierarch's suite. At least he had stepped away from the door, was peering this way and that, as if looking to see whether the intruder who had made such a noise had come in this direction.

Well, she had, but I feared he would not see her. In fact, I practically slipped past under his nose. He stiffened, as if sensing something, but since I was more or less invisible in the semi-gloom of the corridor, he could not detect precisely where I was. And as his head was craned in the direction where his compatriots had disappeared, I lifted the handle to the door, opened it just enough to allow myself to slide through, then shut it behind me.

Not a minute too soon, for even as I slumped against the wall, trying to calm my agitated breathing, I saw my body slowly becoming more solid, as if resolving itself from a dark mist. Within the minute I was fully myself. The spell had done its work.

And now I must do mine.

From my past visits here, I had seen that Besh shared my dislike for having servants underfoot at all times. Yes, he must have the guards, and once or twice I had seen a quiet, unobtrusive manservant going about and lighting the lamps and such, but otherwise, these rooms seemed to be my husband's sanctum, a place where he wished to be left undisturbed. Which was good, because my bag of tricks was quite empty. I had no more means of hiding myself, and so must hope to find my way to where he slept without being seen by anyone.

All was still here, the only sign of life the faint flickering of the flames in the alabaster sconces to either side. Only half of them were lit, and so the place had an odd, dreamlike quality very different from its normal opulence. Although I knew Besh would not be up at such an hour, still I stopped and peeked into his library. Yes, all was dark within, not a single lamp lit, and so I ducked back out into the corridor and resumed my stealthy journey into a section of his apartments I had never seen before. Here, all was unfamiliar, and I hesitated, not sure where I should go next.

But then I saw that the long hallway ended in an elegant staircase which curved its way up to the second floor, and I realized Besh's sleeping chamber must be up there somewhere, away from the library and offices and other rooms where he might, if he wished, grant an audience to a favored member of his court. Of course, if I were truly his wife, I would know very well where his bedchamber was located, and my mouth twisted at the irony of my ignorance, even as I hurried to those stairs, made my way up the steps of gleaming marble inlaid in an intricate diamond pattern, and emerged on the landing.

There was an entrance to a corridor directly in front of me, and so I went down it, passing walls hung with embroidered silks and a few paintings, stylized portraits of past members of the royal family, done in a stiff, formal style that had gone out of fashion in Sirlende almost a century earlier. And that corridor ended in a pair of double doors carved with more of the intricate leaf and flower motifs so popular in Keshiaar.

I paused there, my heart beating so loudly I thought for sure it must be audible even on the other side of those doors. In my heart, I had been worried that there might be another contingent of guards standing here outside their Hierarch's bedchamber, but the hallway was empty, save for myself.

All was still within. Of course it was; I did not know the exact hour, but I guessed that we were nearer to dawn than midnight. Besh would be sleeping. And oh, although I had thought myself quite fearless in coming here, now that the moment was upon me, I found it harder than I had thought to reach out and touch the carved bronze handle on the right-hand door, to wrap my fingers around it and pull it toward me.

But somehow I did force myself to do that very thing, and the door swung outward.

Within, it was not as dark as I had expected. Like my own apartments, this inner sanctum of my husband's had a sitting room immediately inside the entrance, and there the sconces on the walls still glowed, warm light flickering across the frescoes painted on the smooth surfaces. By the window there was a desk, and at that desk sat my husband.

His head lifted as soon as the door opened, and his gaze fell upon me as I stood there in shock, staring at him and wondering why he was not in his bed.

He was the first to find his voice. "Lyarris?" he asked, obviously so discomfited that he had forgotten the distance he usually maintained between us, and used my first name. Abandoning the pen he held, he rose from his seat. "Whatever are you doing here?"

So I would not have the leisure of approaching him as he slept, and deciding the best way to awaken him. Resolutely, I shut the door behind me and took a few steps in his direction before saying, "I needed to speak with you."

"Now? In the middle of the night?" He ran a hand through his hair, and I realized then that he wore a heavy dressing robe of dark wine-colored silk, embroidered in gold. And beneath that…nothing I could see, save an expanse of golden-brown skin, and the smooth, sculpted muscles of his chest.

My breath seemed to go out of me at the sight, and a new kind of heat washed through my body, one I did not immediately recognize. Desire. Yes, that was it. I had never experienced it before, not like this, but as I gazed on my husband, I knew then what it was to truly want the meeting of flesh and flesh that I should have experienced by now…if only my husband had been truly my husband in anything other than name.

He seemed to note my particular attention, and at once tightened the sash at his waist, causing the fabric to overlap more closely. Without precisely meeting my eyes, he said, "And how is it that you came here unnoticed, unremarked? Surely the guards would have stopped you long before you came this far. You should not have been able to go more than two paces from the entrance to your suite."

No, I should not, thanks to the guards you have posted there, making me your own particular prisoner. Then I pushed that thought away, deeming it not precisely fair. After all, guards had stood watch outside my chambers back in Sirlende as well. That was the way of things, when one was a member of a royal household.

I found my voice and replied, in what I hoped were casual tones, "Oh, to be sure, they do an excellent job of guarding the doorway...but I fear they do not pay quite as much attention to the window."

These words seemed to take him aback, and he stood there staring at me, amber eyes wide in shock. "My lady wife, tell me you did not—"

"I did," I said boldly. "There is quite a convenient ledge that runs the entire length of my wing. It was easy as a wink."

A bit of an overstatement, but I was not about to let on just how frightened I had been, with my feet on a strip of stone less than a foot wide, fingers clinging to the spurious safety of a thin tile border.

However, he appeared far from fooled by my nonchalance. Taking a step toward me, then another, he said, "That was quite a stunt, my lady." For the first time I saw the glitter of anger in his eyes, and I swallowed. I knew he was not a man given to any sort of physical violence, and so I did not fear for my person, but I also didn't want him so angry that he would not listen to what I had come here to say. He seemed to gather himself, adding, "But as you have come to no harm, I will let that go for now. I find myself wondering what on earth could have been so important that you could not wait until morning, and send word then that you wished to speak with me."

Now that I was confronted by his very real displeasure, I found myself wondering the same thing. Truly it had been a sort of madness that seized me, in the depths of my desperation and sorrow. I moved toward him as well so that only a few hands' breadths separated us. "My lord, I have been thinking of this man who has been captured, the one Chancellor Tel-Karinoor says was the mastermind behind the attempt on your life."

"Yes?" Besh said, still clearly irritated. "What of him?"

"It is just—just that I have heard things, and I wonder—"

"Heard things?" he cut in. "What sorts of things?"

From the furrowing of his dark brows, I could see that he wished to know where I would have heard anything, trapped in my quarters as I was, with only a brief respite here and there where I would walk in the gardens, or escape to have dinner in company. Not that that was much of an escape, as I had still made no good friends here at court. Everyone was courteous and polite, as befitted proper conduct toward the Hierarch's wife, but I had thought I would find at least one person to be intimate with, as my sister-in-law had found her dear friend Gabrinne. No one had ever approached me thus, however, and if it were not for my late acquaintance with Therissa, I feared I might have started to go mad with loneliness.

Then again, there were some who might think I had already begun to go mad....

"Only that—that perhaps the evidence against him is not so damning as one might think. Is he a man of wealth? Whence came the means to hire mounted mercenaries skilled enough to take on guards from the royal household?"

Besh's frown deepened, and I saw then that perhaps he had not considered such matters...no doubt because his *visanis* had never broached them in the first place. "These are good questions, my lady, and I will ask them of my chancellor in the morning. But I still do not understand why worry over such a thing would cause you to come here in the middle of the night, risking your very person. Surely you can never have met the prisoner, so it is not a personal concern for his well-being."

"Of course I have not," I snapped. "For I cannot take two steps without my movements being overlooked by at least two or three guards or maids or members of your court. But I can still use my ears, and my mind, and I am not the sort of woman to idly sit by while an innocent man is sent to his death, all because your chancellor finds it expedient to do so."

During this speech Besh's jaw had tightened more and more, and when I was done, he retorted, "My chancellor does what is best for the realm."

"No doubt he does, but I fear that in this case what is best for the realm is certainly not best for that poor man being held prisoner in the dungeons." I knew better than to reach out and lay a hand on my husband's arm, but still I moved closer to him, so close I could almost hear the angry beating of his heart. His entire body stiffened, but he did not move away. "All I am saying is that perhaps there are some questions which should be asked. Yes, it would be wonderful to execute this man and say the threat is gone, but if he is innocent, then the threat is still present, and all you will have done is taken a life that never should have been forfeit."

"I will speak with Tel-Karinoor on this matter," Besh said, after a perceptible pause. "I cannot promise anything, but if it troubles you this much, then it should be addressed."

"Thank you," I replied simply. Whether that would change anything, I did not know, but it was better than having him dismiss my concerns outright.

"Now, if you have said your piece, I think it best that you return to your chambers. I will call for an escort."

It was then that I saw the heavily embroidered bell pull hanging in a corner, and I knew he was about to go toward it. Before he took a step, however, I laid a hand on his arm. "Wait."

Another of those flashes of irritation passed over his features. "My lady, it is very late. You will be lucky to get even two hours of sleep ere the sun comes up."

"I do not care for that," I told him, knowing if I did not seize this moment, I might very well never have the chance again.

His expression darkened, although I doubted he could guess the true reason behind my protest. "Indeed?"

"I only want one thing from you," I went on, forcing myself to meet his gaze directly, to not look away. No, I would not beg, but I would ask in a forthright manner, as befitted a princess of Sirlende and the Hiereine of Keshiaar.

"Just one?" he asked, his eyebrow raising slightly. Now he appeared almost amused, his anger from a moment ago seeming to dissipate.

"Yes," I said simply. "I want you to kiss me, Besh, kiss me as a husband should kiss his wife. Only that, and then, if you feel nothing, I will ask for nothing else from you."

His entire frame seemed to go rigid, and although he did not move away from me, I could almost feel the distance between us growing wider and wider, although in truth it was only a few inches. When he replied, his voice was pitched so low that I could barely hear him. "You do not know what you are asking."

"No, I suppose I do not, for you have made certain that I can understand nothing of what is in your heart. But mine, Besh—mine is becoming as dry and barren as the desert that stretches beyond this city. All I ask is a single kiss. Surely a man who controls Keshiaar's riches cannot be so miserly as to deny me that one small thing?"

A heavy pause, and then he said, "Very well. And then we will be done here. Understood?"

"I understand perfectly, my lord," I said, voice calm enough, although my heart had begun to pound in my breast. For of course I hoped that we would most certainly not be done once we had shared that kiss, that somehow my touch would help to break down the barriers he had constructed around himself.

And if it did not?

Well, I did not see how things could be any worse than they already were between us.

The windows were open, and a cool breeze blew in at that moment, sweet with night-blooming jasmine, exotic... enticing. It seemed the perfect moment to step toward him, to close the gap between us. I reached up, my arms closing around him, drawing him toward me. As our bodies touched, I realized that so little separated us. Just a few layers of thin silk, certainly not enough to mask the heat of our flesh. My breasts pressed into him, and I thought I heard him give a little groan, just before he bent down and pressed his lips against mine.

Oh, how sweet the taste of his mouth, how delicious the warmth of his skin! My entire body seemed to catch fire then, and I pushed against him, feeling how hard were the muscles touching my softer flesh. I had never experienced anything like this before, not with Thani, who I had thought I loved. I was melting into Besh, needing his touch, needing to become one with him. My fingers tangled in his heavy hair, and his hands were tightening on my shoulders, pulling me even closer, if that were possible.

How perfect his touch, how exquisite the way our bodies molded to one another's! Surely now he would lift me from my feet, carry me into the bedchamber that lay only a few yards away from where we stood. At last we would be husband and wife, and he could finally abandon the false separation he had allowed to grow between us.

But he did not. Another groan, this one that sounded as if he had torn it from the very depths of his soul, and then he was pushing me away, his eyes blazing, muscled chest rising and falling as if he had just run a mile. I was so startled that I tripped over the trailing skirt of my dressing gown as I moved away from him and began to fall backward, the room swirling around me in a panicked blur.

And then his hand was on my wrist, pulling me back to my feet before I cracked my head on the marble floor. "Are you all right?" he asked, voice rough, quite unlike its usual elegant baritone.

I wanted to fling back at him that of course I wasn't, not after being kissed like that and then just as quickly being rebuffed in the most brutal way possible…but I did not. No, that kiss had not been enough to change things between us. The way he had groaned, though, as if he were having a limb ripped from his body, told me that he was not quite as indifferent as he wanted me to believe. Well, that, and I did not think a man could kiss a woman in such a way and not care. Not completely, anyway.

He wanted to love me…and would not allow himself to do so.

"I am fine," I told him, straightening my dressing gown, which had become quite disarranged. As I did so, I noticed how his gaze flickered toward my half-exposed bosom. No, definitely not as indifferent as he wanted me to believe. It was the tiniest of victories, and one I would not allow myself to enjoy. How could I, when it seemed as if nothing I said or did seemed to make the slightest bit of difference?

But, as I had told myself earlier, I would not beg. I drew in a breath, brushed my hair away from my brow, and said, "You may send for my escort now."

Chapter Fourteen

Despite my agitation, I did manage to sleep longer than the bare two hours Besh had cautioned me about. The sun was quite bright when I finally pushed myself up from my bed and made my way to the window. Looking out, I saw that two guards now stood directly beneath my bedchamber. Their heads tilted upward as I opened the shutters all the way and took in a few breaths of the morning air, which was already beginning to warm. Since there was nothing else I could do, I smiled sweetly at them before closing the shutters again.

Obviously, Besh was not going to allow me to escape my apartments that way again.

I went and gathered up my dressing gown, then put it on. As I did so, a knock came at the door to my bedchamber, and I heard Therissa's voice. "My lady?"

"You may enter," I said formally, as it was late enough that I knew the other maids would be up and about.

She came in and closed the door. This was somewhat unusual, but not so much that Lila or Alina or Marsali would dare to comment upon it. No doubt they had noticed that "Miram" and I had grown much closer over the past few weeks, and that would help to explain why we might be closeted together in such a way.

"Well?" she asked.

"Well what?" I returned, my tone harsher than I had intended. Seeing those guards beneath my window had set me on edge. Not that I had expected Besh to do any less, but even so, their presence sent home the message that my few liberties had been even more closely curtailed. "As you can see, I am whole in body. I did not fall from the ledge, and neither was I captured by the guards. I did make my way to my husband's apartments, and we did have...conversation... but I do not think I have changed his mind about anything."

No, not about freeing the man currently being held in the dungeons, nor about having the courage to recognize me as his wife.

Therissa's face fell, but she said stoutly, "I would give it time, my lady. Your husband is the sort who needs to think things over before he makes up his mind, and you only spoke with him a few hours ago. No doubt he is reexamining the matter and will come to a decision in time. You must be patient."

Ah, patience. Mine seemed to have quite run out, even though in the past I would never have described myself as a hasty woman, or one given to making quick decisions herself. The heat of Besh's kiss seemed to linger on my lips, and I found myself wanting more of that, more of him. I wanted him to stop with his infernal brooding and understand that his heart was quite safe with me.

If Therissa and I had been more intimate—if we were more of an age, as Ashara was with her friend Gabrinne—perhaps I would have related everything that had passed between Besh and myself. But I found I could not speak of how he had kissed me, and then pushed me away. It hurt too much, and I did not want to see her pity. Not now, anyway, while the wound was still fresh.

"I will try," I said. "I did what I could. Now we will just have to wait and see if Besh heard anything of what I had to say."

Her expression was uncharacteristically sober, but then she brightened a bit, saying, "And in the meantime, I think I will do a little information-gathering. By now everyone has become accustomed to me in this guise, and if 'Miram' is now a little friendlier than she used to be, no one has remarked much upon it. So striking up a conversation here and there might be just what we need to gain some additional insights."

I wasn't quite so sure, although I did have to admit that Therissa had a way about her which seemed to encourage people to share confidences. In the meantime, what could it hurt? Her disguise was flawless, as was her command of the Keshiaari tongue; I supposed all her travels had stood her in good stead there, and Ambassador Sel-Trelazar had no doubt given her a few private lessons.

Smiling despite myself at that notion, I replied, "Yes, I think that would be a very good idea. For too many months,

254 ᵔ CHRISTINE POPE

I have had to muddle along with no way of knowing more about my husband, or why he acts the way he does. Even if I am not sure now how I may use such information, it is better that I have it, so at least in the future I might be able to use it to assist me."

She nodded, and then clapped her hands, calling in the other maids to prepare me for my day. I knew it was her way of making sure that no one would think we had spent too much time closeted together, and so I suffered the intrusion of Lila and Alina and Marsali with no further comment. In truth, it felt strange for them to spend so much time preparing me for an audience I would never have; yes, I would be in company at dinner, but they would change my garments for that public appearance, and so what I wore now was in reality of very little importance. But I supposed we all had to do what we could to justify our existence, even if such actions felt very silly in the end.

"Miram" disappeared sometime during this procedure, but I did not worry at her defection. Rather, I was glad, for I thought she had gone to pursue her "information-gathering," as she had referred to it, and I wanted to hear what she would have to say when she returned. In the meantime, I had to do my best to set my expression in placid lines, attending to the neglected writing on my desk as if it were the only thing to concern me, and doing everything I could to not dwell on the pressure of Besh's lips on mine, or the heat of his body as it had pressed against me. I thought then that perhaps I had done myself a disservice, to force such intimacy between my husband and me, for now I found I could not stop thinking of it.

Even in my despair, I could not help wondering whether that kiss filled his thoughts as well…. ·

If my maids noticed anything amiss, I could not tell from either their expressions or their actions. Even if they did, it was not their place to draw attention to my moods, and so I labored away at my writing, even as they endeavored to take measurements of the draperies currently in place so that the new ones would fit correctly. I had to turn a deaf ear to what they were doing, or surely it would have distracted me from the few lines I was able to scratch out in my manuscripts.

At last, though, Therissa returned, dignified and proper as always in her guise of Miram, but something in the look she shot me as she entered my chambers told me that her "fact-finding" mission had not been unfruitful. Our gazes met, and then shifted to the three maids as they busied themselves with cutting panels of the claret-colored silk to make the new set of curtains. Since they were so well-occupied, I did not know how Therissa would manage to get them away so we might speak properly…but I soon realized that I had underestimated her.

"That is all very well and good," she said, surveying them at their work. "But you will have cut all these panels and made no provision to stitch them together. Do you have any thread that matches this fabric?"

The three of them exchanged panicked looks, telling me that indeed they had not considered such a thing.

"As I thought," Therissa went on. "Cut a discreet swatch, and then take it with you to the storerooms."

"All—all of us?" ventured Marsali, the most forthright of the three.

"Yes, all of you," Therissa returned at once. "For it is very important that the color match exactly, and I cannot trust only one of you to make the correct choice. With all three of you involved, I have a better hope that you might be able to pick something that is close."

If they had wished to argue further, one look at Therissa's face seemed to tell them that such protests would be useless. Marsali bent her head, murmuring, "Of course," even as Alina took up her scissors and cut the most discreet of swatches from one edge of a scrap of fabric. Then they pressed their hands together and bowed at the waist toward me, just before scampering to the door so they might travel to the storerooms and match the fabric as best they could.

Yes, the most mundane of tasks, but one that allowed them some freedom to move about the palace. I found I could not judge their eagerness too much, for I thought I would feel much the same way if given a similar opportunity. Indeed, I could not help experiencing the slightest pang of jealousy at the way they were able to slip so easily out of the suite and go about their business. I knew I would be stopped the second I attempted to set foot outside my quarters. Sad, that my maids had freer rein to move about the palace than I, the woman who was supposed to be its mistress.

"Well?" I said, after I had ascertained that they were truly gone. "I suppose it is too much to ask that you might have gleaned something of any importance in so short a time, but I cannot help hoping you might have found a few tidbits to whet my appetite."

"More than that," she said, dark eyes gleaming. "I had already begun to cultivate something of a friendship with the under-cook, who—for reasons I cannot quite understand—has developed feelings of some sort for Miram. Perhaps he merely wishes to take her away from all this."

"A noble ambition," I noted in dry tones. "So what did this under-cook have to say?"

"A good deal. He has worked here in the palace since he was a boy, and is some ten years older than the Hierarch. One thing you may not know, even if you do know that your husband has a brother, is that they are twins."

"Twins?" I echoed. Truly, this was surprising news. In our brief discussion on the topic, Besh had never let on to me that the brother who had betrayed him so heinously was also his twin.

"Yes," said Therissa. "Your husband was the elder by some fifteen minutes, and so of course he was the heir. But their mother was so overtaxed by the ordeal of delivering twins that she died only a few days after her sons were born, and the Hierarch—your husband's father—never sought to replace her."

Such devotion was commendable, I supposed, but I couldn't help thinking that it was rather hard luck for me to marry into a family so fixed on its former spouses. "He must have loved her very much," I said, my tone as neutral as I could make it.

To my surprise, Therissa looked almost embarrassed. She fidgeted with her sleeve, her gaze not meeting mine. "As to that," she replied, "it seems—that is, the late Hierarch was one who preferred the company of men to that of women."

This information took me rather aback, for I had never before heard of such a thing. If any of the men in Sirlende had such proclivities, they did a good job of hiding it. Or at least, hiding it around the royal family. "Indeed?" I inquired, hoping that I sounded calm and not at all shocked. A sudden notion came to me, and though I did not truly believe it, not after the way Besh had kissed me, I added, "Then perhaps that explains some of my husband's indifference to me. If he is at all like his father—"

"Oh, I assure you, he is not. For everyone knows how passionately devoted he was to Hezia, although she did not deserve such affection. And, Lyarris, as I have told you before, I have seen how he looks at you when he thinks no one is watching. If his…desires…lay elsewhere, he would not regard you in such a manner."

This relieved me somewhat, although once again I felt a stir of impotent fury at hearing of how much Besh had loved Hezia. What had it been about her, to inspire such devotion? Could a man ever truly recover from having his heart broken in such a way?

I knew, somewhere deep within my soul in a place I did not want to acknowledge, that I would take even a fraction of what Besh had felt for Hezia. Better to have some part of him than none at all. But he did not seem willing to give me even that much.

"And did this under-cook have much to say of the exalted Hezia?" I asked, not attempting to keep the bitterness from my tone. "For truly she must have been a veritable paragon."

The sad expression on Therissa's borrowed features told me that she heard my pain all too clearly. "She was very beautiful, true. She was the daughter of one Prince Sel-Meladir, a cousin to the former Hierarch. They had been promised since children, and His Most High Majesty loved her even before he married her. But his is not the sort of temperament given to constant flattery and fawning—"

"That much is certain," I injected, chuckling a little despite myself. Truly, if Hezia had expected a husband who worshipped at her feet and praised every little thing she did, then no wonder she had found some disappointment in her marriage and ended up transferring her attentions to her brother-in-law.

Therissa attempted to appear disapproving, but instead smiled slightly before continuing. "Yes, the Hierarch is a man of a more serious mind, far better suited to having a wife such as you, my lady, who are a scholar in your own right. And so, although no one knows much about precisely what happened, it seems she fancied herself in love with Amael Kel-Alisaad, your husband's brother. Apparently he was a more easygoing sort, given to pleasure and frivolous pursuits, and able to provide Hezia with the sort of uninterrupted attention she desired."

"And because he was Besh's twin, when Hezia became with child, no doubt they thought they could conceal the baby's true parentage because she would resemble him either way."

"No doubt," Therissa said. "Not that Aldul—the under-cook—phrased it in that manner. There are limits to what can be said, even in gossip between two servants. But it seems clear enough that was their plan. How the affair was finally discovered, I do not know, for Aldul either did not know himself, or did not want to say. But it was, and so Hezia lost her life, and Amael was banished, for even though he had offended the crown mightily, it is against the law here for a commoner to spill royal blood, and it was asking too much to have the Hierarch be his brother's own executioner."

"I know, for Besh told me that very thing when he—reluctantly, of course—told me something of the story."

That surprised her. "So you knew the details?"

"Some of them. When I discovered Amael's daughter… or rather, she discovered me…I had several questions for my husband."

"I am sure of that. So you have met the child."

"Only once. Besh told me he could not be certain she was his, and so she is being raised in every comfort, but since no one can be sure of her parentage, she is not treated as a true child of the Hierarch."

"Poor thing," Therissa said, her eyes troubled. "Certainly none of this is her fault."

"No," I replied, for I had thought the same thing on many occasions. "But while I do not like it, I do understand what a terrible position Besh has been put in with regards to raising her. She might be his, but from the way he spoke of her, I got the impression he was fairly sure she was not. Very likely Hezia was only intimate enough with him to sow the seeds of doubt."

An expression of distaste passed over Therissa's countenance. "A terrible thing to do to such an honorable man."

Honorable man. Despite how terrible things were between us, I knew he was a man of high principles, which was why I had gone to him the previous night, hoping his true nature would win out over the advice of his visanis. "Yes, it was… but she paid the price for it."

"True. Although I cannot say she was alone in her perfidy. Amael Kel-Alisaad must take his own share of the blame, for I cannot understand how a man could stoop so low as to seduce his own brother's wife." She hesitated before adding, "That is, after what Aldul told me, I have something of an idea *why* Amael would do it, although that does not excuse his actions."

"Was not Hezia's surpassing beauty enough?" I asked wryly.

"I think Amael would have done the same, even if she were plain. Servants are not supposed to speak ill of their betters, but they see much. Aldul says that everyone could tell how Amael put on a good show, saying he was glad that he was the younger child so he would not have the burden of being Hierarch. But no one was much taken in. He was jealous of his brother's position, and so sought to wound him in the one way that would hurt him the most."

Hearing this, much of my present anger toward Besh seemed to ebb away. Poor man, it was not his fault that he had been born first. True, I was a daughter, and therefore had always known that I could never inherit the throne that was my brother's birthright, but even so, I did not think I would have resented him for it, even if I had been born a boy. What would it have been like, to have a brother who was a rival, rather than the good friend I counted my own dear Torric?

"You see, then," Therissa said, her tone very gentle, and I nodded.

"This makes me ache for him even more," I replied. "But I begin to understand. I will—I will try to be more patient, and can only hope that he will forgive my impetuosity last night."

Something in my tone must have alerted her that I was speaking of something more than merely escaping my room by way of the window and stealing into my husband's chambers in the middle of the night. One eyebrow went up, even as her head tilted to one side, and she said, "Precisely how impetuous *were* you, my lady?"

Hot blood surged to my cheeks. "Very, I am afraid. I am not—not normally that forward, but I was feeling so desperate—"

"That is all you have to say," she told me, raising a hand. "I will not pry the details from you. Perhaps he was not as put off as you might believe. And perhaps you gave him something to think about."

Oh, that I most assuredly did. Whether it would change anything, I could not begin to guess.

Dinner that evening was more than a little strained. I made sure that I had been arrayed in some of my very best, although the guests were merely the normal round of princes and courtiers and their wives, with no one of any particular note. And I also made certain that I put on my most serene and dignified aspect, so as to assist in erasing Besh's memory of his wife as a wild-eyed woman who had stolen into his apartments in the dead hours of the night and then flung herself at him with no more discretion than a harlot from the streets.

Oh, damn. When I thought of it that way, I was sure he would never, ever forget.

All I could do was act as if it had never happened. And because I was so calm and polite, discussing only subjects that could not rouse the slightest bit of controversy, such as the weather and the new flowers I had spied a veritable army of gardeners setting out in the courtyard, Besh did seem to relax slightly, whereas before he had been tense, the set of his jaw so stiff I wondered how he could force his mouth open enough to accept a bite of food.

But even with all that, as the meal ended, he turned to me and said, "My lady wife, I fear that I must once again have the guards escort you to your rooms, as I have some business to manage this evening."

Perhaps a few days ago I would have protested. My heart thumped painfully in my breast, but I would not let him see how much it hurt me that he had apparently abandoned the little courtesy I had come to look forward to at the end of each day. I inclined my head, said, "Of course, my husband," and rose from my seat so the guards might take their positions around me and see that I was returned to my chambers with no mishap.

That night I was glad of the maids clustering around me to divest me of my jewels and clothing. Therissa stood off to one side, expression both sad and knowing. We had only been in one another's company for a few days, but clearly she had already mastered the art of reading my expressions, and so she could see things had not gone well.

And although I attempted to tell myself that this was only one night out of many, that I could not predict what Besh would do based on his actions tonight, somehow my heart knew things had changed. In attempting to close the distance between us, I had only made it that much greater.

CHAPTER FIFTEEN

Two days after I had gone to Besh to beg him to investigate the matter further, the prisoner I had been trying to save was executed in front of the palace—in the same spot where Hezia had lost her own life, according to Therissa, who was now in touch with the palace gossip in a way I guessed the real Miram had never been.

I did not attend the execution, of course. No, my husband would not ask such a thing of me, and at any rate, apparently it was not the custom to subject the delicate eyes of the Hiereine to such a spectacle. Neither did he inform me of his decision before having the sentence carried out. Whether he had kept it from me to avoid another argument, or because he did not think it necessary to consult with me on matters of state, I did not know. Not that it mattered one way or another. What were our petty arguments, when an innocent man would be losing his very life?

And even though I tried to tell myself I did not know for certain he was innocent, I could not make myself believe that. Therissa had made another foray into the dungeons disguised as her little bantam rooster of a lieutenant, and could bring nothing back to change my mind, telling me that until the very moment he was led out of his cell to face his own death, he continued to protest his innocence. From what Therissa had been able to find out, he was the younger brother of an ironmonger, certainly not the type to foment rebellion or seek the death of his monarch. On the surface, it seemed clear that he did not have the resources to hire a squad of mounted assassins such as the ones who had attacked us in the desert. But there must have been some convincing evidence, something that Tel-Karinoor's agents had discovered to point at this man above all others as the ringleader.

What that evidence possibly could have been, I had no idea.

In the end it did not matter, for the executioner took his head under the merciless white-hot rays of Keshiaar's springtime sun, and everyone went away, satisfied that justice had been done. The undercurrent of tension I had sensed among the members of the court seemed to have disappeared as well, like poison drained from a festering wound. Now their Hierarch was safe, after all. True, some believed the executed man had associates yet in hiding, as not all of the men who had assailed our camp had been killed that night. Even so, with their leader dead, they most likely did not pose much of a threat.

This was the conversation that swirled around the palace...or at least the conversation as Therissa reported it to me. No one else would speak freely of such things in my presence. Oddly, though, my three maids did not seem to think it amiss that "Miram" and I would have such discussions. Perhaps that was how it had always been here, with the Hiereine isolated from the actual ruling of the kingdom, and her chatelaine being the one to keep her informed. I could not know for sure, as Besh's mother had died when he was only a few days old, and Aldul, the under-cook besotted with Miram, was not old enough to have been alive when the previous Hierarch and his consort reigned.

Once again the days began to slip past, each of such a weary sameness that I hardly bothered to glance at the calendar I had brought with me. Besh treated me with a fragile courtesy that made my heart ache a little more each day, and not once since my ill-fated expedition to his chambers had he escorted me from dinner. Neither had he invited me back to his observatory, even though the clouds of winter and early spring had now quite disappeared.

And I awoke one morning, feeling the heat of the day already seeping through the latticed shutters, and realized I had been here an entire year.

One year. When I had come here late last Averil, I had thought...what? That Besh and I would be experiencing the kind of matrimonial bliss I had seen in my own brother and his wife? That perhaps I would already have given him an heir, or at the very least would be carrying his child?

Yes, I had thought all those things. And not a one of them had turned out to be true.

I sat up in bed and pushed back my covers. They were far too hot now; I would have to ask Therissa to bring me the lighter coverlet of thin embroidered silk that topped my bed during the summer months.

The memory of my previous summer here came to me then…the smothering heat, the endless, weary waiting for the sun to finally dip down below the horizon. At least then I had had my visits to Besh's observatory to break up the monotony of those days, but now, I realized, I had no such pleasant diversions to occupy me.

I did not have him, nor even the spurious comfort of his company.

I was the Hiereine of Keshiaar, and I had nothing.

Tears came to my eyes then. I attempted to blink them back, but there were so many of them, rising from some dark place in my soul, the only free-flowing water in a thousand miles.

Then I heard the rustle of cloth, and a swirl of jasmine-scented perfume, and Therissa's arms were around me. "There, there," she soothed, stroking my tumbled hair. "I know it's difficult, but you mustn't give up. You mustn't."

"Why not?" I raged, lifting my tear-soaked face from her shoulder. "It has been a year, Therissa. A year. If Besh truly wanted me, he would have made me his wife in truth by now. Whatever you saw in him, you must have misjudged. He cannot bring himself to care for me, not even a little bit. Indeed," I added, choking back a bitter laugh, "perhaps I should be glad he is a man of such scruples. Most men in his position would have bedded me by now, whether or not there was any love involved."

She did not pretend to be shocked, but only said, "I cannot begin to imagine how trying all this must be for you. In truth, if I were a bolder woman, I would go up to him and give him a good sound shaking. Perhaps that would at last knock some sense into him."

"I doubt it. Such behavior would only get you a cell in the dungeons, I fear." I wiped my eyes, drew in a deep, shuddering breath. "Perhaps I should ask him for a divorce."

That remark did make her widen her eyes, and she said, "My lady, you are distraught. Such things are very rare, even in Sirlende, and the practice does not exist at all here in Keshiaar. When you are married in the eyes of God, you are married forever."

"So I am bound to a loveless marriage no matter what I do?"

She did not answer, but only cast her gaze downward at the rug beneath her feet.

Her silence was more painful than any words of hers could have been. Overcome, I pushed my way off the bed and went to the window, then looked down at the stolid forms of the guards standing some twenty feet below. They might have been the same men who were there the morning before, or a new group. From this angle, I could not determine any great difference between them.

The very sight of them made the angry heat rise up in me even higher, and I whirled back toward Therissa, saying,

"And I am a prisoner in this very palace that is supposed to be mine! Oh, the accommodations are more luxurious, but even so, I have no more freedom than that poor wretch Besh had executed all those weeks ago. Indeed, perhaps I should ask him to lock me up in the dungeons. At least that way my status will be clear."

She stood up, taking a few hesitant steps toward me. "Lyarris, do not say such things. It must be difficult to remain here, to not have even the limited freedoms you enjoyed as Crown Princess back in Sirlende. But Keshiaar is a very different place—"

"Do you not think that I know that?" I demanded. "And do not tell me how difficult it must be, not when you have the freedom to come and go as you like, putting on different faces and personas as needed. You may go anywhere you like, while—"

And there I broke off, for a notion had occurred to me, one so simple I wondered why I had not thought of it before.

"What is it?" Therissa inquired, although the expression of worry that passed over her face told me she had begun to guess what was in my mind.

"You did as much for Ashara, and so I am asking you to do the same for me—or very close to it. I want you to take on my semblance, and cast a spell so I look like Miram, and that way I can get out and away from here, and breathe in air that is not bounded by gates and walls."

"My lady, no—"

"Are you refusing me in this?" I asked, in what I hoped were my most queenly tones.

Her fingers knotted in the pale fabric of the long over-tunic she wore. "Please, think of what you are asking—the dangers—"

"What dangers?" I scoffed. "Is Tir el-Alisaad such a dangerous place that a woman may not go to the bazaar to shop, or merely walk its streets?"

"It is not that it is dangerous," she replied quietly. "But it is not the custom for a woman to go about alone in the city. When I go to the bazaar, I have two guards with me. So you would not be as free as you might think."

"But I would still be able to escape this wretched palace, would I not?"

A long hesitation. Then she said, reluctance clear in every word, "Yes, you would. I go often to the bazaar, to purchase spices for the sachets with which I scent your wardrobe, or to acquire the compounds used to make the rouge for your lips and the kohl for your eyes. So that sort of an expedition would not seem at all out of the ordinary."

"Well, then," I said in some triumph. Truly, in that moment even going to purchase a few spices and powders sounded wholly exotic to me, as I had not been outside the palace gates since that ill-fated journey to watch the conjunction of the planets. And I had gotten only the briefest glimpse of the capital city when I was first brought here. I had seen nothing when we ventured forth to view the planets in the deep desert, for the palace was built on the extreme eastern edge of the city, and we went out the east gate when we left, our departure unobserved by anyone save a few guards.

That realization shook me somewhat, for it was not as if we had ridden in state through the streets of the capital, letting everyone know that the Hierarch and his consort had ventured forth from the safety of their palace. True, it was not a complete secret, and members of the household knew of it, as they were the ones who had helped to prepare our horses and packed our supplies and so forth. Even so, I had to wonder how the man who had been executed had known where we were going and where we would be.

"What is it?" Therissa asked, apparently seeing my brows pull together in puzzlement.

"Nothing," I replied. I would have to ponder that matter later. Now, I could only focus on my desire to be away from these rooms, whose walls seemed to be closing in on me more with every day that passed. It was true that my escape would be a short one, but it would be enough. And if all was successful, then there was no reason why we could not make the exchange again in a few days or weeks, when once again I felt the need to flee my apartments. "Let us do it this morning, after I have broken my fast. It will be warm, but not so hot as I know it will be later in the day, and that way I will be able to enjoy the expedition all the better."

Her expression was a study in doubt. "My lady, please think on this some more—"

"I have thought on it. As you said, no one will think anything strange of you going out to purchase a few items for the Hiereine. And I know you have managed to bespell your own face and that of another at the same time, so do not tell me you cannot do it."

"I can do it," she began. "However, this is somewhat different from the enchantment I used on Ashara. I only had to enchant her clothing and her hair. I did not have to change her face or body, or the way she walked and talked. I will have to do all these for you at the same time I am working such an alteration on myself, and that is much more difficult."

Since she had already told me she could manage the thing, I did not let her last remark dissuade me. "But it is not impossible."

"No, not impossible." She paused. "But because it will be so much more of a strain on me, you will have to go and return promptly. I was able to keep the spell going on Ashara for hours and hours because I did not have to alter as much of her person. This time, do not go out for more than an hour and a half."

"That little?" Already I began to feel some of my enthusiasm dampen. How much could I see of the city in an hour and a half?

"Yes," she replied. "For you will need some time after you return to the palace to come here to your apartments and change places with me. The city is large, and the bazaar a good fifteen-minute walk from here. Do not think you will be carried there in luxury in a sedan chair. Miram is a servant, and is expected to walk."

"Good," I said. "For being jostled around in a sedan chair in this heat makes me quite sick to my stomach. I look forward to walking."

Her mouth quirked at that. "You may change your mind, after you have spent a few minutes traversing the streets of Tir el-Alisaad."

And she turned out to be correct in that. Oh, it was quite thrilling to have her cast the spell on me while Lila and Marsali and Alina were occupied with scrubbing down the bath chamber, and both thrilling and odd to watch Therissa transform herself into me, right down to the ruby ring I wore on my right hand. It was so very different from gazing into a mirror; I had thought I knew well enough what I looked like, but as I stared at her, I noted the quizzical lift to the eyebrows, a certain sadness in the dark eyes. Was that how I appeared to everyone else, or were some of Therissa's own expressions showing on my features?

I could not say for certain, but clearly the illusion had been well cast, for as I left my bedchamber, I nearly bumped into Lila, who had a bucket full of wet rags in one hand.

"Pardon, honored one!" she gasped.

For a second or two, I wondered why she had addressed me in such a fashion, as the term was never applied to a member of the aristocracy, but only a social better in one of the lower classes. Then I remembered. I wore Miram's face, and so of course Lila would never say "my lady" or "Your Majesty" to me.

"Watch where you are going!" I told her, hoping I had injected enough affronted dignity into the rebuke.

She'd bobbed a curtsey and fled, while I made my way through the halls of the palace, following Therissa's instructions as to where the guards would wait to take her on one of her errands. Sure enough, two of them were standing near an exit off the kitchens, neither of them appearing too happy to be sent forth to play nursemaid to the Hiereine's chatelaine.

Recalling what Therissa had told me to do, I bowed, hands clasped in front of me. If one carefully dissected the pecking order of the servants within the palace, then Miram was rather highly placed, but her relative rank did not come into play when the guards were involved. They were a group set off on their own, following their own chain of command, and therefore demanded a certain amount of obsequiousness, no matter who in the servant class they might be dealing with.

It seemed I appeared humble enough, for they nodded, then opened the door and led me outside. We were in a confined space between the palace proper and the outer walls, one whose primary purpose seemed to be storing refuse until it could be carted away, and I fought to keep from wrinkling my nose and coughing. Surely Miram had been here scores of times before, which meant I could not show any particular reaction to the stench.

Breathing through my mouth, I followed the guards as they made their way to a small gate, one not nearly as fine as that which guarded the main entrance to the palace. From there we emerged into a side street, one lined with buildings two and three stories high, apparently residences of some sort. People were coming and going, all on foot, most carrying parcels and bundles, one chasing a flock of squawking chickens over the hard-packed earth.

It all sounded terribly noisy and chaotic, but that was nothing. After winding away along that street for some minutes, we came out onto a much larger avenue, this one choked with people on foot, men on horseback, carts being hauled by oxen and donkeys, and the odd sedan chair here and there, no doubt carrying some member of the aristocracy from the shelter of one townhouse to another. Or did they even call them that here? My only experience was of the palace, so I did not precisely know what the residences of those who did not reside at court might look like.

What I did know was that, even with one guard in front of me and the other behind, more than once I had to dodge out of the way to avoid being knocked over, and several times I narrowly missed stepping in what the horses and oxen and donkeys had left behind. No wonder Therissa had smiled at my eagerness to walk these streets. She had known precisely what lay in store for me, while I, in my ignorance, had thought it would be refreshing. No breath of fresh air here, that was for certain; I would have been better served to find a well-shaded balcony at the palace and catch a stray breeze there. Perhaps away from these streets, and down at the docks, there was cleaner, cooler air to be had, but I knew I could never ask the guards to accompany me there. I had a reason to go to the bazaar, whereas I had none at all for going to the docks.

Except, perhaps, to find a ship there bound for Sirlende, and to climb aboard, and make my way home, so I might go to my brother and beg his forgiveness for my foolishness. Surely he would take me in, even if he would be very angry with me for the way I had abandoned my responsibilities here in Keshiaar.

No, of course I would never do any such thing. It was only a fantasy born of my despair at my current situation. I would never leave Besh. Even if he did not love me, he would be horribly wounded by such a desertion. I could not do that to him, not when I knew I loved him, despite everything.

So I followed the guards as we wound through the streets, and I told myself there was plenty here to hold my interest—the quick chatter of the people around me, faster, more sibilant than the court speech I was used to, the intricate carving on even a simple drover's cart, the way gold flashed from women's ears and wrists, and from the ears of some of the men as well. This surprised me, for I had not seen any of the courtiers sporting such a fashion. I also noted that none of the women were unaccompanied, that all had a man— husband, brother, father—with them. Even so, they did not seem terribly discommoded by being saddled with an escort at all times, for they talked and laughed with one another, seeming to ignore their companions outright when it suited them, and I had to repress a smile at the sight.

Finally, we came to the bazaar, and my eyes widened in wonder. In my mind I had imagined it as a group of several score stalls and pavilions, taking up a space close to that of one of the parks that were sprinkled through my homeland's capital, but in reality the bazaar was enormous, spanning such a huge

area that I could not even see the far end of it, only an endless sea of canvas in various shades of beige and ivory, broken
here and there by a more permanent stall constructed of sun-
bleached wood. In that moment, I was glad of the two guards
who flanked me, for not only did they provide a welcome barrier against the masses of humanity who flowed in and out of
the bazaar, filling the narrow spaces between the stalls, but they
also led me unerringly to my destination, a large pavilion filled
with basket after basket of various spices and dried herbs, along
with vials of the powdered minerals used for cosmetics.

Therissa had already told me what I should ask for, so
I requested a vial of red ochre for my lips, and another of
galena for the kohl. The shopkeeper, whose name was Isala,
smiled and took the silver coin I handed her in payment,
saying she was surprised that I needed the pigments again so
quickly, as apparently Miram had purchased those items only
a few weeks earlier.

I gave an off-hand shrug, attempting to mimic my chatelaine's somewhat brusque manner, and said, "Ah, well, Her
Most High Majesty would knock over the vials when she was
setting down a book the other day—"

"Oh, my, that would explain it," the woman said, chuckling a little. "I do hope she will take greater care in the future.
That can't have been easy to clean up."

"The maids are still scrubbing the stains out of the carpet," I said darkly.

With a shake of her head, Isala handed me my change.
"It will get better, honored one. The stars are shifting."

They are? I thought. *Perhaps that is a good omen....*

Not that I would know for certain, as I had not discussed the stars with my husband in some months. Realizing I was frowning, I thanked her, then stowed the vials in the small embroidered bag I had brought along for that purpose. Then it was time to fall in behind the guards once again as they led me out of the bazaar.

How I wished I could stop and look at everything—at the hanging lamps of brass, and the cunning figures carved of marble in a dizzying array of colors, and the embroidered pillows, and the mirrors whose frames were inlaid with mosaics of multicolored wood and chips of mother-of-pearl. But because I had come here on a very particular errand, and because I knew that gawking at the wares in the bazaar as if I had never seen them before would certainly invite the guards' attention, I followed them meekly until once more we were winding through the streets of Tir el-Alisaad.

It seemed that we were following a slightly different route this time, for some reason; perhaps the traffic in the streets had its own particular patterns, and so it was easier to head toward the palace along this street rather than the one we had first taken to get to the bazaar. Here there was more foot traffic, and fewer carts, which made the going somewhat easier, although as we walked along, the lane became more and more crowded, until we came to a dead halt.

I could hear why immediately, although I could not see much beyond the shoulders of the people stopped in front of us. A man's voice, rough with anger, was carrying above the murmur of the crowd.

"…And all his protests for nothing! My brother was innocent! You know me, know my family!"

A wave of assent seemed to swirl through the watching people. It seemed clear to me that they knew the speaker… and I also thought I knew of whom he was speaking. Despite the heat of the day, which even now was making the perspiration drip down my back, I felt a chill go over me.

"Do we have the money for even one horse, let alone enough to pay an entire squad of horsemen to attack His Most High Majesty?"

Another murmur, this one seemingly in the negative.

"And yet they ignored my brother's protests, ignored common sense, and took his head anyway, just so they could say the culprit had been dealt with! It's wrong, I say! Wrong!"

Again the crowd shifted and whispered. It seemed they were in agreement, yet afraid to speak up too loudly. And that fear became apparent when the people in my immediate vicinity noted my escort of two guards in the uniform of the palace.

"Quiet, Halmud! There are soldiers here!" someone cried out, and immediately the group began to surge, scattering in all directions.

In that moment I saw the man who had been speaking. He was of medium height, with a heavy beard and equally heavy shoulders, thick with muscles. Dimly I recalled that the executed man's brother was an ironmonger. As his gaze seemed to fasten on me, my guards pushed forward, faces grim. Yes, they had been sent to protect "Miram," but it was more important that they go to take this man who had been speaking openly against the Hierarch.

Their purposeful steps only served to increase the panic of the people around me, and I found myself pushed along with them, flowing with a river of frightened humanity down the narrow street, heading out and as far away from the palace guards as possible. I struggled against them, trying to get back to the spot where the ironmonger stood, but it was impossible. All I could do was move along with the crowd and hope that eventually their alarm would subside, and I would be free to return to the protection of my guards.

That hope proved to be in vain, however. Some minutes later I found myself in an unfamiliar street, surrounded by buildings I did not recognize. Wildly I looked around me, but I could pick out no landmarks to guide me back to where I had started, nothing that told me where I was.

My own panic rose in me, and I forced it down. The last thing I should do now was lose my head. Very well, I was a woman alone on these streets, which in and of itself was bad enough. But if anyone should guess who I truly was....

Heart pounding, I glanced down at my hand. The skin was a pale golden-brown, several shades darker than my own, with the prominent veins of someone who must do much of her own work. Good. So the enchantment still held, but I could not guess how much longer it would last. I had to get back to the palace, and it seemed I must do it on my own.

I glanced up at the sky. The sun was now nearing its zenith, bright and blinding, giving me no real clue as to which way was east. Very well, I would simply have to ask.

This seemed to be a residential street, but even so, I spied some people about. There seemed to be a well of sorts tucked in between two buildings, and women queued there to fill various ewers and basins and buckets with water. None of those women had any male escort, and I guessed they did not require one to go the few paces from their homes to the well and back again. Even better; that way my own unaccompanied state would not draw as much attention.

I approached one of them, put on what I hoped was a friendly but somewhat meek smile—an expression I doubted the real Miram had ever attempted—and asked, "A thousand pardons, but could you tell me in which direction the palace lies?"

The woman, who appeared to be some ten years or so older than I, with gold rings in her ears and expertly painted eyes, shot me a questioning look. "How is it that you do not know where His Most High Majesty resides?"

"Well, I—that is, I thought I did, but I seem to have lost my way."

Her expression shifted from skeptical to somewhat pitying as she appeared to take in my lack of a male companion. "If you are looking for employment, I would advise you to go elsewhere. My own cousin was sacked only a week ago, and with no explanation. It would be better to try someplace else."

"Oh, I am not looking for work," I began, but she cut me off, saying,

"Perhaps not, but you would do well to heed my advice." She lowered her voice then. "And if it is not that sort of work you desire, I can tell you right now that you are not pretty enough to catch the eye of any of the guards."

For a second I gaped at her, and then I realized she must think me some kind of prostitute, to be wandering around the streets unaccompanied. Words failed me for another second or two, until I finally managed, "Very well, but I still would like to know where the palace is."

She lifted her shoulders, pointing with her free hand past the queue at the well. "If you go down this street, and then turn to the right at the first intersection you come to, then you can follow that street all the way to the palace walls. They won't let you in, though," she added, apparently unable to prevent herself from giving me one final warning.

Perhaps not, but I would worry about that when I got there. I thought I would recognize my surroundings well enough once I got closer, and after that, all I would have to do was go to the small side gate in the outer wall, and tell the guards there that I had been separated from my escort. No doubt the two guards were even now searching the streets for "Miram"...or perhaps they had hurried back to the palace once they realized their charge was nowhere to be found. At any rate, the guards on duty would recognize me and let me in.

That is, I had to hope they would.

I hurried off in the direction the woman had indicated, and, sure enough, some hundred paces later I came to an intersection with a much larger street, this one with the familiar ox and donkey carts, and the occasional sedan chair, which told me I must be getting closer to my destination.

They were the preferred mode of transportation for the women of the court, and not something one saw much of in the poorer districts of the city.

As I walked, I could feel the curious gazes of the men and women in the street settling on me. They had to be wondering who this woman was who had the temerity to walk through Tir el-Alisaad without a single male companion as her escort. All I could do was keep moving forward, not allowing my eyes to meet any of theirs. Perhaps they would note the determination in my stride, and let me alone.

This seemed to work at first, and I allowed myself the tiniest sensation of relief. Gradually the traffic on the street lessened, the carts replaced almost completely by men on horseback or women safely concealed in the confines of their sedan chairs. The buildings on either side were very grand, faced with marble and decorated with intricate carvings, banners of colored silk fluttering from their balconies. And there—not a hundred yards off I saw the street come to its end, high walls of pale stone marking the boundary of the Hierarch's palace.

Something not unlike a sob of relief escaped my lips. I hurried forward, gaze darting this way and that as I looked for the narrow lane that would lead me to the gate on the south wall whence I had departed only an hour or so earlier. Nothing seemed familiar, but perhaps it was only because I now approached from a different direction.

I paused then in the shadow of a stately palm, one of a pair that guarded the entrance to a large home with its own wall and gate, although that gate now stood open. Pondering the best place to go next, as my current location did not jog my memory at all, I raised my hand to push a stray strand of hair away from my face.

Red flashed on my finger, and I stared at it for a few seconds, puzzled, until I realized with dawning horror that the flash of red had come from the ruby ring I wore. *I* wore... not Miram.

With a gasp, I looked down at myself, saw not the ivory tunic and skirts that were Miram's normal costume, but my own garb of embroidered red silk with the filmy pale gold wide-legged trousers underneath. The spell had worn off.

Now I knew I must get off this street as soon as possible. Bad enough that a woman in the dress of a palace servant was wandering about alone. In this outfit, I should be recognized almost immediately—if not as the Hiereine, then at the very least as someone who had no right to be out and about without a full complement of guards.

As I hesitated there, not wanting to leave the spurious protection of the palm in its large planter of cast stone, I heard a most unwelcome voice say in incredulous tones, "Your Majesty?"

Knowing there was nothing else I could do, I took a step toward the speaker, lifted my chin, and said, "Good morning, Chancellor Tel-Karinoor."

Chapter Sixteen

"What on earth were you thinking?" Besh demanded, turning away from where he had stood at the window and coming to stand by me, arms crossed over his chest, brow thunderous.

"I-I wasn't," I faltered, my courage deserting me in the face of his very real anger.

His jaw tensed. "You weren't thinking?"

"I—" Damnation. I had rehearsed this speech in my mind at least a hundred times, almost from the very moment when the visanis saw me in the street as he left his house. Perhaps the gods knew why they had decided to twist fate and make me pause in front of the very residence that belonged to Tel-Karinoor, but they had not seen fit to pass that information along to me. At any rate, I had thought I was prepared for this confrontation. What was the worst Besh could do to me, after all? Confine me to my chambers?

We were now in his suite, in his library with the door shut. At least he had the grace to chastise me in private, and not in front of his chancellor. Perhaps it had only been my own fear and worry, but I almost thought I'd seen an expression of satisfaction cross Tel-Karinoor's face when he confronted me in the street, as if he'd been somehow happy to catch me in such a wildly inappropriate situation. Why, I couldn't begin to guess. For some reason, it seemed as if he had never approved of me, and I supposed anything that might make me look worse to my husband would please the chancellor.

"I merely—I needed to escape for a bit."

"Escape? Escape to where?" His tone was not quite as rough now, but I could still hear the thrum of repressed fury within it.

"Nowhere!" I flung at him. "Anywhere! I had no true destination in mind, my husband, only that I needed to be out, away, someplace where I was not breathing the same air I had breathed a thousand times before, or staring at the same walls, or the same faces. Truly, it is enough to drive a person mad!"

To my horror, I felt tears begin to stream down my cheeks, and I put my hands up to my face to conceal my weakness, even as I pushed myself up from the chair and stumbled to the door. Where I thought I was going, I did not know, for the guards standing watch at the entrance to Besh's suite would not let me go any farther than that without his express permission.

But then, wonder of wonders, I heard him approach, and strong arms reached out to enfold me, to pull me against him. His hand touched my hair, almost gingerly, as if he were not quite sure that I wouldn't slap it away. "Shh," he murmured, voice much gentler now, rich and soothing. "It is all right. I am not angry with you. It is only that you could have come to some grief, wandering about the streets like that."

And would you care? I wondered, but in that moment I realized that was a petty thought, and that, wonder of wonders, he must care. Surely if he were indifferent, he would not have been so angry, even though he had said he was not. At least I had been with him long enough to perceive when he was upset.

"I know, and I am sorry," I told him, trying my best not to sniffle. "It is only when I saw the gate open, and no one watching it…." For that was the lie I had told to explain how I had gotten away from the palace grounds in the first place.

"My dear," he said, and my heart wanted to break at those words. How I had longed for him to address me by such an endearment! What had caused his shift in attitude? That he had finally forced himself to examine his feelings when he realized he had come close to losing me? That perhaps he had taken my presence for granted, and at last saw in his heart what it might mean to him if I were not here? "Why did you not tell me how you were suffering? It was never my intention to make you feel as if you were a prisoner here."

"I could not think of how best to talk to you. Most days, it seemed to me that you might as well have been one of those stars you watch in your telescope, thousands of miles beyond my grasp."

His arms tightened around me, and I breathed in the wondrous scent of him, warm skin and something fragrant and spicy, as if his wardrobe had been scented with dried orange peel or something similar. "Lyarris...I am sorry for that. It was never my intention to cause you pain."

"Then what was it?" I asked, determined to learn something of why he had held me away from him all these months. "Every day I racked my brains, trying to think of what I might have done to offend you, and how best to get you to speak with me, treat me as your wife. In the beginning, I thought perhaps we were growing closer, but...."

"That was my fault, and none of yours," he replied, loosening his grasp so he could step away half a pace and look directly into my face. "My way of protecting myself."

"Because of Hezia." I did not bother to keep the bitterness out of my words.

"Yes, because of Hezia," he said heavily. "Some wounds take a very long time to heal."

"How much more time do you need?" I wrapped my fingers around his, gazed up into those extraordinary amber eyes. "One year? Two? Ten? Am I supposed to be patient and wait however long it takes?"

Heavy black lashes swept over his eyes as he glanced away from me. "I had told myself after her that I would never love again. Not like that. And then you came to me. They had told me you were beautiful, but I had thought that was merely a pleasant fabrication, a lie told to make the marriage contract even more appealing. But you were—you are—and beyond that, you are strong and wise…but not so wise that you protest staying up until all hours to look at the stars with me."

"If I am all those things," I said, taking care to keep my tone light, for what he had said struck at my very core, and I wanted to weep all over again, "then why this eternal distance? Simply because you would not grant yourself permission to ever care again?"

"No, it was more than that." A long pause, as he returned his gaze to me and seemed to study my features for an endless moment. "I was told—that is, my chancellor informed me that you had been engaged in Sirlende, and that you had thrown off your betrothed as soon as you were given the opportunity to become my wife. I did not want to risk becoming close to someone whose affections could be so easily transferred, even though as time went on, it became clear to me that you were not that sort of woman at all. It was difficult for me to reconcile what I had heard with the truth of the person before me."

The chancellor. Always the chancellor. What was his stake in all this? In truth, I could not begin to guess, for surely the welfare of the kingdom was his greatest responsibility, and doing whatever he could to keep the Hierarch and his new wife apart did not seem to agree with that responsibility at all. A ruler without an heir of his body was never good for a kingdom. Tel-Karinoor's scheming was something my husband and I would have to discuss, but I thought it better to clear up one misconception first.

"Besh," I said, pausing as I saw one of his rare smiles steal over his face when I used the familiar form of his name. Thank the gods. It had quite slipped out, but it seemed that he did not mind at all. "While it is true that I had to break my engagement to the Duke of Marric's Rest to become your wife, it was not without a good deal of soul-searching. I cared for him—yes, I cannot lie and say I did not. But when I examined my feelings, I realized it was more because he was handsome and pleasant, and rather an outsider to court politics, a quality I found very appealing. It was not enough, however, to make him what I considered to be my ideal husband."

"And my qualities were?" Besh inquired, mouth quirking slightly, although he did not quite smile all the way. "But you had not even met me at that point."

It did sound rather dreadful when put that way. "True. But Ambassador Sel-Trelazar spoke so highly of you, spoke of you being a man of learning, one who did not scorn the pursuits of the mind, and I thought in that we were far better suited. If we could not have love, *real* love, I hoped at least we would share respect and friendship, which is more than many princesses can hope for in their royal matches."

He was silent, appearing to think it over, then said, his tone almost harsh, "So you would settle for respect and friendship, if nothing else was offered? That did not seem to be your intent when you came to my apartments several weeks ago."

"I was desperate!" I cried. "I only wanted to speak to you in private at first, but I would be lying if I said I did not want to force your hand in some way, attempt to see if you had feelings for me but were only hiding them."

Again he said nothing. After my heart had thudded two or three times in my breast, he took my hands, turned them palm up, and pressed his lips first against the one, then the other. My blood began to race at even that gentle pressure, although I willed myself to be calm, to see what he intended to do next.

I did not have to wait long. His fingers wrapped around mine, and he pulled me up against him, his mouth seeking mine, filling me with the sweet taste of him. It was not so very different from that other kiss, in the heat and the power of it, but this time he did not push me away, only held me close, our bodies pressed together. Even through the heavy brocade of his tunic, I could feel his arousal, but it did not frighten me. No, I wanted that part of him, too. I wanted everything that he could teach me.

Eventually he did pull away, but just enough so he could speak. "I am a fool."

"No—" I began, and he held up a hand.

"I am, for depriving myself of that all these months. How can I ever make amends?"

"I can think of one way," I said, casting a significant glance upward to the second floor, where I knew his bed-chamber was located.

This time it wasn't a smile that lit up his face, but an outright grin. "Ah, my lady wife, my thoughts have run in the same direction. But allow me a small opportunity to woo you—a private dinner here, with no one else intruding, and then the wedding night you should have had long ago."

I appeared to consider. "Well, if I have already waited a year, then I suppose a few more hours will not make much of a difference." I tilted my head to one side, then asked, "And will it not cause a fuss, for you to cancel a public dinner already planned?"

"Oh, I will not cancel that one. The guests can come, as they always do, but they will find their host conspicuously absent."

"Very daring of you, my lord."

He bent and kissed me again, kissed me so thoroughly that the room quite began to spin around me. I would have been content to stay there in his arms forever, his mouth against mine, but after some minutes he drew away, saying, "There is one matter that troubles me, though."

"Only one?"

The quip did not seem to move him, for his expression remained serious. "It is not good that you found the gate open and unattended. That is an unforgivable breach of the security here at the palace, and I must have the situation investigated and the negligent parties punished."

Oh, dear. I had hoped he would have let that particular part of my story slip by unremarked. Loath as I was to reveal the true nature of my escape from the palace, I could not allow some innocent to be punished because of my actions. And really, attitudes toward magic here in Keshiaar were not quite the same as they were in Sirlende. Therissa was in no way at risk of being punished with death, or even banishment.

Besh might not completely approve of what I had done, but I knew he would not take any action against the woman who had helped me.

"As to that"—I paused, then forged on ahead— "I might not have been entirely truthful as to how I managed to get outside the palace walls."

An eyebrow lifted. "Indeed? Then precisely how did you manage it?"

"No one left the gate open. I walked out in the company of two guards, and the guards whose duty it was to watch the gate made sure it was closed securely behind us."

"And how did you convince the guards to simply walk through the gate with the Hiereine of Keshiaar?"

"Because they did not know it was me. They thought they were with Miram, my chatelaine."

He rubbed his chin, watching me closely. "Explain this."

"The woman everyone thinks is Miram is—is not Miram," I went on, hoping I had not just made a terrible mistake in deciding to reveal her identity.

"Then who is she?"

"Her true name is Therissa Larrin, and she is aunt to the Empress of Sirlende."

A lift of the eyebrows, and he said, "I would say that if she is such a relation, then she should have been greeted with honor…but I think that if she has managed to disguise herself so well as your chatelaine, then there is something more here than you have told me so far."

"There is." We were not so far apart that I could not take his hands in mine, holding them tightly, as if that contact might help to make him understand why Therissa's and my subterfuges had been so important. "Mistress Larrin is quite an accomplished wielder of magic, specifically of illusions that alter one's appearance. And so she took on Miram's identity, so that she might be here for me as a friend, since...." And here I faltered, because I was not certain how to proceed without sounding either pitiable or desperate.

"Since what?" Besh prompted, his tone gentle, as if he already had begun to understand.

"Since I had none."

His fingers closed on mine, and he pulled me close, kissing not my mouth, but my forehead, his lips lingering there for a long while before he murmured, "My dear, I am so very sorry for that. Since you had brought no ladies-in-waiting with you, I had thought you did not mind being alone—"

"And I thought I would not, save that Chancellor Tel-Karinoor sent my Sirlendian maids away, and so I had no one from home at all." I looked up into his face, saw only concern there...concern perhaps mixed with regret. "Mistress Larrin is the kindliest of souls, and came to provide what support she could."

"And how is it she even knew of your predicament? For truly, all these months you have carried on with such dignity and serenity that I find it difficult to believe anyone could have looked on you and seen that you were in any distress."

I hesitated before answering; I most certainly did not wish to bring any trouble down upon the good ambassador, for I did not know how Besh would look upon his relationship with Therissa. But neither did I wish to lie, so I said,

"She met with Ambassador Sel-Trelazar as he was passing through Tarenmar in South Eredor, and as they had been great good…friends…for some years, he told her something of my situation here. And so she traveled to Keshiaar to offer what support and friendship she could."

Besh did not question me further on their relationship. I guessed he knew exactly what I had meant when I referred to them as "friends." "It must have been quite a burden to her, to maintain such a spell day in and day out. But what happened to the real Miram?"

"Oh, Mistress Larrin paid her off, saying she had come into a great inheritance, and Miram went off to enjoy her money far away from any relations who might attempt to lay claim to it."

He actually laughed at that. "Ah, so Miram had a happy ending. I had rather feared that you would tell me this Mistress Larrin had her kidnapped and taken away to be a slave in Seldd, or some such."

"You know I would never countenance such a thing," I said severely. "And neither would Mistress Larrin. She is truly all that is good, and it is so very unfortunate that the laws in Sirlende regarding magic are so severe that she could not remain there to be an aunt to my sister-in-law, as the Empress has no other family in the world." *Well, not any she wishes to acknowledge,* I thought, although her stepsisters apparently have improved markedly now that they are living away from their mother.

"And fortunate that we do not have such laws here, I suppose," Besh remarked. "While I cannot say I precisely approve such a subterfuge, I can see why you thought it was necessary. And so this last time you escaped the palace while disguised as Miram, and she took on your appearance, so as to make everyone think you were safely in your quarters."

"Precisely that. I did not think there would be any harm in it, as I intended to go to only one stall in the bazaar, and I had the guards with me, of course. But there was a disturbance in the street, and we were separated, and I could do nothing but attempt to make my way back here as best I could."

"Ah, yes, that 'disturbance.'" He let go of my hands then, moving with restless steps toward his desk, where he rummaged amongst the papers there and seemed to peer down at one of them. "'Seditious speech and fomenting rebellion' was how the captain of the guards phrased it, once his soldiers had made their report."

"Well," I began, then paused. The execution of the iron-monger's younger brother was probably still a sore subject, and I saw no way to bring it up without appearing to criti-cize my husband, or at the very least his chancellor. Then again, I knew we would have to discuss the matter at some point. "The ironmonger did lose his brother, and for reasons he finds difficult to understand."

"What is so difficult to understand about being found guilty of treason, and losing one's head for it?"

This was a side of Besh I did not much like—expression severe, implacable. No doubt he was anticipating another argument on the subject. That was the last thing I wished for, especially now, when so many of the barriers between us seemed to be breaking down, but to let it go would make me a hypocrite, and I would not be so weak.

"I suppose it is not so difficult, if the charges of treason had any bearing in fact."

"I saw the evidence. You did not."

"And what was that evidence, pray?" I crossed my arms and stared up at him, refusing to look away, even as his brows lowered and his lips thinned.

"Documents showing he had paid for a group of mercenaries from al-Sirtan," Besh said, naming a province in the far south of Keshiaar known for its unruly population. The rule of law did not lie as heavy that far from the capital.

"Paid off how? I will confess to not being completely familiar with the finances of the artisan class, but I find it difficult to believe that the younger brother of an ironmonger would have the resources to hire a squad of scullery maids, let alone a fully mounted and heavily armed troop like the one that attacked us that night."

My husband's mouth compressed further. "Indeed, my lady wife, if I had known you were such a passionate defender of the downtrodden, I would have assigned you as the man's legal representative."

"And perhaps I would have done better by him," I retorted, then shook my head, going to Besh and laying a hand on his arm. "Dearest, I don't wish to quarrel with you over this. But even I can see something dreadfully wrong about the evidence...about everything." Should I leave it at that, or bring up my misgivings about the *visanis?* We were already arguing, however, and so I decided it was better to press forward. "I cannot say what his motivations might be, but I fear that somehow Chancellor Tel-Karinoor created the evidence so there would be an easy conviction."

Besh stared at me as if I had gone mad. "Why in the world would he do something like that?"

"I don't know," I said, taking care to keep my tone level, so I would not sound like a hysterical woman flinging out unfounded accusations. "Neither do I know why he would dismiss my Sirlendian maids, nor why he would do his best to give the impression that I was a light-minded woman incapable of deep devotion, so you would not risk coming to care for me. I do not know any of these things, but they have happened, and so there must be some motivation behind them, even if we cannot say for sure what it might be."

During all this Besh had listened with his lips pressed firmly together, jaw taut, as if forcing himself not to interrupt me. When I was done speaking, he waited for a few seconds, watching me carefully, as if attempting to see some truth in my face. Then he said, voice tight, sounding very unlike himself, "I had not thought of it that way. But when you present all the information together...." I saw him take in a breath, and give a shake of his head. "I fear the matter bears some looking into."

Relief spread through me, relief that my husband was a reasonable man, not one to ignore logic and instead cling to his ideas of what should be. "I think that might be a very good idea, my husband. But leave it aside for now, to be taken up on the morrow. We have more interesting matters to occupy us today."

His eyes lit then, as if he had just recalled our planned assignation tonight. "I very much look forward to all of those…matters. In the meantime, though, I fear I have several appointments that cannot be pushed aside. Every hour will be a century, but I will have an escort bring you here at dusk, and we will share a dinner."

"And so much more," I added, smiling as I went on my tiptoes to kiss him quickly. Not a deep, passionate kiss, but rather a promise of what would come later.

He saw the kiss for what it was, returning it lightly, then saying, "I will have the guards take you back to your chambers, but you will return here soon enough. And after that" —he paused, as if to give his next words greater emphasis— "you will not have to return to your apartments ever again, if you do not wish to. We can make our home here, together."

Joy surged within me at those words. It was no small thing, to invite me to share this place with him, for truly it was his private retreat from the world. And I knew in Keshiaar, as it was in Sirlende, that the Hiereine always had her own suite. It was quite a break from tradition, one he was willing to make for me.

"I would like that very much," I told him, not trusting myself to say much more, for I could feel the afternoon's emotions beginning to overcome me.

He took my hand and raised it to his lips. "Then I will make sure that some of your things are brought over as well. Until dusk, my dearest wife."

"Until dusk," I murmured, then took my leave of him, my heart full and my mind racing ahead to all the coming night promised.

Of course Therissa was waiting for me, her expression anxious, for I had been taken straight to see my husband upon my discovery in the street, and so had no opportunity to speak with her and let her know what had happened. What she had done to conceal her own transformation back into "herself"—well, Miram, at any rate—I did not know, but as the three maids were quietly stitching away on the new draperies as I entered my apartments, it seemed she must have done a good enough job of it.

At once the maids abandoned their sewing and bowed, even as Therissa hurried forward, brow puckered in confusion. "My lady...?"

"All is well, Miram," I said, with just the slightest dip of my head in her direction so she might know I would discuss matters further with her when I had the opportunity. "But I am having a private supper with His Most High Majesty this evening, and so I think it best we start preparing right away, after I have had my luncheon." Indeed, I was quite famished by then, for it was now almost two hours past noon, and the time when I should have eaten had come and gone. "Something light, however, so as not to interfere with my supper," I added.

"Of course, my lady. I will see to it directly." As she spoke, I could see the beginnings of a smile beginning to play around her mouth, despite her best efforts to suppress it. It was quite obvious she understood the ramifications of that "private supper." Then she turned to Lila and Marsali and Alina, her manner suddenly brisk. "Lila, off to the kitchens to fetch a tray for Her Most High Majesty. Marsali and Alina, go begin to run a bath so that it will be ready when she is done eating."

They all scampered to obey, Lila heading for the door, the other two going to the bath chamber. After they had gone, Therissa shot a questioning eyebrow in my direction.

"I see you managed to escape unscathed, my lady."

"I did, thank you." In an undertone, I added, "It was touch and go for a bit, but in the end it was all for the best, as my lord husband and I have reconciled, and all is as it should be."

Her face lit up so much at this news that even Miram's plain features were transformed, and I began to understand what the under-cook might see in her. "Oh, that is so very good to hear. I was so worried—"

"All is well, and I see you managed everything here in my absence, so pray, let us not speak of it further."

She seemed to understand, her gaze darting in the direction of the bath chamber, where Alina and Marsali were at work, then nodded. "Of course, my lady. I will begin to lay out your garments. Something very special, I think?"

I smiled at her. "Yes. This will truly be my wedding night."

A bob of her head and a smile, and she was off to inspect my wardrobe. A few minutes after that, Lila returned with a tray of cheese and fruit, and some of the nutty-flavored flatbread I liked so much. Usually my luncheon was more substantial, but as I was eating late, I did not want to be weighed down too much. It was enough to calm the pangs in my stomach, and that was all I required.

Afterward, it was time for my bath, and I luxuriated in the rose-scented water for a long while, glad to get rid of the stink of the streets, which felt as if it still clung to my hair and skin. Then the long process of drying my hair, and applying rose-scented oils, and the ritual painting of my face—belatedly, I realized I had left the little bag with my purchases down in Besh's study—and at last the donning of my garments one by one. First the under-blouse of filmy silk, and then the billowing trousers of silver tissue, and at last the tunic of white damask with its intricate edging of silver trim sewn with crystals and pearls.

Therissa settled the headdress of silver and diamonds on my head, murmuring, "Truly you are the most beautiful bride I have ever seen, my lady. I cannot tell you how happy I am at how all this has worked out."

"Thank you, Therissa," I said, in equally low tones, so the maids could not hear how I had used her real name. But I was so grateful to her for so many things, I wanted to use the name she had been born with, and not the one of her subterfuge.

A quick smile as her gaze shifted away from me, clearly checking to see if any of the three girls had heard what I had said. But as they were occupied on the opposite side of the chamber, rinsing out the bathtub and putting away all the scented oils and such, it seemed they had not noticed anything out of the ordinary.

At least we were not yet in high summer, when dusk would come very late. As I had bathed and been dressed, I had noted the way the light coming in through the windows seemed to slant further and further to the west, becoming deep gold and then russet-colored, reminding me of the shifting shades in my husband's eyes. Now I stood, adjusted the fit of the tunic minutely—it was lower-cut than some of my others, and I thought Besh would not mind that at all—and glanced one last time at the window. It seemed to be dusk, and I wondered when the guards would arrive to escort me to his chambers.

But then there came a knock at the door, and I could feel my blood begin to tingle with anticipation. Marsali hurried to the outer room to open the door, and I began to move in that direction as well, telling myself to maintain a dignified pace and not run to greet the guards, so there would be no delay in going to my husband.

I heard Marsali squeak, "Most High Majesty!" before bending over and bowing so deeply I thought she might topple forward altogether.

My pulse raced. Had Besh truly been so impatient that he had come here to be my escort himself? How very… importunate of him. Somehow I managed to keep my head high as I went to meet him, although my cheeks flushed with sudden heat.

He seemed to fill the doorway. Just behind him I could make out the forms of at least eight guards, and I wondered at such an escort, when we never had more than four with us at any given time.

"Good evening, my husband," I said, then raised my eyes to meet his.

All the heat that had flooded my veins seemed to turn to ice. Yes, those were Besh's eyes, warm amber framed in sooty lashes, and those were his straight black brows. But the nose was not quite as well-defined somehow, and the mouth was not his at all. This one seemed to smirk at me, and I had never seen Besh smirk in the entire year I had known him.

So alike, and yet different.

The man who faced me was Amael, Besh's twin brother.

CHAPTER SEVENTEEN

So many panicked thoughts ran through my mind that I was not sure which one to give voice to first. As I stared up at the man who so resembled my husband and yet so horribly was not him, he grinned, asking, "My lady, are you always so silent?"

Somehow I pushed the words from my dry mouth. "What are you doing here, Amael?"

The grin did not slip at all. "Why, I have come to claim what should have been mine all along. And since you, dear princess of Sirlende, are part and parcel of that birthright, I am taking you as well. Guards!"

They surged around him, heading toward me. The one in the lead carried a length of rope and a coarse linen bag. Guessing their intentions, I stumbled backward, even as Marsali looked on in horror.

Through the blood pounding in my ears, I heard Therissa gasp, "My lady—what is this?"

I knew there was no hope of escape for me. The guards were almost upon me, and even if I had attempted to flee, their longer legs would have brought them to my side in a second or two. No, there was only one person here who might make it away safely, as she still stood at the door to my bedchamber—that same bedchamber I had slipped from only a few nights earlier.

"Therissa, run!" I cried in Sirlendian, praying that neither Amael nor his guards understood the language of my homeland.

And bless her, she did not hesitate, did not protest. She knew my only hope of rescue lay in her escape.

So she bolted back into the bedchamber and slammed the door behind her.

"Get that woman," Amael said lazily, as if he did not much care what might happen to her. One of the guards went to the bedchamber entrance, found the door locked, and promptly kicked it in. The carved wood splintered, and I winced.

"She's gone out the window, Most High Majesty," the guard said.

Most High Majesty? What insanity was this? The only way Amael could claim that title was if his brother was dead....

No. No. I could not allow myself to believe that. In his vanity, the erstwhile prince had probably instructed his lackeys to address him thus, whether or not it might be true.

"Well, go after her," Amael commanded, before turning to the guard who held the rope and the bag. "And you, secure Her Majesty. We must be gone from this place."

I backed away. "You will never succeed in this mad plan. You must know that."

"No, I think not. Do you not hear that?" He paused, and I realized I could hear indecipherable shouts and the far-off steely clash of sword against sword. "That is the sound of my brother's rule ending. Now take her."

The guard stepped toward me, even as one of his compatriots came around from the other side, grabbing my wrists before I could begin to pull away. Never had I been handled so roughly, but that was not the worst of it. A second later, the first guard dropped the bag over my head so I could see nothing, although I did hear a faint metallic clink that must have been my headdress falling to the floor. At the same time I felt the rope being wound around my wrists, the coarse fibers cutting cruelly into my flesh.

And then, worst indignity of all, I found myself being hoisted off the floor and thrown over the guard's shoulder like a sack of meal. I gasped, then coughed, feeling the wind get halfway knocked out of me. That did not seem to bother my captor, though, for immediately afterward he began to move. I heard heavy boots tromping all around me, and then we were out of my chambers, walking with some speed down the corridor.

As we went, I could still hear the muffled sounds of battle, although Amael and his cohort seemed to be taking a route that kept them out of the thick of it. A few minutes later, we seemed to emerge from the palace and walk some distance. Because of the sack over my head, I could not get a very good indication of which direction we were headed, or how far we had gone. It did seem that we had not traveled very far before the boots of the men around me began to echo off polished marble floors rather than hard-packed dirt. We climbed a series of steps, and then I felt myself being deposited on an upholstered piece of furniture of some sort. The boots moved away, and then the bag was lifted from my head, and I saw Amael's hateful smile. In the shape of his mouth, so unlike that of my husband, I thought I saw an echo of Nadira's pout, and realized then that she must indeed be Amael's. Poor child. I could only hope that her character would be quite different from that of either of her parents, both weak in their own ways.

I could spare her no further thoughts in that moment, for I knew I had to concentrate on the man who had taken me, and the place he had brought me. Wherever we were, it was of a luxury to equal that of the palace, for past the form of my kidnapper I saw a large room with columns of carved marble, and sconces of worked brass and alabaster similar to those I had seen in Besh's suite. But no, I could not think of Besh now. I had to tell myself that he was safe, that he and his men were fighting to put down this coup. All I could do now was keep my wits about me and not allow the usurper to gain the upper hand.

Still smiling, he produced a curved knife set with gleaming topaz and garnet from his belt. He held it in front of me, and I forced myself not to react, to only sit there and gaze back at him with as stony a face as I could muster. Then he stepped toward me, lowered the knife…and cut through the ropes binding my wrists together.

Although I wanted nothing more than to rub my chafed skin, now bruised where the ropes had pressed a bracelet into my left wrist, I made myself sit there, hands resting quietly in my lap. I would not let him see how I had been hurt.

But he seemed to notice, for he shoved the knife back into the curved scabbard at his belt, then took my hand and lifted it so he might inspect it more closely. "A thousand apologies, my lady, for the hurt my soldier caused you." His fingers tightened on my flesh, and I forced myself not to wince. "So beautiful and delicate a prize deserves better handling."

"Then perhaps you should have instructed your henchman not to hoist me like a sack of flour," I snapped, pulling my wrist from Amael's grasp. Perhaps it would have been better to sit calmly and let him handle me as he wished, but I knew I did not have that much self-control.

He threw his head back and laughed, as if I had just told him a very good joke. His laugh was nothing like Besh's, either, but had a note of malice in it, something piercing that made me want to wince. "Ah, I think you have more spirit than I was led to believe. Trust me, my lady—you will come to enjoy me far more than you did Besh the scholar…Besh the milksop."

"I somehow doubt that," I returned, my tone dripping acid. "For I enjoy the company of a real man, not a sneak who hides in the shadows and betrays his own brother by sleeping with his wife."

That was far bolder a statement than I had planned to make, but I could not take the words back now. Something about the man who stood before me set every nerve on edge. And I knew I would have felt that way even if we had met under different circumstances.

"You are not one to mince words, are you, Lyarris? I may call you that, mayn't it?" When I said nothing, but only continued to stare up at him, my mouth tight, he said, "I think I shall. It is a lovely name, lovely and exotic, just like you. Your skin is like purest cream, did you know that? I shall enjoy drinking it in, just like the cream it resembles."

My stomach heaved, but I forced myself to sit still. He could stand there and say whatever he liked…as long as he made no move to touch me again. If he did that, I very much feared I would be sick. Once I thought I could speak without my voice shaking, I asked coldly, "What is it you want, Amael?" I would not call him "my lord." He did not deserve that courtesy.

His expression grew thoughtful. "What do I want? My brother's throne, which will soon be mine, thanks to the valuable assistance of Tel-Karinoor."

So my instincts had been correct. Oh, if only I had pressed my husband on the subject of his *visanis!* Perhaps I would not be sitting here now. But the mistakes of the past cannot be mended, and so I must do what I could to salvage the situation. "And why would the chancellor take such a risk? For already he is a man of great power."

"Great power, but not great birth. You are new here, dear lady, and from what I have heard, you have not learned everything about those around you. Tel-Karinoor was not born a prince, but the son of a humble scholar. His brilliance advanced him far beyond his simple beginnings, but that did not make his blood less common. My late father had promised to give the *visanis* a grant of nobility, making him a peer, but then had the misfortune to die before that promise could be fulfilled, and dear Besh knew nothing of it. He and our father were not all that close, as you may or may not have heard. But I knew of the promise, and told Tel-Karinoor that he would be a prince of the realm once I was Hierarch."

During that entire speech Amael wore a self-satisfied smile on his face, one I wished I had the courage to slap away. Oh, what treachery those two had hatched together! For now I saw the motivation behind it, I had no doubt that it was Tel-Karinoor or his agents who had hired the mounted band of thugs to attack our party in the desert, and his work to scapegoat the poor ironmonger's brother as well.

"You will never succeed," I said. Now I could hear my voice shake, despite my best efforts to keep it steady. "My husband has a vast army at his command."

That smug smile did not waver at all. In fact, it broadened, as if he had heard the tremor in my voice and derived a good deal of pleasure from it. "True, those men fight in the Hierarch's name…but it is the chancellor who passes on his commands. And what do you think those commands would be? Perhaps that His Most High Majesty's treacherous brother has returned to Keshiaar, and that he must be put in the dungeons immediately? Remember that he and I are so very alike, and most of those men would have only seen Besh at a distance, if at all."

I listened to all this without moving, although my heart seemed to sink in my breast, heavy as a stone. What if the unthinkable had happened, and the very men who were supposed to protect my husband had instead made him a prisoner in his own palace? True, they were forbidden by thousands of years of tradition not to spill royal blood. Amael, however, had no such strictures restraining him. Once Besh had been secured, his brother would only have to go to the dungeons and....

No, I could not think of that. My husband was strong and resourceful. I had to believe he had not been caught. If I allowed myself to think otherwise, I would surely go mad.

"Your plan seems to rest on a goodly number of 'if's,'" I said, still in that cold, clear voice which did not quite sound like my own. "But laying that aside, I do not see what you want with me."

"Oh, I think you know exactly what I want," he replied, lingering on the last word, gaze intent on my face...until it shifted lower, to the curve of my bosom as revealed by the low-cut tunic I wore. "It is more than that, of course. Your marriage to my brother has not been consummated, and therefore is not valid. You did not know that, did you?"

I shook my head, words failing me in that moment. Why had no one spoken of this to me?

Because Besh would not, and most likely Therissa did not know. And who else have you in this place to act as your friend and confidant?

Seemingly amused by my stricken silence, Amael went on, "A small detail, one which my brother neglected to tell you. Oh, in the eyes of the world, you were husband and wife, but because you were not that, not truly, I can marry you now, and there will be no talk of bigamy. And what should it matter to you? One brother is as good as another, after all. At least, Hezia thought so."

"Do not speak of her to me," I retorted, glad I had something else to distract me, rather than the horrifying notion that not only was I not Besh's legal wife, but that this creature could make me his, simply because of some ridiculous loophole in the law.

"Jealous?" Amael inquired in arch tones.

"Hardly. But as it seems clear to me that she was your equal in treachery, I do not wish to waste any breath on her."

"Treacherous?" He raised an eyebrow, then shook his head. "No, I would not say that, not precisely. You see, she wanted to love my brother, but as he found it expedient to ignore her—and Hezia must needs always be worshipped— she went elsewhere for the attention she craved. Indeed, her needs became rather tiresome after a while. I cannot say as I miss them all that much."

I had thought I was past being horrified, but hearing Amael speak so callously of the woman who thought herself in love with him, who had given up her life because of that love—well, once again my stomach roiled. I shut my eyes, wanting to take away the sight of the monster who stood before me, the monster who intended to steal my husband's throne and make me his wife.

"Oh, my dear," came that monster's voice. "Do not waste any tears on her. She knew the risks she was taking."

Since so much was wrong with that statement, I knew there was no way I could begin to answer it. Instead, I opened my eyes, looking past him and at the chamber around us. "Where are we?" I asked abruptly. "A townhouse of your own?"

"No, this humble abode belongs to the *visanis*. He thought it best that we be somewhere nearby, yet safely out of the chaos at the palace. No doubt he will be joining us here soon enough, once my brother has been captured."

"I fear that will not be happening anytime soon," came a familiar voice as the door opened to reveal Besh standing there, a bloody sword clenched in one hand.

My heart leapt, and I began to rise from the chair where I sat. Amael's hand, heavy as iron, descended on my shoulder, holding me in place.

"Be careful, brother," he warned. "For I have your lady wife here, and as much as it would pain me to cut this exquisite throat of hers, I will do it if you do not leave this place at once."

Besh's gaze shifted toward me, and his mouth tightened. "Are you well, my lady?"

"Yes. He has not hurt me."

"Yet," Amael said, fingers digging into my shoulder. No doubt I would have bruises there to match the ones on my wrists.

"Do not be hasty," came Besh's voice again...and yet it did not issue from the man who even now advanced a pace

316 - CHRISTINE POPE

or two into the room, but from a second figure, identical in every way to the one who had first appeared, down to the blood-covered sword he held in his left hand.

Left hand. But Besh was right-handed....

Oh, Therissa, I thought. *So you did make your escape, and somehow found my husband. But what did you two plan to do next?*

Over the past few weeks, I had grown accustomed to the way Therissa could casually assume the appearance of anyone she wished. Amael, however, was not quite so nonchalant.

"What sort of deviltry is this?" he demanded, staring with disbelieving eyes at the two copies of his brother.

"Perhaps it is no deviltry at all, but only the product of your own guilty imagination," said the Besh on the left, the one I knew was my husband. If it were not for Therissa holding her sword left-handed, I would never have been able to tell them apart.

"I bear no guilt," Amael replied. "You do not deserve to be Hierarch of Keshiaar. And what gave you that title? A mere accident of birth?"

"I am inclined to believe that God knew what He was doing when He made sure I was born first," said the Besh on the right in droll tones, and I knew it was Therissa who had actually spoken. My own husband would never have said anything so self-important.

Amael, however, did not appear quite so discerning. "Indeed?" he asked, lip curling. "So now you think you were anointed by God to rule this land? A man so incompetent he could not get his first wife with child, or even bed the second one?"

In his anger, he had lifted his hand from my shoulder. Besh—the true Besh—did not respond to his brother's hateful words, but only called out, "Now, Lyarris!"

I did not stop to think. I knew he was telling me I must seize my chance in this one moment, while Amael was distracted and had let go of me. By instinct, I kicked out with my left foot, catching him behind the knee. He stumbled, cursing, and I pushed myself out of the chair and away from him, taking shelter behind one of the pillars that lined the room.

As soon as they saw I was free, Besh and the disguised Therissa moved forward, approaching Amael with careful, measured steps. "You are caught," Besh said. "I have brought guards loyal to me, and all the traitors in your employ have been killed—as has the treacherous chancellor who gave me poisoned advice for so many years."

From my hiding place, I could hear Amael curse under his breath, but he did not falter. Perhaps in that way he was like a trapped wild animal, too crazed with fear and anger to surrender. He stood straight and tall, meeting his brother eye to eye…before pulling the dagger from his belt and hurling it directly at the man he resembled so closely.

I screamed, and saw the second Besh, my dear Therissa, throw herself in front of my husband, shielding him with her body. The blade sank into her side, and she collapsed to the ground with a cry of agony, her assumed form melting away, leaving only the limp body of a woman behind.

"Ah, so you would allow a witch to shelter you?" Amael sneered.

Besh appeared stricken, but then I saw his jaw clench. "That woman is worth ten thousand of you, Amael." Sword up, he advanced on his brother, even as I ran from behind the pillar and sank down on the ground.

So much blood. The dagger still protruded from her side, so I grasped it and pulled it out, then threw it away. Her face was blank and quiet, and I thought, No, no, gods no, before laying a finger to her neck so I could feel the pulse there. It still beat, but quickly and faint. I did not have much time.

The silver tissue of my trousers would be useless as a bandage, but the tunic I wore was of thick silk damask, heavy but fine. I grasped the edge and pulled with all my might, managing to tear away a large strip. It would have to do.

As I pressed the makeshift bandage against the wound in Therissa's side, I heard Amael say, "But brother, I am unarmed. Surely you would not be such a dastard as to strike down a man who cannot fight back?"

Voice grim, Besh replied, "Normally I would not. But your actions have already shown you to be beyond the pale, and therefore I will not treat with you the way I would a worthy man. But you can still stand there and accept your doom with dignity, and perhaps preserve something of our family's honor."

For a second or two, Amael hesitated, eyes fixed on the bloodstained sword in his brother's hand. Then he seized the chair I had occupied only a few minutes earlier, and flung it at Besh.

But it seemed Besh had anticipated the move, ducking out of the way. The chair crashed to the floor only a few feet from where I cradled Therissa in my arms, and I flinched. Then Besh was moving, sword a blink of silver in the light from the sconces on the walls, flashing so quickly I could not quite comprehend what was happening. Then followed a heavy thud, and I realized the sound had come from Amael's head hitting the carpet. His body toppled next, falling over to lie next to his head in a great spray of blood.

I believe I flinched, for I had never been witness to such personal violence before. This was different from the battle at the oasis…and yet just, for Besh had merely done what the executioner could not. Far more important to me, however, was the woman lying limp against me, her blood oozing past the fabric I held and staining my now ruined clothing, the beautiful pieces I had put on with such anticipation earlier that day.

Besh approached, then knelt down on the carpet next to me. "Is she—"

"She is still alive, but I do not know for how long. You must send for a doctor."

A half-familiar voice said, "No need for that. Let me see her."

Blinking, I looked toward the doorway and saw the last two people I would have expected: Besh's former tutor Alim, along with Nezhaam, Besh's dear friend. Alim hurried forward, a satchel clutched in one hand.

"So you are not only a man of learning, but a man of medicine as well?" I asked as he came to kneel beside me.

"They are not mutually exclusive," he said, his tone wry, although his gaze was serious enough as he opened the satchel and pulled out a sharp knife, along with a quantity of fresh, clean gauze. "But let me see what I am working with here. Go ahead and let go, my lady. I daresay you have saved this woman's life, but now let me finish the task."

Blinking back tears, I released my death grip on the bandage, pushing myself to my feet as I watched Alim cut away Therissa's blood-soaked tunic with quick, efficient movements. There was so much blood that I could not see how deep the wound actually was, but I was startled to see Alim give a grim smile and then nod as he reached into his satchel for a bottle of clear liquid, which he poured over the wound.

Although I had thought she was completely unconscious, Therissa twitched and moaned softly. I sent a questioning look at Alim, and he said, "The wound is not deep enough to have cut into any of her organs, so, while it looks alarming, it is not as bad as I feared."

"That is good," Besh added, coming to stand by me, Nezhaam a few paces away. "So she will survive?"

"I believe so." Alim continued to work as he spoke, cleaning the wound, then fetching a long curved needle and a length of some kind of stiff thread from the satchel. He poured more of the clear liquid over the needle, threaded it, and began to stitch the wound closed.

It was rather a gruesome procedure, if a necessary one, and so I was glad that my husband captured my attention, taking my hands and turning me slightly so I would not have to see Alim working on my fallen friend.

"He will take care of her," Besh said, raising one palm to his lips and kissing it, and doing the same with the other. "Mistress Larrin could not ask for better aid, and well she deserves it, for I do not think I have ever seen a woman with such courage." He smiled grimly, then added, "And…you are quite well? You did not suffer any hurt?"

"Nothing more than a bruised dignity from being flung over the shoulder of one of the guards and carried here like a sack of potatoes," I replied, thrilling at his touch, despite my various bumps and bruises, despite my ongoing worry over Therissa.

A slight chuckle. "Well, if that is your only wound from this day, then you have fared better than many." His expression darkened, even as Nezhaam approached. "Your report?"

Nezhaam straightened. Gone was the happy-go-lucky man I had known from our journey to view the conjunction; his expression was unsmiling, his mouth tight. "This house has been cleared completely, and although the traitors who followed Tel-Karinoor have not all been caught, I have no doubt they will be by morning. The palace is likewise safe, although I fear your servants will have quite a time of it putting things to rights."

Although Besh nodded, he did not look entirely happy. "How many lost?"

"We are still making a count, my lord, but I believe it will be above two hundred by the time we are done."

For a few seconds, Besh said nothing. I could see his gaze rake the room, linger on the body of his brother, and then move to where Therissa lay, Alim's needle glinting as he worked to close the wound Amael had inflicted. "How does Mistress Larrin fare?"

"She has lost a good deal of blood, but she seems strong and healthy enough," Alim replied, not looking up from his work. "However, I do not think she should be moved very far."

"We will take her upstairs when you are done," Besh said. His amber eyes glinted, and he added, "This house will do well for her convalescence. After all, my chancellor has no further need of it."

CHAPTER EIGHTEEN

The final tally was some two hundred and eighty souls dead, most of them the turncoats who had thrown in their lot with Amael and Tel-Karinoor. Even so, there were many loyal men who had given their lives in defense of their Hierarch, and the realm mourned their loss while at the same time reeling from the brief but bloody revolt.

Although Besh and I had made a vow to each other that we would become husband and wife in more than just name, I did not want to selfishly attend to my own pleasures when my dear Therissa was in such a bad way. True, Alim had saved her life, but it would be some time before she was up and about, and I told Besh I wanted to tend to her and make sure she was well on the road to recovery.

"I understand, dear wife," he told me. "After all, I have made you wait all these months. It is certainly not fair for me to begrudge you a few days."

I smiled and thanked him, and inwardly sent a quick prayer of gratitude heavenward, so the gods might know how indebted I was to them for sending me such a wise and understanding husband. And so I sat at Therissa's side, noting how the cheery flush that usually filled her cheeks was gone, and her face was somehow thinner than it had been a few days earlier.

But then she opened her eyes and smiled at me, and said, "So you have decided to play nursemaid, Hiereine?"

Since she had used that title, I knew she was teasing me. Inwardly I cheered at seeing her recovered enough to make a joke, but I said in mock-severe tones, "It is the very least I can do, Mistress Larrin, seeing that you saved the life of the Hierarch and kept this realm from falling into utter ruin."

"Well, then," she replied. "I suppose it is all right for you to be a nursemaid for a little while." Almost as soon as the words left her lips, her eyelids fluttered shut, and she fell asleep again. That did not unnecessarily disturb me, as Alim had said she would sleep a great deal as her body fought to recover from the wound and the blood loss it had caused.

But the next morning when she awoke, her eyes were bright, and she took in her rich surroundings with lively interest. "It seems I have moved up in the world," she remarked.

"You are in the house of the late *visanis*," I told her. "Alim thought it best you make your recovery here, as there was a danger of your wound reopening if you were moved too far. And, as my husband pointed out, Tel-Karinoor had no more use for it."

She smiled then, albeit weakly. "True. It is a pity you were busy being kidnapped, for watching the Hierarch run that viper through was highly satisfying."

Besh had not told me exactly what had happened, only that he had dispatched the traitorous chancellor. However, Nezhaam had given me more detail, had described how my husband came upon the *visanis,* and was taken by such a cold rage that he slaughtered all six of the men who accompanied Tel-Karinoor, and then plunged his sword into the older man's black heart with such force that the blade was buried up to the hilt. I shivered slightly at the recollection, but managed to say, "I had no idea you were so bloodthirsty, Therissa."

"Indeed I am not, except when someone richly deserves it."

I could not dispute that, so I only said, "Indeed, that must have been quite a blood thirst, for I could swear that the blade you held was not exactly pristine."

A long sigh, and she closed her eyes for a moment. "Self-defense, my dear Lyarris. And before you ask, yes, I have learned something of how to handle a sword over the years. A woman on her own should know how to protect herself."

"You are a woman of many talents, it seems."

"As are most women, I find. It is only that my talents are perhaps somewhat different from most." She shifted slightly in the bed, wincing a bit, then regarded me closely for a few seconds. "It was good that you had already proven the ledge outside your window as a handy escape route. The guard pursuing me could not quite figure out where I had gone—at least, not until I had a healthy lead on him. And as soon as I reached the balcony, I took on the guise of one of the guards, and so was able to make my way more or less safely through the palace to your husband's quarters. The clash between his men and the traitors was just beginning then, but they had not yet reached him. So I was able to warn him, and we made our escape." Putting a hand to her head, she offered me a weary yet cheerful smile. "It was touch and go for a bit until we met up with Nezhaam and a squad of loyal guards, but your husband acquits himself very well with a sword. You should be proud of him."

"I am," I said at once. "And of you, dear Therissa. Goodness, what a tale I will have to tell when I write my brother next!"

"You will need to edit the account a good deal, I think. I cannot imagine your husband will be too overjoyed to have an account of such treachery in the heart of Keshiaar sent straight to the Emperor of Sirlende."

She did have a point there. "Oh, dear," I replied in some dismay. "I had not thought of that." Pausing, I considered the problem, then added, "But then again, my brother has a goodly number of spies here at court, so I have no doubt that he will get a true account one way or another."

"And no doubt he will not be overjoyed, either, to have you reveal such a thing to me."

I began to protest, but then I saw the dancing light in Therissa's eyes and knew that she was teasing me again. "And I am sure that you know who every single one of them is, so there is no reason to play the innocent with me."

Her mouth curved in a smile. "As to that, I will say neither yea nor nay."

In that moment, I heard something of a clamor downstairs, and I stiffened, worried that somehow some of the rebels who had not yet been caught had returned here to cause mischief. But then I heard my husband's voice, accompanied by one that sounded quite familiar, although I couldn't quite place who it might be.

Therissa seemed to know, however, for her eyes widened, and I saw her reach up to smooth her hair—quite unnecessarily, as I myself had run a brush through it not less than an hour earlier. There was a sound of heavy feet in the corridor outside, and then the door to Therissa's chamber, which I had left partway open to catch the fickle morning breeze, opened all the way. Besh peered in, smiling.

"Normally, I would not intrude, Mistress Larrin," he said. "But as my wife reports that you are doing much better, I thought you might like to have a visitor."

He stepped aside, and in stepped Ambassador Sel-Trelazar, looking quite fit and hearty, although his brow puckered with worry as he gazed down at Therissa. However, he had not forgotten himself quite enough to forget to acknowledge me; he bowed, hands pressed together, and said formally, "Most High Majesty, I am pleased beyond measure to see you so well."

"Thank you, Ambassador," I replied. "But I think there is someone here who is even happier to see you than I am, and so we will leave you to speak in private."

"A thousand thanks, my lady." And that seemed to be all the niceties he had time for, as he turned from me at once and went to the bed, taking Therissa's hand in his.

This was their time to be together, and so I did not linger. But even as I shut the door, I saw Therissa's face light up so much that one would never have guessed she was recovering from a grievous wound, and I felt my heart fill with happiness for her.

I saw Besh waiting for me in the corridor outside, a smile of his own illumining his face, and I went to him, then took his hand. "That was well done, my husband. How is it that the ambassador came here now?"

Besh lifted my hand and pressed it to his lips, then released it. "This is the time of year when he usually returns to Keshiaar to make his report. No doubt he did not expect to find that so much had happened in his absence, but when I told him of how bravely Mistress Larrin had acquitted herself, he wanted to come and thank her in person."

"Indeed," I said, my tone dry. I knew Besh was aware of the relationship Sel-Trelazar and Therissa shared, for I had told him of it myself. "How very thoughtful of you."

"I felt it best, especially now that I have requested the good ambassador stay here in Sirlende and give up his traveling days. I find I am in need of a new *visanis,* and I cannot think of anyone with a better heart or mind to take that position."

Indeed, I had not thought my own heart could grow any more full, but it seemed to swell further in that moment. I flung my arms around Besh, going on my tiptoes so I might kiss him and show him my gratitude for his thoughtfulness. Yes, guards stood on either side of the door to Therissa's chamber, and more watched the head of the stairs, but in that moment I found I did not care who was watching.

"Ah," he said, after I had pulled away and he had recovered his breath. "I shall have to play matchmaker more often, if that is how you intend to reward me."

"I look forward to rewarding you, my husband," I replied with a sly smile, and he gathered me into his arms and kissed me again, and again, and I knew we would not have much longer to wait.

And so it was that Malik Sel-Trelazar, lately appointed visa-nis to the Hierarch, and the Lady Therissa Larrin, lately of Sirlende, were wed one fine spring evening in the house that had been made theirs by royal decree. True, they were married with the lady still in her sickbed, as Alim had not yet given his approval for her to be up and about, but the new chancellor and his bride did not want to wait.

"For you know how people will talk if he stays here, and I an unmarried woman," Therissa told me with a wink, and I could only laugh, knowing she spoke the truth. It did not matter that the former ambassador was near fifty, and Therissa not quite forty-five. People would talk, and Malik Sel-Trelazar had vowed that he would not leave Therissa's side until she was fully healed, so a discreet wedding seemed the best course of action.

Besh and I left them to their happiness, and returned to the palace. It had been some ten days since the abortive rebellion, and the servants had done a truly remarkable job in restoring the interior to its former pristine state. One would never know that many scores of men had died here not quite two weeks earlier.

But I did not want to think of that. Tragic for the families and loved ones left behind—yes, even of those who had been lured to Amael's side by promises of riches and easy advancement. In time, though, the kingdom would heal, and the entire affair would be only a footnote to history.

As we walked, I noticed that the guards were guiding us toward Besh's apartments, and my heart began to beat a little faster. We had not spoken of that delayed "wedding night"— at least not formally—but our unspoken agreement had been that we would be together after I knew that Therissa was truly out of danger. Her bedside wedding to Malik Sel-Trelazar seemed to confirm that she would be with us for a good long time to come. There was no reason to delay any further.

One of the guards opened the door for us, and Besh hesitated, inquiring, "Will you dine with me here tonight, my lady?"

We had shared some light refreshments at the Sel-Trelazar home, but I knew that was not precisely what my husband was asking of me. By following him inside, I had agreed to be with him wholly, completely. I knew there could be only one answer to his question.

"It would be my greatest pleasure, my lord."

A brilliant smile illumined his face, and he took me by the hand and led me inside, shutting the guards and the rest of the world out as he closed the door behind us. Almost at once he drew me to him, bringing his mouth down to mine so he might taste my lips. I tasted him as well, heat building within me, an urgent, needy fire that must be quenched.

"Come," he said simply. We walked past his library, and past the large room he used sometimes to meet with his advisors and generals, and past sitting rooms and parlors. At last we came to the great staircase, but he did not hesitate there, instead guiding me up to the second story. In the open area on the landing had been set out light refreshments—grapes and cheese, and thin slices of cured meats and fine little pastries sweet with honey and almonds. Next to the trays sat a decanter of wine, deep, deep red. He poured a glass for me, and I came and took it from him, then waited while he poured himself some of his own.

"To the wisest and most beautiful Hiereine this land has ever seen," he said, lifting his glass toward me.

I could feel the blood rush to my cheeks, but I raised my glass and replied, "To the bravest and handsomest Hierarch this land has ever seen."

He laughed then, and drank, and I followed suit, letting the sweet, rich wine linger on my tongue and then slip down my throat, bringing with it a subtler warmth to echo the one that already lay coiled in my belly and seemed to throb along every vein.

"I am sorry it took so long for us to come to this," he added, voice quiet, although something in me thrilled at the intensity in it.

"Then that will make us appreciate it all the more," I told him, swallowing more of my wine before setting the glass down on the table next to the decanter. Yes, the wine was all very well, but I had had enough of waiting.

Besh seemed to sense my mood, for he placed his glass next to mine, then came to me, lifting me in his strong arms. I clung to him, and we moved into his bedchamber, almost twice the size of mine, with an equally enormous bed, all hung with red silk. Seeing that bed made it all the more real, and I stared up at him as he deposited me upon it, my mouth dry.

Perhaps he noted my sudden anxiety, for he asked, "Are you ready—*truly* ready, my love?"

All hesitation fell away as I gazed up at him, at the sculpted planes of his face, at those amber eyes, glowing with love...and need. "I am ready, Besh. Please...make me your wife."

He needed no more encouragement than that, for at once he was lying next to me, mouth on mine, hands running over my body, awakening sensations I had never before experienced. In that moment, he was the world, the endless night sky, the entire universe. And I took him into me, our bodies joining in perfect joyful conjunction, and I knew I would never feel alone again.

Some hours later, after we had wandered out to sate our appetites with the delicacies the servants had left behind, Besh turned to me, eyes holding that certain glint I had come to recognize.

"My lord, as much as I have enjoyed this evening, I do not think I am quite ready to do that again."

He laughed then, and picked up his goblet and drained it with one large swallow. "My lady wife, I would not think to impugn your…stamina. However, that is not precisely what I had in mind."

I did not care for any more wine, and instead sipped at some of the lemon-flavored water that had been provided along with the headier drink. "So what do you have in mind?"

"Let us get dressed."

Puzzled, I followed him back into the bedchamber, discarded the dressing gown he had loaned me, and climbed back into the costume of blue and gold I had worn earlier in the day. My hair was beyond repair, so I pulled it into a hasty plait and reassured myself that there would be no one around, save a few guards, to see my disheveled state.

While I was dressing, Besh did the same. When we were both ready, he extended a hand to me and I took it, reveling in the rush of warmth that went over me at the touch of his fingers against mine. We had done far more intimate things during the last few hours, and yet I was happy beyond measure that something as simple as holding hands could send such a thrill through me.

"Come along," he said.

We went downstairs and out through the front doors to his apartments. Immediately the guards fell in behind us, but Besh seemed to pay them no mind, so I did the same. From his suite, he moved through half-lit corridors, twisting and turning until we emerged in the moonlit gardens, the air still warm, but in a soft, gentle way, like a lover's caress against one's cheek. Then I knew where we were bound, for he chose the path that led to the observatory, taking me past fountains sparkling in the moonlight and flowers whose fragrance seemed twice as sweet as during the daytime.

At last we came to the observatory doors. Two guards hastened forward to open them for us, but by some unspoken signal they remained outside while we entered. Inside, all was blind dark, and I almost bumped into Besh when he stopped a few paces from the door.

"Do you want me to light one of the lamps?" he asked.

"It depends," I replied. "Are we here merely for privacy, or to watch the stars?"

Although it was utterly black in there, I thought I saw a glimmer of his teeth as he smiled. "The latter. There is something I wish to show you."

"Then do not bother with the lamp. I trust you to guide me."

I felt his mouth press against my fingers, and then we were moving forward again, going to where I knew the telescope stood. Sure enough, my eyes had begun to adjust to the darkness, and I could see the cylindrical bulk of it pointed up toward the opening in the observatory's domed roof.

"I set it up earlier today," Besh said. "All you must do is look through the eyepiece."

Moving with care so I would not bump the instrument, I took up my position as he instructed, then gazed upward. There, encircled in brass and swimming in darkness, I saw a bright, flaring light almost pearlescent in its radiance. It seemed to pulse with its own rhythm, almost as if it were alive.

"What is it?" I breathed.

"That, my love, is a star being born. It was not there two nights ago, but suddenly blazed forth in the night sky. I thought it a good omen."

"It is the very best of omens," I said, turning away from the gleaming newborn star so I might face my husband.

He clasped his fingers around mine, pulling me close, and I felt his lips touch the top of my head, gentle, warm. "You are a very great gift, my lady wife. I never thought I would be allowed such happiness, but God has seen fit to grant it to me."

Had I ever felt so safe, so loved? I thought not. Some part of me wanted to weep for joy, but I fought back the tears, instead saying, "After all the sorrow you have suffered, you deserve happiness, my love."

He kissed me then, kissed me with all his strength and his passion and his brilliance. How long we stood thus, I do not know, but at last he released me and said, "Here in Keshiaar we have a saying: 'I will love you for a thousand nights and one more.' I will love you, Lyarris, for those thousand nights, and the thousand after that, and so on, until the very end of time."

Truly, in that moment I had no words, no way I could reply, except to kiss him again, and again, and so let him know that I would be his, and he mine, forevermore.

The End

CPSIA information can be obtained at www.ICGtesting.com
Printed in the USA
LVOW07s0349291214

420711LV00008B/481/P